MARS ONE

Also by Jonathan Maberry

Scary Out There

THE ROT & RUIN SERIES
Rot & Ruin

Dust & Decay

Flesh & Bone

Fire & Ash

Bits & Pieces

THE NIGHTSIDERS SERIES
The Orphan Army

Vault of Shadows

MARS ONE

Jonathan Maberry

SIMON & SCHUSTER BFYR

NEW YORK LONDON TORONTO SYDNEY NEW DELHI

SIMON & SCHUSTER BFYR

An imprint of Simon & Schuster Children's Publishing Division
1230 Avenue of the Americas, New York, New York 10020

SIMON & SCHUSTER BFYR is a trademark of Simon & Schuster, Inc.
For information about special discounts for bulk purchases, please contact Simon & Schuster Special Sales at 1-866-506-1949 or business@simonandschuster.com.
The Simon & Schuster Speakers Bureau can bring authors to your live event. For more information or to book an event, contact the Simon & Schuster Speakers Bureau at 1-866-248-3049 or visit our website at www.simonspeakers.com.
Jacket design by Laurent Linn
Interior design by Hilary Zarycky
The text for this book was set in Aldine 401.
Manufactured in the United States of America
First Edition
2 4 6 8 10 9 7 5 3 1

Library of Congress Cataloging-in-Publication Data
Names: Maberry, Jonathan, author.
Title: Mars One / Jonathan Maberry.
Description: First edition. | New York : Simon & Schuster Books for Young Readers, [2017] | Summary: "A teenage boy leaves for Mars as a colonist with the Mars One space program and grapples with what he's leaving behind to do so" —Provided by publisher.
Identifiers: LCCN 2016011449 |
ISBN 9781481461610 (hardback) | ISBN 9781481461634 (eBook)
Subjects: | CYAC: Mars (Planet)—Fiction. | Space colonies—Fiction. | Love—Fiction. | Science fiction. | BISAC: JUVENILE FICTION / Science Fiction. | JUVENILE FICTION / Family / General (see also headings under Social Issues). | JUVENILE FICTION / Action & Adventure / General.
Classification: LCC PZ7.M11164 Mar 2017 | DDC [Fic]—dc23
LC record available at https://lccn.loc.gov/2016011449

This is for Neil Armstrong. On July 20, 1969, I was an eleven-year-old kid sitting in front of a flickering black-and-white TV, watching the impossible happen as you stepped out of the lunar module to put a human footprint on another world.
It was one small step for man, one giant leap for mankind.

And, as always, for Sara Jo.

Acknowledgments

Space travel happens in a vacuum. Writing does not. I've been unusually fortunate to have as advisers some of the world's more notable astronomers, medical doctors, astrophysicists, and space technologists. When I get the science right, cheer them. When I get it wrong, yell at me.

My heartfelt thanks go to Dominick D'Aunno, physician adviser to NASA; the good folks at the Johnson Space Center in Houston; Brother Guy Consolmagno, SJ, president of the Vatican Observatory Foundation; and Lisa Will, professor of physics and astronomy at San Diego City College.

MARS ONE

PART ONE

BLUE MARBLE

Astronomy compels the soul to look upward
and leads us from this world to another.
—Plato, *Republic*

Chapter 1

She said, "You're going to die up there."

"You're going to die down here," I said.

We sat there, holding hands, trying not to cry. Failing like we always do.

I said, "Izzy . . . I'm going to *Mars*."

"Mars doesn't want you," she said. "I do."

Chapter 2

My name is Tristan Hart.

When I was ten my parents told me that we were going to Mars. Not Mars, California, or Mars, Pennsylvania, or even Mars, Texas—which is a ghost town we visited once.

No . . . *actual* Mars. The planet. Millions and millions of miles away from Earth.

That Mars.

I believed them too, because ten-year-old kids believe pretty much everything their parents tell them. I was still pretty sure Santa Claus was real. Or real-ish. So Mars? Sure, why not?

Then I was sixteen. I didn't believe in Santa anymore. Or the Easter Bunny or much of anything.

But I believed we were going to Mars.

The Mars One, an independent international space program, sent a bunch of robots up first and tons of supplies. People were next. Originally it was going to be four people, but they got tons of extra funding from reality-show producers all over the world and now there were forty of us going. The first wave, they called it. Colonists.

It was a one-way trip. No one was coming back. They'd send other colonists every two years. If . . .

If we make it.

If we didn't die.

If we could make it work.

If we became Martians.

I was sixteen. I'd turn seventeen in outer space.

If I lived long enough I'd celebrate my eighteenth birthday on another world.

Mars, man.

We were going to Mars.

And no matter what happened, we were never coming back here.

Never.

Ever.

Chapter 3

I still went to high school. The people running the Mars One project sent us back to school for six months before we were to leave. Parts of each month, anyway. We had to go for long training weekends, but most of that time we were back in school. Me to my hometown school in Madison, the other three to schools in their countries. They want all four of the teens who are going to be "habituated to age-appropriate social behavior enforced by peer interaction." Which is their way of saying they want us to be normal.

Or, the way my friend Herc put it, "They don't want to be stuck in a tin can with freaks."

"Pretty much," I agreed.

"Way too late for that."

I sighed. We tapped pop bottles. Sipped. Watched the clouds sail slowly across the Wisconsin sky. We were sprawled on bleachers on the north side of the track outside of our school, James Madison Memorial High. It was September 10 but it felt like mid-July because of a freak heat wave that turned everything into a sauna. Humidity and temperature in the eighties. Forget anything that involved moving.

Sweating was a theme. The only easy thing to do was talk.

"And this is really happening?" asked Herc.

"Yeah."

"Going to Mars."

"Yeah."

He shook his head, grinned, and took a long swallow.

"Oh, please," I said, "if you're going to give me the same old 'you're going to die up there' speech, save it. I'm tired of—"

"Nah," Herc said. "Even *I'm* tired of hearing that crap and I'm staying here."

"Okay."

"I'm just wondering what you're going to do about *them*?" He used his bottle to point to the crowd on the other side of the chain-link fence, behind the cops and their wooden sawhorse barricades. The sunlight flashed on hundreds of cameras—cell phone and professional. Broadcast towers rose above the seven news vans parked on the street. There was a bunch of protestors, too. There always were, ever since Mars One started. Some were just whack jobs who seemed to like to yell at anyone who was doing something interesting. Some were people who wanted to try and get onto the news, even if it was via a photobomb. Some, though, were religious nuts who seemed to think going to Mars was somehow against God. Not sure how that worked, though. Those protestors were always there.

What I was looking for were the really scary ones, the ones

who always wore white robes and red bandannas, the ones who called themselves the Neo-Luddites. Those guys were freaky, but I knew they wouldn't be on school grounds. The Neo-Luddites usually only showed up at official mission events or sometimes when we were filming an episode for one of the reality shows.

The Neo-Luddites were a deeply weird kind of extremist group. Not exactly religious—I mean, they weren't fundamentalists the way you'd think. It's hard to explain them because they mostly talked about what they *didn't* believe in and what they were afraid of, but not really much at all about what they *did* believe in.

As far as I could tell there were two kinds of them. Most of their group wasn't violent. They were organized and persistent but they didn't cause a ruckus at events. But there was a smaller bunch that was way dangerous. No one in the press or military or in Mars One could seem to decide it they were an official part of the Neo-Luddites or a separate splinter group who just used that name. But that bunch didn't just stand around and wave signs. They sent an actual hit team out to place magnetic limpet mines on the hull of one of the SpaceX sea-launch stations. The bombs had some kind of special trembler switch that was triggered by the exhaust blast when the SpaceX team test-fired one of the new Falcon Heavy rockets. Seventeen people were killed—blown to bits—and another thirty were hurt, some really bad. The four-person

Neo-Luddite team was killed too. No one can tell if it was a suicide attack or if they got caught in their own blast by accident. Dead either way. The authorities used DNA from some of the body parts they fished out of the water to identify one man who was known to have ties to the Neo-Luddites, and when accusations were made the Neo-Luddite goofballs didn't deny it. They didn't admit it either. What they did was post photos of the murdered SpaceX people on their website with the heading: "BETRAY THE TRUST—PAY THE PRICE!"

The Trust . . . ? They never came right out and said what that meant. Everyone on the news had been beating each other up with theories.

That was the first attack. After that the Neo-Luddites were tied to some other bombings—of a parts manufacturer making equipment for Virgin Galactic, an electronics firm building a guidance system for SpaceDev, a metallurgy plant making hull sections under contract to ARCA Space Corporation, and the chemical processing plant in China that makes fuel for the Shenzhou program. More people were killed, and every program upped its security game by a factor of ten. Definitely Mars One did. The mission shrinks grilled every single candidate six ways from Sunday. Lie detector tests, wave after wave of psych evals, questioning by cops from Interpol. It was scary as hell. All through it I felt sweaty and guilty for no reason. If they'd leaned any harder on me I'd have confessed to everything up to and including the assassination of Abraham Lincoln.

There was a movement going around to have the Neo-Luddites declared an actual terrorist group. Some of them definitely were, which was why I always looked to see if there were any in the crowd wherever I went. I'd seen them a bunch of times, but always the quiet ones. None of them had chucked a bomb at me, so I'm putting that in the win category.

Scared me, though. What if they went after my folks? Or Izzy?

I wasn't the only person losing sleep over it. I just wished it made some kind of sense.

Today, though, it was the usual suspects. Nobody to be scared of.

The sun baked us all. I sighed and rested the cold bottom of the pop bottle on my forehead.

When I didn't say anything, Herc snorted and sat up. He was about my size: five ten, lean, built for running. We both ran track. I was faster, but he could run all day. He wore cargo shorts and a T-shirt from the church a cappella choir he was in, the Preach Boys. "They're going to dog you every day until you light the candle, you know that, right?"

"They've been dogging all of us since the mission administrators at Mars One announced the final team three years ago," I said.

"Yeah, but you and the other kids are the real story."

"How do you figure that?"

"C'mon, everyone else is an adult. They're legal, which means they can vote, get married, whatever. They have a choice. You guys are minors. You're going because your families are going. A lot of people think that's messed up."

I pulled my shades down to look at him over the lenses. Herc's family emigrated from Mexico two years before he was born, and he had dark brown hair and his skin was a medium tan. I was eighth-generation American white boy, but I took a tan that made me darker than him. A lot of it earned when our Mars One training teams were in the Bahamas doing underwater drills in space suits.

"You think it's messed up too?"

He shrugged. "You want me to lie or do you want to hear what I really think?"

"You always tell me what you really think. So . . . sure, fire away."

Herc took a few moments with that, glancing at the reporters and gawkers, then back to me, then up at the sky. "I wish I was going too," he said.

I waited for the grin, the punch line. But his face didn't change.

"You serious?" I asked.

"God's honest truth, Tris."

The buzzer rang. Lunch was over. I did a slow sit-up and swung my legs off the bleacher.

"You're crazier than I am," I told him.

"You asked."

A dragonfly buzzed around me and then whizzed off.

"Saw your mom on the news," Herc said. "She looked pissed."

"Mom always looks pissed."

"Nah, your mom's cool. She's just intense."

"I guess."

The news story last night was about the series of technical problems they'd had with one of the rockets. Technically they weren't *our* rockets—Mars One was leasing them from SpaceX—but my mom was the chief mission engineer, so it was her job to make sure everything was totally up to code. She didn't allow for mistakes. She didn't even allow for "margin of error." As she'd said a million times, "In space you get one try to do it right or you're dead." Herc was right; she was intense. She was also almost always right.

"That guy from CNN was riding her pretty hard," said Herc. "All that stuff about sabotage and stuff."

"Not happening." I yawned and stretched. "We have better security than NASA. I'm serious."

"Yeah, maybe," said Herc, "but people are saying that someone's trying to stop you guys from flying."

"People are always saying that."

He shrugged. "Whatever, dude. You're the one who's going to be sitting on a big tank of highly flammable rocket fuel, not me. If you blow up, can I have your Xbox?"

"Don't take this the wrong way, man, but bite me."

"Yeah, yeah."

We stood up. So did the two private security guys who were assigned to me. My dad called them Frick and Frack. Their real names were Kang and Carrieri, but I called them that only when I had to. They were here to protect me and they'd apparently had their personalities surgically removed along with any trace of a sense of humor. On any given day they'd say about ten words to me.

In a strange little pack, we walked off the field and back toward the school. Even from that distance I could hear all those cameras going *click-click-click*.

Chapter 4

I didn't really want to go inside because it was the Wednesday Powwow, which was the insanely corny and culturally insensitive 1950s name they *still* used for the weekly assembly at Madison High. I mean, really?

The big problem was that I *was* the afternoon assembly. Or the star of it, anyway. Since I'd come back to school from underwater training, the principal had approached the Mars One directors and my folks to get permission for me to talk to the other kids. Everyone thought it was a great idea. Terrific PR, a learning experience, blah-blah-blah.

I wasn't crazy about being the center of attention. I wasn't exactly shy, but my ego still fit into the box it came in. Even being part of this mission hadn't made it swell. The mission shrink said I was "remarkably well balanced." If she only knew the stuff that really went on inside my skull I'd get kicked off the trip.

Which Izzy would love.

But I had a great game face. I looked like Joe Middle-America. A healthy, reasonably intelligent, reasonably sane, reasonably okay-looking, reasonably talented sixteen-year-old who some media fruitcake decided should be the "face" of Mars One.

Me.

I mean, it was nuts. There were better-looking people going. Even the other teenage guy, Luther, was hotter than me—or so Izzy's friends kept saying—and both of the teen girls, Zoé and Nirti, were smarter. Actually Zoé was freakishly smart, so maybe she didn't fit into the equation.

Herc and I both knew why I was picked, though, and it had nothing to do with me being the average guy on the mission—or the Everybody, as our mission PR guy kept saying. It wasn't that.

It was because of Izzy.

Because of Izzy and me.

We'd been in love since we were twelve. If I weren't going, then you could bet cash money we'd end up married. Our chemistry was perfect. People saw us together and they started to smile, even if they were having a bad day. Maybe we glowed, I don't know.

We tried to keep our relationship on the DL because it was hard enough between us knowing that there was a sell-by date on what we had. But it got out, because no matter how smart we tried to be with our social media we weren't sly enough. Our bad. Now we were the star-crossed lovers. Paint that in big letters across the sky. That phrase, in one form or another, had been on every news feed, print magazine, cable show, and meme since the story broke.

I was the handsome hero who was going off to conquer a new world.

Izzy was the tragic heroine left behind with a broken heart.

I'm not joking, the media people put it like that. Actually they made it sound even worse than that. There was even an e-book out called *The Girl He Left Behind*. Completely unauthorized, but it had pictures of both of us and all sorts of wild stuff about how this was the greatest love story of the twenty-first century. We got offers from forty different producers to do reality shows, and after telling each other we would never in a million years do something like that, we caved. They put a whole bunch of zeroes on those offers. Izzy would be set for life, and I'd actually be able to donate a big chunk to the Mars One project.

Making tough and complicated decisions like that was part of why the principal and teachers at my school wanted me to talk to the kids in the Powwow. To try and stop the rumor mill from grinding us all down. Like that was going to work.

The other reason was better.

They wanted me to cut through the crap that was all over the Internet about what we were doing and why. The mission PR people put together a 3-D presentation for me with all the right talking points. I agreed as long as the whole thing wasn't about Izzy and me.

She promised me it wouldn't be. Her smile looked like molded plastic when she said that, though.

"Why are you making that face?" asked Herc as we approached the door.

"What face? I'm not making a face."

"Yeah," he said, "you are."

"What kind of face?" I demanded.

"Like you haven't taken a good dump in two months." He clapped me hard on the shoulder. "You got to lighten up, Tris, or you're going to explode long before you crash-land on Mars."

He was laughing as we went inside the building.

I wasn't.

And for the record, I don't make faces. He was way wrong about that.

Chapter 5

The assembly room was packed. Pretty sure every kid at Madison was there; all the teachers, too. The place was crammed with people in every seat, others standing in the aisles. Somewhere a fire marshal was having a meltdown.

Frick and Frack made a path for me through the crowd—sometimes using manners, sometimes glaring nuclear death at people until they got out of the way. They escorted me to the stage, where the principal and all of my teachers waited. The teachers stood in a line to shake my hand, which felt weird. The adults all took the mic to talk about me as if I were someone else, telling the kids I grew up with how special I was, how brave, all that stuff. I stood there and could feel my face grow red-hot. By the time my science teacher got finished talking I wanted to crawl off the stage and hide in the boys' room. I'm not going to call him a liar, but the version of Tristan Hart he was hyping sounded like a cross between Captain America and Stephen Hawking.

Izzy was there in the front row, flanked by her squad of ninja killer girlfriends, all of whom seemed to think I was the world's worst person because I was breaking up with her by fleeing the planet. That's how one of them put it on Twitter. Fleeing the planet.

Jeez.

I smiled down at Izzy and even though she had tears in her eyes and tried to look mad at me, she smiled. Nobody smiles like Izzy. It's everything every corny love song and poem ever said. Sunshine and magic. No wonder her face was on more news feeds than mine.

But then the speeches were over and the applause faded out. A screen dropped from the rafters with a hiss and they dimmed the lights until it was just me and the screen and absolute silence.

"Hi," I said. "Thanks for coming out."

They went nuts. I probably could have said "penguin farts" and gotten the same reaction. That's when I saw the signs. Well, pictures on sticks. Big red disks. Some were painted; some were done in Magic Marker. A few were laser printouts of photos.

Mars.

Hundreds of them, dancing in the dark, lit by cell-phone lights. It was like the whole night sky was filled with nothing but the planet Mars. Here and there I began to see something else. Flashes of white and silver. Spaceships. Some were the *Huginn*, the ship my family would be on, and our sister ship, the *Muninn*. But there were all kinds of ships bobbing up and down. The starship *Enterprise*, the *Millennium Falcon*, TIE fighters, Death Stars, flying saucers.

Some of the kids banged their spaceships into the red planets around them. Making a joke. Silly colonists going to crash into the ugly red planet. Ha-ha. A bunch of kids had their hands up to ask questions even though I hadn't started my talk yet, and some of them just yelled things out.

The principal stood so straight and stiff she looked ten feet tall, and the expression on her face scared everyone into shutting up.

"I appreciate your enthusiasm," she said in a way that meant she clearly *didn't*, "and I'm sure we all want to hear what Mr. Hart has to say. But we will do it in a quiet and dignified manner as befits James Madison Memorial High School."

I caught sight of Herc in the second row, laughing as he mouthed the words *Mr. Hart*.

A row ahead of him, Izzy's girls gave me the same squint-eyed glare as always. Izzy smiled at me, though, and touched her fingertips to a necklace I'd given her last year. It wasn't expensive and it was kind of corny—half a heart, which fit perfectly with the one I wore on a silver chain under my shirt. I touched my shirt over the other half of the heart, to show her I understood. She nodded, still smiling.

Funny how a smile can be beautiful and heartbroken and loving and angry all at the same time.

The room was silent now, so I took my cell phone out of my pocket and connected the Bluetooth to the projector, accessed the mission presentation, and tapped a key. The empty silver screen suddenly turned black, and within seconds stars began appearing. Slow, the way they do when the sun is down but there's still reflected glow hiding the lights. Venus climbed high into the western sky, and Jupiter, too, but not as bright. Saturn hung in the south-southeast. And then the camera panned. It was clearly video from one of the space stations. The curved edge of a planet crept into the right side of the screen. Growing, getting bigger, changing from arc to circle as Earth came into view. Swirls of white clouds, brown landmasses, the green of the big rain forests, and the ten thousand shades of blue of the oceans. The screen had multiple layers for a no-glasses 3-D view, and what the audience saw was a world. Our world. Not distorted by flatness, but massive and round, ripe as a blueberry. It seemed to move outward from the screen and fill the whole auditorium with an image so high-res that you could see the rolling waves on the ocean, the shift and swirl of clouds.

I said, "This is where we live. Earth. This is where our life began."

The image shifted again as the moon crept out from behind it. Much smaller, gray and white and black, pocked with craters from a billion meteors, its dusty coat making it look older than our home world.

I said, "In 1969 three men left Earth and traveled 233,884 miles through space. Two of those men landed on the moon."

The image tightened focus and showed a CGI re-creation of Apollo 11's clunky and awkward lunar module settling down in the Sea of Tranquility. The CGI gave way to actual footage of a foot in a clunky white boot stepping down into soft dust. An audio clip replayed Armstrong's historic words, "One small step for man, one giant leap for mankind."

I said, "Neil Armstrong was the first human being to leave his footprint on another world. Think about that. No one else in the history of . . . well, *history* is going to be able to say that. Imagine how scared he was. Imagine what it took for him to even agree to go, let alone to step out of the lander and put his foot on the surface of the moon." I paused. "I think about that all the time. I have ever since I was little. Thinking about it used to make me cry. Go ahead and laugh, but it's true."

Actually, no one was laughing. The room was absolutely silent.

There was a collage of images now showing Armstrong and Buzz Aldrin placing the American flag on the moon, then other astronauts driving in a moon buggy, and then other missions, including the first Chinese moon landing. This montage ended with a high-def picture of the moon colony base.

"Almost a year ago Chinese astronauts established a base on the moon, making them the first people to colonize a world other than Earth."

The focus tightened to show the layout of the colony—a

big domed structure surrounded by ten smaller habitats, all of them linked by corridors.

"Right now there are more than fifty active space programs around the globe, ranging from NASA here in the States to other government-funded programs to private groups. Some of them are involved in projects to mine asteroids for raw materials. Some are working to build more and better space stations. Within fifteen years there will be six new moon colonies, including an American colony. But the moon is a place to build a base, mine raw materials, and use as a way station to other places. You can't turn the moon into the next home for the human race. It's a dead world. There's no atmosphere, no water ice, and you couldn't terraform it—which means you can't use any kind of science or technology to make it into a mini-Earth. Maybe in a thousand years, but not now. Not with what we know."

Behind me the image changed. The camera began pulling away from the moon, away from Earth, moving fast so they dwindled in size, becoming small, smaller, and then burning as dots no brighter than the millions of stars scattered across the black screen.

"You see those stars?" I asked, still following the script. "Many of them are actually whole galaxies composed of hundreds of millions of stars and maybe ten times as many exoplanets. Worlds so far away we'll never see them, never visit them. There could be life there, civilizations, cultures. But we'll probably never know. It's too far away for us to go and for them to come here."

One point of light began to dominate the sky, growing brighter as the camera moved toward it. The brighter it got, the more the color changed from the blue-white of a star to the rust-colored red of a familiar world.

"This is Mars," I said. "This is the only planet we know of right now—the only planet we can *reach*—where people will be able to live."

I went through the sales pitch for Mars One. I'd heard this stuff a zillion times, and maybe some of the other kids in the audience had read it online or heard about it from the teachers, but even so, everyone was paying attention. Except for the amplified sound of my own voice the big auditorium was dead silent.

I told them that in November, less than two months from now, forty people in two spaceships would take off for Mars. Those ships would be in space for seven months, and then the colonists would descend to the surface in special landers. Habitats would be waiting for us, sent by earlier rockets and assembled by robots. We'd take up residence and from that point on we'd be Martians. We'd live there for the rest of our lives. We'd be the first human beings to set foot on another planet.

I explained that Mars One was an international nonprofit organization that was funded by donations from all over the world. Billions of dollars. The project had kicked off in May 2012, and in 2013 they'd opened it up to volunteers. If anyone expected there to be a shortage of people willing to do this, they were wrong. Thousands and thousands of people applied. Most were cut during the screening rounds. Too old, too fat, too skinny, too sick, too locked up in politics, too crazy, too eager, too emotionally unstable, too antisocial, too social, too indifferent. It's a long list.

People were also cut for reasons that seemed weird until mission doctors explained it. One former basketball player was cut because he had a kidney stone once. That was a big no-no because in micro-g, bones lose mass as calcium is leeched out of them. That increases the risk of kidney stones by a lot, and they're bad enough on Earth. In space a kidney stone could be fatal.

I shifted gears back to how, by 2015, they had the list carved down to one hundred candidates. This Mars 100 went into intense training to build their fitness and health, to sharpen their minds, deepen their knowledge, expand their imaginations, balance their emotions, and hone their judgment. The idea was to send four people up in the first ship, with plenty of supplies being sent before and after. Then twenty-four months later another ship would bring four more people. And on and on. Building the colony slowly. Reducing the overall risk by keeping the number of colonists down.

Then things changed. There were new studies released that

seemed to prove that four people could never make it work. There were more risks associated with a small group, including a lack of manpower if worst-case scenarios required muscle and hands on deck to mine for resources, do emergency repairs on the habitat, or hunt for water sources. So they redesigned the ship to take eight. Then it was twelve. Then twenty.

And then the Keppleburg-Lansky Study was released. That was this massive, multifaceted psychological and sociological study on the potential negative effects of "nongenerational dynamics." What that means is that people would work harder at survival if they were trying to keep their families alive. It meant that there would be a higher quality of life. Or, as Herc once described it to one of the other kids in school, "If you don't have someone to do this stuff for, you're gonna go bongos."

It was the Keppleburg-Lansky Study that opened the door for select families to volunteer for the mission. There was a list of restrictions a mile long. Had to be couples with only one child, and it had to be families where everyone *wanted* to go. If anyone from a candidate family backed out, then the whole family was cut. That was only fair, and in a weird way it helped people think more deeply about their decisions. I know my family did. We talked about it so many times, and we went through it with psychologists, family friends, even neighbors. This wasn't the time for a rash decision. Or, as Dad put it, not the time for a sentimental decision. No one went just because the rest of the family was going, and no one was being pressured into it.

Does that mean we didn't have doubts? Of course we did, we're not insane. There were a lot of times I wanted to bail. Even got as far as talking it over with my folks. They said it was my choice. They could have been mean about it, they could have laid guilt trips on me or pressured me, but they didn't. Just the opposite. They gave me every possible out.

But Mars, man . . . it was out there waiting. And corny as it sounds, it was calling to me.

When I told my folks I was definitely going, we all got a little weepy, and then we got the giggles. Not sure what was funny, but we totally lost it for like a day. First Dad would start laughing and Mom would try to get him to stop, then I'd lose it, and so would she. Next time it was her. Or me.

I went over a lot of this with everyone in the assembly. I could tell from their faces that most of them thought I was totally nuts. Not saying they were wrong.

But . . . I did want to go. And I told them that.

They believed me.

I looked at the faces of the two people in that room who meant the most to me—Izzy and Herc—and I could tell that they believed me too.

Silence fell again and I stood there for a moment, awkward and unsure of what to do next. So I said, "Any questions?"

Everyone started yelling at once.

Chapter 6

The questions came hard and fast and I answered as many as I could.

A tenth grader whose name I didn't know asked, "There's no air on Mars. How are you going to breathe?"

"Good question," I said, because it really was. "Water and compressed air are actually heavier than you'd think and it would take way too much fuel to bring enough for all of the colonists for two years. We'll have enough to get us set up, but our first priority is to build habitats that are also processing plants and labs. They'll not only keep us safe, but it's how we're going to produce breathable air and drinkable water. There's plenty of water ice on Mars and mining that water is the key to people being able to live there."

"What if there's not enough?" asked another kid.

"There's enough," I said with more confidence than I felt. *Cerberus*, our Mars rover, had absolutely proved that there was water ice on Mars, but we were warned that we would need to actually *be* there to prove that we could mine it, melt and purify it, draw oxygen from it through electrolysis, and filter large quantities for drinking, hygiene, cooking, cleaning, and about a thousand other uses. "There's also water ice in the regolith, which is what they call the Martian soil. We'll extract it, and we'll get nitrogen and argon from the air." I explained that the air humans breathe isn't pure oxygen but a mix of gasses. The rover's sensors found the presence of the gasses we needed to make a breathable mix in the thin Martian atmosphere.

A girl from my homeroom asked, "Tris, I keep reading about all the radiation. Won't you all get cancer?"

"That's not the plan," I said. "And that's another reason we need the water, because our habitats and space suits are designed to use water as radiation shielding."

"I heard you were going to live in caves," said a kid from my gym class. He said it like an accusation, though.

"Sure. Caves will protect us against radiation too. And from temperature shifts. But first we have to find good ones."

"What's a *bad* cave like?" asked a girl I didn't know.

"Too shallow, not enough flat ground, unstable rocks. We want a shelter not an adventure." That line was cribbed from one of our training sessions, but it got a laugh, so I stole it.

"What about terrorists?" asked someone from the back, and that stilled the room for a moment. "What if those Neo-Luddite guys try to blow up your spaceships?"

I took a moment deciding what to say, and I could feel the weight of everyone staring at me. Our mission PR people didn't want us to talk about the Neo-Luddites at all, but I couldn't just blow him off.

"Look," I said, "if you're asking me if I'm scared of the Neo-Luddites doing something, then sure. Who isn't? We all are. But if you're asking if I think they *will* do something . . . then no. I really don't. We have great security and we have—"

Herc cut me off by yelling at the top of his lungs: *"Mama Hart will kick their ass!"*

Everyone burst out laughing and then began applauding. Everyone knew what my mom was like. I saw one of the teachers pushing through the crowd toward Herc, eyes shooting laser beams. Herc was going to log some detention time for that, but knowing him, he'd think it was worth it.

There were more questions after it all settled down. Questions about the ships, about why Mars is red (iron oxide), if there are canals (no), are there people (not as far as we could tell and probably not), if there's anything alive there (we hoped to find bacteria or something), about the geology (Olympus Mons is the largest volcano in the solar system and the second-highest known mountain), how long the days are (24 hours, 39 minutes, 35.244 seconds), how long the Martian year is (687 Earth days), would I be able to see Earth from Mars (yes, it would be a small white dot), about why we were going (we were running out of room on Earth), about the technology (it was badass), about everything from what we were going to eat to how we take a dump in zero g. Sometimes the questions got even more personal—like about how I could leave Earth, how I could leave my friends, about religion, about Izzy. I passed on some questions and got booed by a few bozos, but I answered as much as I could for as long as I could. But it was clear that I was going to crash long before they ran out of questions.

Finally the principal stepped up and did her air-patting thing until the room went quiet again. She held up a stapled sheaf of papers and said it was a timeline I'd created so everyone would understand how the Mars One thing worked. "The entire file will be on the school website, so make sure to download."

I was beat, sweating, trembling a little. Izzy looked like she wanted to drag me off the stage and run away with me to hide. Sounded good to me.

Then Herc shouted out a question and it froze the room. "Tristan—are you going to forget us?"

It felt like a punch to the heart, and from the look on Herc's face it was obvious his question surprised him, too. Everyone looked at me, wanting an answer. No . . . they needed one, and at that moment I couldn't explain why.

I needed that same answer.

I came to the edge of the stage and looked at Herc, at Izzy, at the sea of faces. All the kids I knew and those I'd never get to know.

"No," I said. "I'm never going to forget you. I'm still going to have e-mail, vid-chat, and all that. You guys are my friends and you always will be. Distance isn't going to change that.

One way or another I'm going to take you all with me."

Silence washed over the room like the ocean surf. They stared at me. The teachers stared too. Herc stood up first and raised his hands above his head. He let loose with a piercing cry. "Wooooooooooot!" And then he began clapping. Hard, heavy, fast.

Soon everyone was on their feet and there was new thunder.

In the front row only one person wasn't standing or applauding. Izzy was folded down into her seat, bent forward with her face in her hands. I couldn't hear the sound of her sobs. But I felt every single one of them.

Mars One Timeline
By Tristan Hart
James Madison Memorial High School
Madison, Wisconsin

In 2011, Dutch entrepreneurs Bas Lansdorp and Arno Wielders decided they wanted to realize their dream of establishing the first human colony on Mars. Some people thought they were nuts and said so all over social media. But the naysayers were the minority. Most people thought they were brilliant visionaries. My dad says they were a little of both, but since we're going to Mars on their ships, apparently we are too.

2012: Lansdorp and Wielders created Mars One, a nonprofit international corporation to facilitate the Martian colonization project. They held meetings with several major governmental and private aerospace component suppliers in the USA, Canada, Italy, and the United Kingdom. This was the phase where they worked out the budget (big), timetable (short), and logistics (insanely complicated) to make their dream a reality.

2013: The official Mars One Astronaut Selection Program was launched at a pair of press conferences in New York and Shanghai. Potential candidates were invited to apply online. Hundreds of thousands of people applied. There were several increasingly challenging layers of screening and testing to find those candidates best suited to the project. Candidates underwent physical and psychological testing and participated in solo and group challenges. The Mars One astronauts had to be able to endure the hardships, learn the science, and work as a team but also show that they could function independently. It was a lot easier to get cut from the program than to make it to the next round.

This was when my family joined the team, but they were put on a kind of standby. They had a kid and wanted to bring me along, but the Keppleburg-Lansky Study hadn't been released yet. If the study hadn't come out in favor of families going, then we wouldn't have one-way tickets to Mars.

So, meet the family.

My mom, Jean Stettner-Hart, is a PhD professor of mechanical engineering who's logged a lot of time on the International Space Station (ISS) and in all kinds of low-orbit space missions. She was a contractor for NASA and advised them on their moon projects, and she worked for Elon Musk's SpaceX. (Insider tip: SpaceX is our biggest competitor even though Mars One leases rockets and launch sites from them and hired them to build our two transit vehicles—the *Muninn* and the *Huginn*.) My dad, Cornelius Hart, is a botanist. He's also been in space a lot, working to prove that he can grow just about anything, even in micro-g.

2017: The candidates began full-time training, and it was really tough. During that phase the Mars One team had to identify those candidates who were the best choices to be on the first colony ship. They were separated into groups and trained in extreme locations on Earth that offer challenges as close as possible to those on the planet Mars. That included reduced-gravity training underwater and in isolation in places like a submersible, an island, and the Arctic desert.

This was also the year the Mars One project underwent a kind of growth spurt. Instead of sending four people up in one rocket, the project was expanded to send forty in two much bigger rockets. And that's when my parents got approval to have me come along. They told me this on my tenth birthday. Some kids get skateboards or pool parties for their birthday. I got to become an astronaut.

2020: They launched the Mars-bound demonstration mission and the communication satellite. This was done to prove to investors—and everyone else, I guess—that the Mars One project could successfully launch a spacecraft and put it in stable orbit around Mars. The payload included the first Mars One communication satellite has since relayed videos, telemetry, and other data from the Martian surface. We learned a lot from that satellite.

2022: Our second launch sent up a rover that's like a more advanced version of *Curiosity*, which NASA launched in 2011. Ours has a whole different set of instruments and tools aboard and better communication equipment. The new rover surveyed the terrain and nearby cave systems so the mission planners could pick the best possible location to establish our colony. The rover did tons more tests on the radiation in different areas to look for ice in the Martian regolith (soil). It also explored the liquid water NASA detected on the surface of some mountain slopes.

2024: Six cargo missions were launched. This was our main haul of equipment and supplies. The payloads included another rover, two big living units (habitats or "habs"), a couple of life-support units, and tons of food and equipment.

2025: All of the cargo landed safely on Mars. Whew! They landed about ten kilometers from what will be our outpost. The rover located each payload and collected the equipment. Once the second rover was activated, they set up the outpost for us so that we'll have a place to live when we get there. The rovers have all sorts of mechanical arms and are synched with autodeployment systems built into the cargo payloads. The rovers are slow, though, which is why they were sent up more than a year before we even take off. One of the most important jobs for the rovers is activating the Environmental Control and Life Support System (ECLSS). Just charging the batteries that will run life support in the hab takes months. The rovers also set up solar panels to act as backups to the hab batteries. The habs themselves are inflatable, and no, they aren't like bouncy castles you see at carnivals.

The ECLSS will extract water from the regolith by evaporating the subsurface ice particles in an oven. The evaporated water is condensed back to its liquid state and stored. Some of the water will be used to produce oxygen. Other gasses, like nitrogen and argon, will also be collected directly from the Martian atmosphere to mix with the oxygen because what we humans breathe is nowhere near pure oxygen. It's a mix of gasses. Earth air is 78 percent nitrogen, less than 1 percent argon, and the rest is oxygen. The ECLSS needs time to collect those gasses, mix them, and store enough for the colonists once we get there.

The rovers will also collect tons of regolith and use it to cover the habs as radiation shielding. Mars doesn't have an ozone layer, which means radiation is always going to be much higher. Dirt, even Martian dirt, will help keep us safe.

2026: The first crew to land on Mars starts their journey from Earth. That's us. The Mars Transit Vehicle will be sent up into near-Earth orbit in stages and assembled by a team at a space station called the Lucky Eight. My mom is the chief mechanical engineer—known in the biz as a "toolpush"—so she'll oversee the assembly of the transit vehicles.

Cargo for the second crew is launched to Mars in the same month we take off. The next wave of colonists will launch a year after we head out into the big black.

2027: We land on Mars. Wish us luck!

Chapter 7

Izzy was waiting for me by my locker, surrounded by the ninja death squad. As I went over, one of her girlfriends said something behind her hand, but Izzy shook her head. The clan of doom moved reluctantly away, but they gave me stares that I'm pretty sure took a full year off my life. I told Frick and Frack to give me a moment and they took up station across the hall.

Izzy turned to me, shaking her head. "This is all so surreal, isn't it?"

"It's definitely not normal," I agreed.

Her eyes were red from crying but she'd fixed her makeup and brushed her black hair. We hugged and when Izzy put her forehead against my chest I could feel how hot she was from crying. Then she pushed back from me, sniffed, and gave me a rueful smile.

"All I ever do is cry," she said. "I'm such a stereotype."

"You have the best heart," I said. What I didn't add was, *and I'm breaking it.* That would be too obvious, and it would be lame.

"You were great in there," she said. "Smart and funny."

"I rambled a lot."

"You did. A little. But everyone needed to hear that stuff, Tris." She cocked her head. "You get that, don't you? You get why they need to hear this from you?"

"I think so."

Izzy leaned against the row of lockers. She wore a pale yellow tank top under a loose white cotton blouse, old blue jeans, and boat shoes with a flower pattern. She looked ready for a walk on a boardwalk, but Madison, Wisconsin, was a long way from the ocean. She had a few little braids hidden in the ink-black waves of her hair, which I said that I liked once, so she did that for me. She was so pretty and looking at her always made me smile.

Well, almost always.

"We've been hearing about this in the news and in homeroom for years," she said. "Ever since we all knew you. But it's not real, or it wasn't, I guess. I mean, you're here for part of the school year and part of the summer, you're back for Christmas and Thanksgiving, but mostly you're gone. Most of the time you're a face on TV or on the Internet. They even sell mugs and hats and T-shirts with your face on them. The president talked about you during the State of the Union address. So . . . you're not really real to everyone, Tris. And what you're doing is definitely not real."

I started to say something but she shook her head. She wasn't finished.

"That all changed in there," she said, nodding toward the

open doors to the empty assembly hall. "You couldn't have had that conversation with everyone one at a time. But somehow you managed to talk to all of us like *we* mattered, like *we* were part of it."

"I—"

"And at the end? When Herc asked that question? God! I wanted to kill him because that could have messed it all up."

"No, it was a good question," I said.

"That's exactly what I mean. It's the question everyone's afraid to ask you. But everyone's *wanted* to ask. Even the people who don't love you. Even people who don't really *know* you. You're going to another planet. You're one of us but you're leaving us forever. I know it's hard for you and it's scary and intimidating, but it's hard for us, too. Not just me and Herc, but everyone. How are we supposed to think about things, about the ordinary details in our lives, about day-to-day stuff, when someone we know has left us and walked right into a history book?" She turned to rest her back against the cool metal of the locker and then kicked backward. "I'm not saying this right."

"Yes you are. Herc's been saying it for weeks. I'm the ultimate story topper. I'm a hometown kid who went to live on Mars."

Izzy's blue eyes searched mine. "That's only part of it. And it's not normal grief. Not like when Billy Carlin died."

Billy was a senior who'd gone to his older brother's college frat party, gotten drunk, and then run his car into a tree at ninety miles an hour. Billy was in a coma for three weeks and then died. Billy had been one of those kids everyone thought would be something. Smart, and he knew everything about computers. Then he was gone, taking all of his potential with him and cutting all his connections with the rest of the kids at school. It was hard, and it was scary because some of the kids I knew were starting to drink. Billy's death could have been any of them. It wasn't the teachers, cops, and special assemblies that made nearly everybody pull back from drinking like booze was radioactive. It was the thought of Billy being killed. We all saw the car on the news.

"I'm not dying," I said. "And this mission isn't me doing something irresponsible."

"No," she said, her face getting a little red. "It's you doing something they don't understand. And stop being dense because that's not what I'm talking about anyway. I'm trying to tell you that you *helped* everyone today. Saying that you'd stay in touch and all . . . that really meant something."

I pretended to punch buttons on my phone. "I'll text ya."

"No, I mean it, I'm serious," insisted Izzy. "You need to do what you said you'd do. You need to talk to us."

I nodded, getting it. "I'm playing around now, Iz, but I wasn't messing with them. Or with you. I'm always going to stay in touch."

I looked around. The hall was mostly empty because the

next period had already started. Frick and Frack stood like statues, their eyes staring at nothing but probably seeing everything. Not sure if they could hear our conversation or not. It bugged me that it was so hard to have any real privacy. But then again, once we left Earth we'd be leaving privacy behind too.

Izzy's cell tinkled to let her know she had a text. She looked at the screen, then sighed, long and heavy.

"Let me guess," I said. "The interview?"

She made a face that was equal parts disgust and anxiety. "The interview."

I sighed too.

Mars One was funded by all sorts of donations, grants, and crowdfunding events, but the biggest chunks of money were from the producers of television shows. There are all kinds of deals in place. Some for the general mission, others based on aspects of it—there's even a show about gardening that my dad and another botanist do. There are shows about the engineering, the philosophy, the history of Mars, and space programs in general. And on and on. More than half of the crew members have contracts for their own shows, separate from the ones directly licensed by Mars One. Like the one Izzy and I have. A lot of agents and lawyers are making a lot of money keeping it all straight. Depending on how the deals were cut, some of us are contractually required to split the income with Mars One and some are merely encouraged to be generous.

Most of us are cool with donating because, hey, the more money the group has, the more supplies, modern tech, and support we'll have on the mission. Bottom line is that without those shows we'd all be staying here on Earth watching reruns of old *Star Trek* episodes.

Izzy originally said she would rather be eaten by a pack of rabid Yorkies than ever even consider being part of a reality show.

But . . .

One of the cable stations made her the kind of offer that takes your breath away. Two million dollars for the first year, and depending on ratings, a big jump from there. The potential was forty to sixty million, which included money from product endorsements.

I know she didn't want to do it. The whole reality show thing seemed cheap and intrusive and a billion miles away from "real." But . . . millions of dollars? That money would change everything. She would be set. She'd have the best of everything. College, a house. She could travel, which is something she always wanted to do but her family couldn't afford. All of that would change if she said yes. The show would follow her life after I left. But the deal had a catch. Izzy had to get me to agree to a series of interviews before the launch date. The story, the producers insisted, was Izzy *and* Tristan. They said they needed me for context and validity and other crap. Izzy didn't want to ask me, I know that. So yeah, I signed on and *Tristan and Izzy* became a real show.

Tonight was the first of the interviews. Sigh. Just because you make the right choice doesn't mean you have to be happy about it.

Izzy said, "I'm sorry."

"It's all cool. We'll be amazing. We'll act like movie stars and the TV people will fall all over themselves."

"You're crazy."

"Look at my life choices," I said. "I'd have to be out of my mind."

That made her laugh so I kissed her. Nothing too crazy because Frick and Frack were still there. A peck. She moved her head forward as I pulled back, wanting more. So did I. Her eyes said, *Later.* I grinned my answer.

The whole school seemed to go quiet except for the low, muffled jumble of teacher voices behind closed doors.

"Don't you have a class now?" I asked.

She gave me a sour look. "They gave me a note. I think they felt bad for me. So I'm allowed to take the rest of the afternoon off."

"Cool."

"They always let *you* take off early," she said, and punched me lightly on the chest.

"That's because I'm a spaceman hero, champion of the people, and media superstar." I gave her my best celebrity smile. The fake one I use for photo ops. All bright white teeth, lantern jaw, and deep-water tan. Herc says it makes me look like a used-car salesman, but what does he know?

"Oh, please." Izzy laughed. She grabbed my head in both hands and pulled me in for another quick kiss. "I'm hungry. Feed me."

"Steak and lobster at the best restaurant in town?"

"No. Something greasy and fried. I need hot sauce and salt and gluten and dairy and saturated fats and lots of cholesterol."

"I'm not supposed to eat that sort of stuff, you know."

She gave me a wicked grin. "Do you care?"

"No," I said, "I pretty much don't."

We ran laughing out of the building and into the parking lot, where a black SUV was parked.

Chapter 8

So, okay . . . I guess I need to talk about the whole "Tristan and Isolde" thing. Let's get a few things straight.

First, everyone who interviewed us asked if we started going out together because of our names. That answer is no. Big honking no. I never even heard of the story of Tristan and Isolde until after we'd been going out for two years. I mean, it's not like they teach twelfth-century French poetry in middle school. Did I know the story now? Sure. Everyone who knew it had told me one version or another. In the old poem, Tristan was a young knight from Cornwall, England, who fell in lust with Iseult (one of the spelling variations), who was an Irish princess. They drank a potion that made them fall madly in love, but they never really got to spend their lives together. And they died unhappy and heartbroken.

The History Channel did a whole special about it, complete with clips of us from the news and studio interviews. They pointed out that it's probably based on an eleventh-century Persian story about Vis and Rāmin, and it's possible it influenced the origins of the legend about Lancelot and Guinevere. On the special they tried to make all these parallels between what Izzy and I have and what happened in the story. It's a real stretch.

In some of the stories Tristan and Iseult get together in the end. In most they die, apart or in each other's arms. There's betrayal, adultery, murder, and all of that.

That's not Izzy and me.

Chapter 9

The interview was set up in Izzy's living room, which Mrs. Drake had cleaned so hard everything looked like real people didn't actually live there. The network techs had lights set up and power cords stretched everywhere. The whole Drake family was dressed in "casual" clothes, which means they were clothes picked by the wardrobe staff to make them look like ordinary folks. They *are* ordinary folks, but no one on TV is allowed to look *ordinary* ordinary. They have to look *TV* ordinary, which isn't the same thing. TV ordinary makes everyone look like uncomfortable plastic people.

The director put Izzy and me on the couch and put a box of tissues on the side table nearest me. The idea, I knew, was for me to have to hand her a tissue every time she got emotional. Exploitive and obvious? Yup.

"I'm *not* going to cry," growled Izzy, but her eyes were already wet.

The reporter who was interviewing us was pretty famous. Her name was Mindy; she was a scholarship kid at MIT who became a runway superstar, then the host of a reality competition show about robotics and AI. She was smart, no doubt, but the show was ruthless. You know the kind, where all the contestants go from being "wow, it's so cool we're on TV" to trash-talking each other as they get closer to the finale. Whatever. The ratings made Mindy a reality show star.

My folks sat in the dining room, but they could see us from the table. Mom had the kind of blank face you see on TV shows about poker champs. Dad had his notebook out and was doing a drawing of the flower arrangement on the table. What's the expression? Same planet, different worlds. They had to do reality show stuff too, and they did a good job with it—Mom was always very technical and kind of dry; Dad talked about plants as if they were philosophical concepts and made a lot of jokes. They understood the need for the shows in terms of funding, exposure, and support for Mars One, but when it came to *Tristan and Izzy*, neither of them was happy with it. They thought it was too much of an intrusion into my life, even taking into account the financial benefits for Izzy. Dad called it a necessary evil. Hard to argue.

Herc sat halfway up the stairs. He wasn't scheduled for an interview, so he was dressed in raggedy jeans, flip-flops, and an ancient Milwaukee Bucks tank top that used to belong to his grandfather.

"Okay, if we're all ready?" said Mindy brightly.

Izzy took a breath and said, "Yes."

I grunted.

The lights came on and the cameras began recording.

Chapter 10

Mindy started out slow. Kind of nice. Like in boxing where the other guy taps with a few light halfhearted jabs to see how you're going to move. That way he knows where to plant that hard right.

"Izzy," she said, "you've known Tristan since the seventh grade. Were you friends from the start?"

"No," Izzy said. "We were in some of the same classes."

"He was famous even then, though, wasn't he?"

"Sure. Everyone knew about Tristan Hart. He's always been in the news. Ever since they announced the four families that would be part of the Mars thing."

"How'd that make you feel? Knowing someone who was famous?"

Izzy shrugged, then grunted softly when Mindy flared her eyes. Izzy jerked as she realized she hadn't actually answered the question. The interview wasn't going out live, but we'd been told to give "full and complete" answers. No grunts, no silences, no dead air.

"How'd I feel? God, I hated him at first," Izzy said.

Mindy jumped on that like a cat on a limping mouse. "You *hated* Tristan? Why was that?"

"He was so egotistical." As she said that I caught just a hint of that little Izzy smile I knew so well. "He was all 'Look at me, I'm going to Mars. I'm going to be famous. I'm special.'"

Izzy paused, but there was something about that pause that prevented Mindy from jumping in.

"But then," said Izzy, "I got to know him." Another pause, during which she cut a look at me, then glanced at Mindy, and then looked right into the camera. "And it was all an act."

"An act . . . ?" prompted Mindy.

"Sure. Tris was acting tough, acting big, but it was all hype, all show."

"And why would he act like that?"

"Because he was scared out of his mind. Why else?"

The camera shifted from her to focus more tightly on my face. Mindy looked like she was going to have kittens right there on the floor. Happy ratings kittens.

"Does that make you angry, Tristan?" she asked. "People always talk about how brave you are. What do you think about Izzy saying that you were scared? *Were* you scared? Are you?"

Maybe there was a better PR way to handle it. I'm sure the mission people would have wanted me to use one of the zillion scripted responses they gave to everyone on the crew. I knew a lot of them by heart, and I'd used a bunch.

But using them now would feel like a cheat. Besides, these people wanted a "reality" show, so maybe they should get that. Something real. Izzy's comments already started it spinning that way.

I said, "Of course I was scared. I was scared then, I'm scared now, and I'm pretty sure I'm going to be scared for the rest of my life. I have nightmares about this stuff. I'll probably have nightmares while we're in space. Even if I were an adult, I know I'd be scared. Everyone on this trip is terrified. We're using tech that no one's really proved yet. We're doing something no one's ever done. How could we not be scared?"

"We talked about this a lot," said Izzy, shifting her focus back to Mindy, making it a conversation. Selling it. "When we first started getting interested in each other, we talked about it. About how dangerous it was."

"Dangerous in what way?" asked Mindy.

"In every way, I suppose. Once we started hanging out, we knew we liked each other. A lot."

"A lot," I agreed.

"And we knew that it was kind of stupid to get involved because there was no . . . no . . ." Izzy fished for the word.

"No 'hope'?" suggested Mindy, but Izzy shook her head.

"That's not it. There was nowhere to go with it. We tried to be adult about it. I mean, we're still kids, so I guess we're still trying to be adult about this. The thing is, though, I'm not sure being 'adult' would really be any better. Tristan's introduced me to a lot of the other crew members. We've been to parties with them and lectures. And we had separation counseling sessions. Those were mostly for people who were leaving family behind, but I asked if I could go too."

"And they let you?"

"Of course they did. The mission people aren't cruel. It's not like they're trying to kidnap Tristan and everyone else. They seem to understand how bad this is going to feel once the rockets take off. They're trying to do whatever they can. It's just that . . . well, what can anyone really do? I love Tristan and he loves me, but in two months he's going to go and there's nothing that will change that. In two months I'm going to be here and all I'll ever see of him is on a video screen."

Mindy had a look on her face that would have scared a great white shark. "And how does that make you feel?"

Izzy seemed ready to answer the question, but then she hit a speed bump. We'd both known this would be tough but we'd talked about it so much that maybe we tricked ourselves into thinking we had it locked. Now that we were saying it, though, in front of her folks and mine, in front of Herc, in front of the camera crew and Mindy—and knowing this would be edited and shown to millions of people—it suddenly got bigger. More real. Instead of walking through a minefield where we knew how and where they'd placed the mines, it suddenly felt like walking barefoot on broken glass.

"It makes me feel like he's dying," said Izzy. "It makes me feel like I'm dying too."

A tear broke and fell down Izzy's cheek and she brushed it angrily away.

And yeah, I handed her a damn tissue.

Chapter 11

Herc walked home with me. His family lived one block over from mine. We took the long route, neither of us in a hurry.

After a couple of silent blocks, Herc said, "I saw the interview with that Indian chick, Nirti, last night. Did you watch it?"

"No."

"You've met her though, right?"

"Like a thousand times."

Herc nodded. "She's hot."

"I guess."

He cut me a look. "Don't even, Tris. You can't tell me you're so hung up on Izzy that you can't see how smoking hot Nirti is. The other one too. The blonde. Wow. No way you can look me in the eye and tell me they're not insanely hot. Both of them."

"I didn't say they weren't, but—"

"You and them, in a little spaceship. You can't tell me you won't be thinking about hooking up. Maybe not now, but sometime." We walked for half a block. "You know that's what *they've* got to be thinking," he said. "Either you and Nirti or you and what's her name?"

"Zoé."

He shrugged. "Zoé, whatever. You know they're hoping you'll hook up with one of those girls. And by 'they' I mean the mission people."

"I don't think so."

"Why not? You're going to colonize a planet, dude. Someone's got to hook up and make a bunch of little Martian rug rats."

"First . . . no. And second, there's another guy, you know," I said. "Luther Mbede."

"Yeah, yeah, I know," said Herc. "They had his interview two weeks ago. African dude."

"South African," I corrected. "He's Zulu, which is part of the—"

"Nguni people. Right. Like I said, I saw him." Herc stooped and picked up an empty plastic Coke bottle, rose, jumped, turned, and made a shot into a trash can on the corner. "And he scores!"

I made hissing sounds like crowds cheering. We continued walking.

"That Luther kid's better looking than you."

"That's not news."

"He'll get first pick of those girls."

"You say that, man, but you haven't met those girls. Nobody's going to *pick* either of them. Besides . . . it's not a meat market, you know. And they're not sending us all that way just so we can hook up."

He laughed and shook his head. "Dude, sometimes you are so dumb."

"No, man, it's just that you don't understand the science. They really don't want us to have kids up there. I'm not saying 'ever,' but not anytime soon. Not until we figure out how."

He stopped and stared at me with a half smile on his mouth. "Um, say, son, do you want to have *the* talk? You know, the whole facts of life? You see, when a man and a woman love each other they—"

"No, dumbass, I'm saying we don't think it's *safe*."

"Safe? You lost me. Are we talking alien STDs?"

"No," I said, and explained that one of the mission candidates was cut last year because her religion didn't allow her to use any kind of contraception, and as of now there was no known way for a woman outside of Earth's atmosphere and gravity to carry to term with even a tiny guarantee of delivering a healthy, normal baby. There were apparently a lot of theories about how microgravity would prevent bones, nerves, and other tissues from forming. My point is that the colonists who went were supposed to live there but not to breed there. Not until they knew we could have normal pregnancies and healthy babies.

He thought about that and looked sad for a moment. "Wow. That really kind of sucks."

"I know."

"No, wait, this whole thing is about *colonizing* Mars, right? Or did I miss something?"

"That's the plan."

"Without babies? Without reproducing? Don't get me wrong, Tris, but that is the stupidest idea I ever heard of."

"It's complicated," I said. "They're pretty sure they *will* figure it all out, it's just that they don't have those answers yet."

He looked pretty upset. "One minute I'm thinking this is an interplanetary booty call and now you're telling me this?"

"They'll figure it out," I insisted.

"Yeah, but what if they don't? What if you're all sitting up there and they don't science up a solution? What are they going to do then—keep sending bunches of people to replace those who die off? How's that *colonizing* anything?"

I didn't have an answer to that. None of us did. The scientists here on Earth and the ones going with us seemed convinced there would be answers. Practical answers. And soon. But "soon" is a weird word and it doesn't have a shelf life.

We stopped outside my house. There was a SOLD card in the slot of the wooden Realtor's sign. We stood there for a moment, looking at it.

"Getting close," he said after a while.

"I know."

Overhead the stars were as bright as headlights. Herc

sighed and punched me lightly on the arm. "See you tomor-row, Tris."

"Yeah," I said, "see you."

I walked up the three steps to my porch and turned to wave at him, but Herc had his back to me. He was staring at the SOLD card. Then, without saying a word, he slapped it out of the slot and let it fall to the grass. He walked away without looking back.

I let the card lie where it had fallen.

Chapter 12

That night I lay on my bed with the lights off and music playing. It was a playlist Izzy made for me last summer. One hundred tracks of space and science-fiction music. Most of it was stuff I'd never heard of and would never even have bothered to listen to if it wasn't for me going into space. Some of it really old, some of it funny, some of it pretty weird, some of it corny, and some of it like a knife in the chest.

Was it masochistic of me to keep playing it? Maybe. I don't know. I was taking the playlist with me.

The last crickets of the season were pulsing in the darkness outside my bedroom window. Downstairs I heard Dad say something and Mom laugh. Couldn't hear what he said, but she laughed really loud and kept laughing for a long time. No one else I knew could make Mom laugh. It was hard enough to get her to crack a smile. Dad could, though. He was quiet and off in his own head a lot of the time, but it didn't mean he wasn't paying attention and didn't know what was going on.

They were so different that it was sometimes hard to understand how they ever fell in love. Maybe it was Dad's sense of humor and the optimism that came with it.

Besides, we'd all need to be able to laugh on Mars, too.

All the lights were off in my room and I was sprawled on the bed staring up at the cosmos. Stars and planets swirling across my ceiling.

It was something Mom rigged up for my twelfth birthday and I never took it down. A little laser projector sat on top of my bookcase and it splashed the image in a continuous loop. It was the stars as seen from Mars, a high-def video capture from one of the rovers. Earth was a tiny white light. The sun was larger, but not much.

The song that was playing was from some guy who used to be famous a long time ago. Elton John. The song was "Rocket Man." I sang along with it 'cause I'd heard it a hundred times. The singer was saying how Mars wasn't a good place to raise kids. Jeez.

Mom's laughter died away downstairs. The crickets were a soft background sound, and somehow they seemed to work their way into the song.

I lay there and sang the old song. Softly, though.

Not too loud.

Chapter 13

September burned away so fast.

I spent as much time as I could with Izzy. And with Herc. The closer we got to the launch date, though, the harder it was getting for all of us.

Mom kept trying to divert me from being morose by giving me weird technical problems to solve. One day I came home from school and found a note telling me to go down to the basement. The washing machine was completely disassembled. Every single part down to the last nut and screw. And not laid out nice and neat. The parts were all mixed up. And there, sitting on top of my toolbox, was a timer. She'd rigged it to start counting down as soon as the cellar light went on. There was a note.

Fix it.

That's Mom. She'd allowed me four hours to fix the thing. I did it in three hours and twenty-two minutes. She came home while I was cleaning my tools, put a load in the washer, added soap and softener, kissed me on the cheek, and went upstairs.

A couple days later I found she'd done the same thing to

the big-screen TV in the den. Only this time she'd deliberately broken three really important parts. When she came
home Dad and I were watching last night's DVR'd episode of
Tristan and Izzy. He'd helped me dismantle Mom's computer
down to the last microchip.

Life at my house.

Chapter 14

Izzy and I recorded more than twenty episodes of our show.

That's a weird thing to say. *Our* show.

And we were hits, too. We hit the number one slot with episode seven.

We were five minutes into episode twenty, where Izzy and I were at the Madison High Reach for the Stars Fall Carnival. Mindy told us the show would be about nostalgia. She wanted Izzy and me to walk around the carnival and go on some rides so they could get B-roll of us having fun. She said they'd edit it into a montage. Corny, but we understood what they wanted. Since they couldn't get footage of us during the last couple of years of our relationship, they wanted to see us having fun and being "normal kids." Herc was there with that week's girlfriend, Spice, a black girl who'd moved out here from Philadelphia. She played field lacrosse and had the most infectious laugh I'd ever heard. And, yes, Spice was her real name, which I thought was incredibly cool.

There were some protestors outside, because there were *always* freaking protestors. But there were a lot of cops and a lot of security provided by Mindy's producers. I saw one guy with a red Neo-Luddite scarf and a MARS IS DEATH placard, but a minute later I saw that a cop with a big German shepherd was following the guy to keep an eye on him. Nothing happened.

Actually, for the first, like, ninety minutes of the carnival the producers let us have some fun. There were rides, including a Tilt-A-Whirl, which I dug and Izzy did not, and a great haunted house, which Izzy loved but which made me jump halfway out of my skin. We dropped some cash to play the game where you pop balloons with darts and I won a stupid-looking stuffed penguin for Izzy, but she gave it to a little girl whose dad couldn't hit the board let alone the balloons.

Because Mindy's people were using those ultracompact digital cameras, they were able to put a dozen camera people in the crowd and caught everything: us, our friends, the goofy space decorations all around the place. The carnival was set up in the sports field and spilled over into the parking lot. It was a dollar to get in and the money was for a food bank, so the organizers were happy with the enormous crowd that showed up.

The trouble started when the handlers brought us over to where Mindy was waiting. There was a crowd of people around her and five of the production team's camera techs.

"Uh-oh," said Izzy when we were still twenty feet away.

I said, "Yikes."

"Make a diversion so I can escape."

"Nice try, but if I have to do this, so do you."

"I hate you."

"I know."

She squeezed my hand and we walked over to Mindy, who met us with open arms, like she hadn't seen us in years.

"Tristan and Izzy," she cried, and from her tone it was clear her mic was on and this was all part of the show. "I hope you've been having a wonderful time here at the Madison High Reach for the Stars Fall Carnival."

The crowd clapped and yelled and whistled. I saw that Herc and Spice were front and center. He had a funny look in his eyes. Almost a warning, but there was no time to give me any real message. It was too late for that.

"We have a special surprise for you both," said Mindy brightly, which caused Izzy to squeeze the bones in my hand hard enough to hurt. Mindy shifted her focus to me. "Tristan, since this is your last carnival on Earth, and your last week of school before you begin final training for the Mars One colony mission . . . I thought you'd like to have the chance to say good-bye to some of the special people in your life."

I was totally unable to say anything. I think there was a grin on my face, but it was probably a wince. My heart started hammering.

"Tristan, perhaps you will remember Tommy Callahan?" said Mindy triumphantly, and she yanked a skinny kid out of the crowd with all the flourish of a magician pulling a rabbit from a hat.

"Hey, Tris," said Tommy.

"Tommy—?"

He grinned shyly and offered his hand. I shook it, then before either of us knew it we were hugging and slapping each other on the back.

I heard Mindy telling the crowd and the TV audience that Tommy Callahan was my first friend back in pre-K and all the way through second grade, but that his family had moved away. I never heard from Tommy again, and now here he was.

Maybe if it was just Tommy we could have had some fun talking about the trouble we got into in first grade. But it wasn't just Tommy.

It was eight other kids from grade school, the twins who used to live next door to me, several of my teachers from grade and middle school, the entire soccer team from our old neighborhood, and the old lady whose grass I used to mow. The girl who I liked in sixth grade, and the girl I liked after that, and the girl who introduced Izzy and me.

With Tommy it was a real surprise. Fun and heartbreaking, but mostly great.

Then the fun went away. Izzy kept trying to get between me and those people, and Herc did too. But Mindy owned this moment and we were under contract and the reunion went on and on.

The version you probably saw on TV was cut down to an

hour. Less if you count commercials and the carnival montage. But the whole thing lasted for two or three thousand years. They call it ambush journalism. I call it mean. Mindy knew it embarrassed me too.

I remember once in English class, when the teacher was talking about the different kinds of journalism, she said there was an old expression news reporters used. It explained how they picked the kinds of stories that would get the best ratings:

"If it bleeds, it leads."

And Mindy came at me with a knife.

Chapter 15

Herc, Spice, Izzy, and I sat on Herc's porch.

Him and Spice, Izzy and me. It was late and the crickets were out again. More of them now. No stars, though—there were too many clouds. Herc had his GoTunes set to random and our background music shifted from Latin acoustic to dance pop to classical.

"Well," he said after a long silence, "that sucked ass."

"Yes, it did," I agreed.

Izzy's fists were still clenched and I could see small muscles at the corners of her jaw flex. She was so freaking mad.

"I should *never* have agreed to let that psycho . . ." She tried to find a word bad enough to describe Mindy, and even though Spice and Herc offered plenty of suggestions, Izzy finally shook her head and made a wordless sound of total disgust.

"It was mean," said Herc.

Spice shook her head. "It was cheap."

We all nodded.

"It'll kill in the ratings," she added.

We sighed and nodded again.

Aside from the parade of old friends, teachers, neighbors, and other random people, Mindy also hit me with a list of "lasts." Last carnival was the start of it, but there was last cotton candy, last hot dog, last group photo with my entire first-grade class, last trip on a carnival ride, last handshake by the mayor of Madison—which, actually, was also the first handshake with him. And a lot of other lasts, most of them really cheesy. And some of them weren't actually going to be "lasts." Even though I was leaving Madison High this week, I'd still be home for another few days. I intended to have more pizza, more Cheetos, more time with Herc and some of my friends. More time with Izzy. This was staged as last, and because it was staged it felt wrong. Like Spice said, it was cheap.

"Was any of it fun?" asked Spice.

"Not much."

"I'm sorry," Izzy said again. "This is all my fault."

"How is it your fault?" asked Spice, and Herc explained about the agreement with the reality show people. She freaked when Izzy chimed in and told her how much money they were paying. Most of it was going into a trust account that she'd get half of at eighteen and the rest at twenty-one.

Herc laughed and kissed Spice on the cheek. "Would you sign me up for something like this if they offered you that kind of money?"

"Boy," she said, "if they gave me *half* that much money I'd perform surgery on you without anesthesia."

"You're not even a doctor," he protested.

"How does that matter?"

We all laughed at that. Herc's laugh sounded a little uncertain. Then he raised his bottle of iced tea. "Here's to ratings."

That episode *did* kill it in the ratings. Number one show on TV that night, both in shows watched live and recorded to watch later. That would mean a big bonus check for Izzy. For me, too, and for Mars One.

We sat there for a while, talking about it some, not talking about anything a lot. We were up past curfew, but Spice called her mom and cleared it for her to come back late. Her older brother would pick her up.

"I hate that this is how people are going to remember you," said Izzy, still fuming.

"Pretty sure they're going to remember him taking off on a rocket," said Herc.

"Oh, sure, of course . . . but they'll remember this, too. Tristan looking like a deer in the headlights and trying to remember everyone's names, even people he barely met when he was little."

"That's great," I muttered. "My legacy is me looking like future roadkill."

"Could be worse," said Herc, and then he grunted. "Well, no . . . not really."

"Thanks."

Spice sipped her tea and asked, "What legacy do you want?"

"First, I'm not dying. I'd kind of like to clear that up first."

"We know," said Herc. "You keep telling us that."

"No," Izzy said, jumping in, "you know what he means. The show . . . the way Mindy did it . . . it was *like* Tristan is dying. It's like he got to attend his own wake."

"Tristan Hart's Make-A-Wish Family Special," suggested Herc. "Download a coupon for a free box of tissues."

"This isn't getting better," I said glumly.

"Then make it better," said Spice. We all looked at her. "That's what I meant when I asked what kind of legacy you want. Just because Mindy ambushed you doesn't mean that she gets the last word. You're *not* dead, Tris, and you still have some time before you leave for pre-mission training. So . . . you're famous, you have all that sponsor money and your cut of *Tristan and Izzy*, and you want to change how people remember you, right? What kind of footprint do you want to leave?"

I stared at her. The others did too.

"My girlfriend," declared Herc, puffing up his chest with pride, but Spice elbowed him hard enough to deflate him.

"Not your girlfriend yet, Romeo."

"Almost," he said.

Her grin was sly. "Almost."

Izzy took my hand and studied my face. "Why are you smiling like that?"

"Am I smiling?" I asked distractedly.

Chapter 16

It's a really interesting question, the whole legacy thing. I'm good with tools and I can fix almost anything, but my "legacy" wasn't going to get fixed with a socket driver or welding torch. No. There had to be another way to make a difference, and there was something that I'd been bouncing around in my head for a while now.

Here's the thing—all of us with reality shows or speaking engagement contracts already forked over big chunks of cash to the Mars One program, but not every cent. Because of the sponsorship deals and the growing income from *Tristan and Izzy* I had a boatload of money left over after my contributions to the mission. It was a ridiculous amount and that's what I wanted to use to create a legacy that would actually matter.

Before I told Izzy and Herc, I wanted to clear it with my folks. Not sure what reaction I expected, but my dad gave me a hug. Then he held me at arm's length and studied me with wet, glistening eyes.

"And I had such high hopes that you'd grow up to be a thieving, coldhearted, money-grubbing captain of industry," he said. "Your uncle Scrooge will be so disappointed."

"I'll try to be crueler, sir," I said in a sniveling little voice. "It's just that I'm a soft touch for the widows and orphans."

"Bah," he said. "Humbug."

Mom pulled me away, shaking her head at the two of us, and gave me a quick, firm hug. She was a little misty-eyed too, but she was all business. She set up a videoconference call with our lawyer and the branch manager of our bank. The lawyer asked me if I wanted to go public with this, and he actually brought up the legacy thing too. He suggested that the reality show people might even make me an offer built just on this.

I said no.

Mom asked the lawyer and the banker if I could still manage my "legacy" during the mission. At first they both said yes, but then they got quiet and looked at me. We all thought about the realities. Once we were on Mars everyone on the mission was going to be seriously busy at ten thousand different jobs just to make sure we could survive. I might be too far away, too busy, and—let's face it—too out of touch to manage it myself.

Dad asked, "What about a proxy?"

"A what?" I asked.

"That could work," said the lawyer. He explained that a proxy would be someone appointed via a legal document called a power of attorney. Once this was set up, our lawyer would oversee the trust of what I wanted to call the Hart Foundation. And I asked if Izzy and Herc could be officers of this new corporation.

"Not at first," said the lawyer, "but if you desire it, I can act as temporary officer until they come of age, and thereafter serve as adviser. Would that work?"

Yeah, it would. We set it up so Izzy would become an official officer of the trust when she turned eighteen and would be paid a salary of one dollar a year. When I told her about it, she agreed without hesitation and didn't even have to ask why she was only paid a dollar. She was already rich and didn't need any cash from the trust beyond what was legally necessary.

She wasn't the CEO, though. I wanted that title for Herc.

But . . . when I told Herc that he was going to be the CEO of the Hart Foundation, and that he'd be paid one hundred thousand dollars per year beginning at age eighteen, he freaked out. Not a happy freak-out, though. He was absolutely furious.

We were in my living room and he said, "I'm not doing it for the money, you total . . ."

Well, there was more, but I'd be embarrassed even writing it down. You get the point. It took me all day—with Izzy and Spice helping—to get him to calm down and listen to reason.

"With the contracts I have right now," I said, "and all those stupid product endorsements, by the time I get to Mars I'm going to have forty million dollars in the bank. A third of it's already going to be given to the Mars mission, but the rest is mine to do with as I please. And I want to know that something good's going to come out of it. It was your girlfriend who asked me what I wanted to have as my legacy. Well . . . this is what I want."

"But why me?" he bellowed. "I'm just a kid."

"You're my best friend."

"I'm *sixteen*! How do you know I won't blow it all on crap? Mansion in the Hills, solid gold skateboard, lots of drugs . . . ?"

"Oh, please . . ."

"Money is the root of all evil, Tris. You could be turning me into a supervillain right here."

"Then use some of it to buy a hollowed-out volcano."

We were in my living room. Spice and Izzy were sitting on the couch. I was in the lounge chair and Herc was standing in the middle of the floor like a prosecutor trying to tell a jury to put a criminal in jail. His brown face had turned beet red.

"This is so . . . *nuts*!" he protested.

"No it's not," said Izzy.

When he turned to glare at her the lamplight caught the glitter of tears in his eyes. "And what am I supposed to *do* with that kind of money?"

I grinned at him. "We can work that out."

"There are a lot of food banks in Madison," said Spice.

"There are four shelters in town for abused women and children," said Izzy.

"We all know some kids who could use some help paying for college," I said.

"But why pay *me*? That hundred g's should go to that kind of stuff," insisted Herc.

"Because," I said, "there are ten zillion charities out there, man. You know how much of a pain in the ass it's going to be to figure out which ones need the cash?"

"And which ones are scams," said Spice.

"And who knows what might come up," said Izzy. "Hurricanes and tsunamis and all sorts of disasters. Somebody has to take the time to figure it all out."

"Read my damn lips," he roared, "I'm *sixteen*."

"Yeah, so what?" I asked. "You're almost done with junior year. Go to college, take some business courses. Figure it out."

Herc stood there, looking at me, looking at the girls, looking at his own hands. Looking up at the ceiling as if there were answers painted there.

Then he sat down in the middle of the living room floor, put his face in his hands, and burst into tears. A heartbeat later we were all in a pile around him. Crying.

Laughing too.

And that was the last thing it took to give me what I needed in order to truly accept that I was never coming home.

To be okay with it.

To be happy with it.

Chapter 17

I spent the last few days in Madison going to a lot of parties.

A.

Lot.

Of.

Parties.

If I laughed too loud, danced too crazy, talked too much, or made a fool of myself . . . so what?

Only two days really mattered.

The next-to-last day was when Herc and I went around and did all the "lasts." Not for the cameras. For us. We threw a lot of balls at Thunderbird Lanes. Neither of us set any records and neither of us cared. We rode our bikes along the newspaper route we used to share and even stopped to say good-bye to a couple of our old customers who'd been cool to us. The ones who gave us tips or boxes of cookies at Christmas. We bought bottles of water and fish tacos and ate them on the seesaw at the elementary school. Then we played b-ball at the park to burn off some of the calories. I beat him twice and he creamed me four times. We sat on swings in the public playground and named every girl we ever thought was cute when we were little and talked about the ones who'd turned out really hot. Herc's a gentleman and he didn't comment on Izzy, which is why we didn't have a last fistfight.

Frick and Frack had to follow us everywhere. Mostly they let us have fun, but when I borrowed Herc's skateboard they rushed in and literally dragged me off of it before the wheels even started to roll. They yelled at me for being stupid, for risking my neck, and—maybe more to the point—for risking the whole Mars One project. If I broke my leg I wouldn't go on the flight, and that would mean they'd have to shuffle everyone around, blah-blah-blah. I got it. I tried to convince them I was too good on a skateboard to get hurt on a simple stunt like that, but they weren't buying it. Didn't help at all that Herc snorted out loud when I said that.

After that Herc and I walked around for a while and finally settled down on the porch steps at my place. For the last half hour we sat in total silence except for crickets and the sound of cars on the street. Then Herc stood up.

"Got to go," he said.

At first it surprised me, because I figured we'd be out there for hours. Or maybe go inside and play last video games. But Herc really wanted to go. It was only later that I realized he wanted to be the one who left. On his terms. I guess that made sense. It showed how smart he is about things.

We hugged and shook hands and did not say good-bye.

Instead, as Herc turned to walk home, he said, "See you 'round, Tris."

"Yeah, man," I said. "See you 'round."

Chapter 18

Then it was time to say good-bye to Izzy. I walked over to her place. Frick and Frack followed twenty feet behind me. It was thirteen blocks to her house. I tried not to think about unlucky numbers. I tried not to think about how much this was going to hurt. I arrived at her house absolutely scared out of my mind. Izzy was waiting for me on the porch. So was Mindy and her camera crew.

And there had to be at least a thousand people on the streets.

Seriously, kill me now.

Chapter 19

When Mindy saw me she broke out in the widest, whitest, scariest smile I've ever seen on a human face. The kind of smile that would make a velociraptor freeze in its tracks.

She stood on the pavement at the foot of the three steps leading to Izzy's porch. She wore a dress that was some kind of weird blend of swirly gold and silver. Pretty sure she was trying to capture the space travel vibe, and I bet that dress cost more than my mom's car. She sicced a couple of cameramen on me and they rushed up, hitting me with LED lights even though it was still daylight.

"Tristan Hart!" called Mindy in a voice that was amplified by small speakers mounted on the porch rail. The crowd broke into wild applause and I caught sight of a producer waving his arms to make them keep it up and keep it loud.

Then someone in the crowd started chanting my name.

"Tris-TAN . . . Tris-TAN . . ."

The rest of the crowd picked it up and soon the windows of every house on the block were rattling with the sound of my name. Louder and louder. I'll bet a million bucks that the first guy to start that chant was planted there by Mindy.

Izzy was still on the porch, her eyes filled with horror and her face turning as red as . . . well, as red as Mars.

She mouthed the words *I'm so sorry.*

I smiled at her.

Mindy thought I was smiling for the camera. Whatever.

The producer working the crowd began patting the air to quiet everyone down. They were trained better than most dogs and the street got so quiet Mindy's voice banged off the walls. A tech toned it down.

I saw that seeded throughout the crowd were the usual protestors. Maybe a few more than we normally got when we were taping an episode. And now that I thought about it, the number of those whack jobs had been increasing with every episode. Originally we had one or two; now I could count maybe thirty of them. Impossible to say if they were the ones who thought we were going to hell or if they were part of the Neo-Luddite group. I didn't see any red scarves. Some had signs like DON'T GO! or YOU TAKE YOUR SINS WITH YOU. Blah-blah-blah. It pissed me off that they were here and that there were so many of them. The closer we got to leaving, the more of them showed up. Not just here but everywhere one of the mission people lived. I didn't get why it mattered so much to them. If they thought we were wrong, so what? Our mission wasn't going to affect anyone but us. No one was being forced to go with us. Even the four of us kids were totally down with it. No one was a victim and none of this was an insult to anyone's beliefs.

So . . . what the heck?

Security couldn't refuse to let them join the crowd, and unlike the carnival, this was a city street, so unless they started something, they had as much legal right to be here as the fans of the show.

I suddenly felt a hand on my shoulder and I turned and looked up at Frack's stony face. His eyes were fixed on the nearest protestor. "You want to bug out, kid, say the word," he said. It was almost the only conversation we'd ever had. Frick closed in on my other side, his eyes roving with disapproval over the crowd.

I smiled at them and shook my head. "Thanks . . . but I'm good."

Frick and Frack gave me identical robot nods, then turned toward Mindy. If it's possible for faces to clench like fists, theirs did. I'm pretty sure that if I'd asked them to kneecap her, they would have. Frack gave my shoulder a small reassuring squeeze, let go, and stepped back.

"Tristan," Mindy cried, walking toward me, still grinning, holding her hand out, "the youngest Martian!"

It took me a moment to realize she was right. I was younger than Luther by two months.

"Today's your last day," said Mindy. "How's it feel?"

I cleared my throat and tugged my shirt down, trying to look cool and normal.

"Well . . . ," I said, "it's my last day *here*. We won't be leaving Earth for a couple of weeks, though."

"Oh, I know, and *Tristan and Izzy* will be following you every step from here on," she said, making a promise sound like a threat. "But it is your last day at home. And it's the last time you'll ever see Izzy Drake."

I wanted to tell her that she was wrong. I'd talk to Izzy on Skype every day between now and liftoff, and on the mission we'd vid-chat as often as possible once the ships were out in the black. Even when I got to Mars and we had the time delay, we'd only be twenty minutes apart. I'd see Izzy for the rest of my life.

For the rest of our lives.

I wanted to say that, but I knew this was all for the show, and the TV people didn't want actual truth. They wanted the version of it that would keep the ratings high and keep those advertising bucks pouring in. Besides, nitpicking like that would be a dick move.

"I know," I said, making it sound almost as heavy as it felt. "As much as I want to be part of this mission, it's so hard to say good-bye to all of this."

I waved to the crowd as if they were all BFFs.

They went totally nuts.

Mindy beamed her approval at me. I forced my mouth to smile back at them, thinking of Izzy and Herc and the Hart Foundation.

There was more of the interview, but it was all what you'd expect. Mindy kept asking the kinds of questions that left me having to give "heartfelt" answers. It was like being asked to bleed on cue.

Which I pretty much did.

Then it came to the part where Mindy led me up to the porch. The process was surreal. Everyone on the street fell silent again, but this time there was an energy in the air that's hard to describe. Like the flutter in your chest on Christmas morning when all of the presents are still wrapped and the whole day is waiting for you to dig in. That kind of excitement but without the happiness. Without the joy, I suppose.

I wished I could do this with just Izzy. That was the only way it could be right.

But Mindy and her network weren't going to let that happen. They wanted every drop of blood, every tear. There were cameras everywhere, microphones everywhere, eyes on everything we did.

Izzy stood there, frozen.

Mindy hovered like the specter of death.

It was going to be up to me to say something. I could make the moment or break it. If I screwed it up I wouldn't be around to help Izzy clean it up. I had my escape plan all set.

She didn't.

Damn it.

On the way over here I'd rehearsed a hundred different

things to say. Cool lines, big speeches, lies that would sound good, sound bites that would burn the Internet. But as I stepped onto the porch, all of that turned to dust. I couldn't remember my own name let alone the speeches I'd written in my head. All I could do was reach out with both hands, take hers, and say the only words that made any sense to me.

I said, "I love you, Izzy."

Then I pulled her to me and we hugged. The crowd began applauding, then yelling, and finally screaming. I even heard a sob break from Mindy. But I didn't care. Izzy felt so good in my arms and I had to be the biggest idiot in the history of the world. This was the end and no speeches were ever to going to make it hurt less.

We clung to each other like we were drowning.

Chapter 20

Mindy did everything humanly possible to turn our last day together into a living hell. Seriously. She arranged for Izzy and me to sit at her computer and go through our pictures. Izzy was smart enough to have made a special folder of only those photos she wanted to share. Not that we had anything spicy, but we'd both taken a lot of stupid, silly, and personal selfies.

Mindy sat us on the couch in Izzy's living room and asked us questions from a script. It wasn't a regular interview, with one question logically following another. These were questions designed to generate sound bites. It's like on those competition shows where they cut away from that day's challenge to the contestant sitting in a room—usually wearing different clothes—commenting on what was going on in their head at different stages of the process. They do it all the time on makeup effects shows, robotics shows, and all that. Something happens on the screen, but instead of a voice-over they do a quick cutaway and the person says something like "The clock's ticking and I don't know if I'm going to finish the gearbox in time." And "That's it, I think this is going to send me home." Or "Roger is being a real jerk the whole time, and that makes me want to crush him in the final reveal."

"Tristan, what did you feel the moment you first saw Izzy?"

"Izzy, Tristan is very handsome. How good a kisser is he?"

"Tristan, the two girls going with you to Mars are very pretty. Which one do you think would make the best match?"

"Izzy, how does it feel to know that Tristan will be in a tiny spaceship with two smart and pretty girls?"

On and on and on. No script to follow. No warning as to what was coming. Mindy said she wanted honest reactions. As we sat there, Izzy gripped my hand hard enough to crush titanium. Pretty sure I'd never have full use of that hand again.

We thought it was never going to end, and it was taking up a lot of that last day. It wasn't fair. Sure, I get it that they *bought* this time from us, and that for Izzy and Herc it would make their lives better. But it was our last day, our last time together. And this wasn't any way to say good-bye.

Finally it was Izzy's mom who came to the rescue. She walked into the shot and stood between us and Mindy, fists on hips, back as rigid as a steel strut.

"Stop the camera," she growled. And it was a growl, too. Even I flinched and I wasn't the target.

"Mrs. Drake—" began Mindy, but she was cut off.

"We've been at this all afternoon. My daughter is tired and she needs a break. She will *have* a break right now."

When Mindy tried to protest, Mrs. Drake unloaded at her. She didn't curse, but she used what my English teacher would have called "figurative and descriptive language" to suggest what Mindy could do with her camera, her camera crew, her expensive and ridiculous clothes, and the horse she rode in on. It was really impressive. I wanted to stand up and applaud but Izzy's death grip had tightened even more.

Mindy was formidable but when Mrs. Drake was in gear she was ten times more fierce. So Mindy pasted on a totally false smile that still managed to outshine the camera lights. "Let's all take a break, shall we?" she said brightly, as if this was her idea, and wasn't it wonderful that she cared so much for us kids. The cameras were still rolling, and Mindy turned and waited for Mrs. Drake to step out of the shot. "Tristan, Izzy, I know you'd like to have a few moments alone." She made it sound kind of sleazy, like Izzy and I were going to run upstairs and tear each other's clothes off. Then Mindy looked directly into the camera. "We'll be back for the last good-bye between these young lovers. You don't want to miss this."

After three seconds, the producer said, "And we're out."

The lights turned off, the Drakes seemed to deflate as they exhaled their tension, Izzy finally released what was left of my hand, and Mindy—still smiling—turned to us.

"One hour," she said flatly. Then she turned away, clearly dismissing us lesser beings as she pulled the cameraman over into a whispered conversation with the producer. I couldn't hear what they were saying, but I bet it had a lot to do with editing out anything Mr. or Mrs. Drake had to say before they aired the episode. That *wouldn't* be ratings gold.

As Izzy stood up her mom hugged her and kissed her forehead. Then she smiled at me and placed a warm palm on my cheek.

"The sun's going down," she said to me. "You know where the best view is."

Chapter 21

The best view of the sunset was from the sloping roof outside of Izzy's parents' bedroom window. It faced away from the street and there was a space between two oak trees that let us see the horizon. Izzy grabbed a blanket and spread it over the shingles and we lay down on it, snuggled side by side, her head resting on my biceps, our left fingers entwined.

It was not my last sunset on Earth. I still had the last couple of weeks of training and mission prep in Amsterdam. But it was *our* last sunset, and this wasn't for the cameras.

The sun seemed to want to show off just for us. It was a massive orange ball, more like a summer sun in the humid autumn sky, and there were streaks of clouds to catch the colors. Sometimes a sun goes plop over the edge of the world and there's nothing really to look at. Other times the sun spills everything out of its paint box and goes totally nuts. This was one of those sunsets. The kind that any photo of it looks Photoshopped. So real it looked fake.

So gorgeous.

Even after the sun was down the light show kept going. Long streaks of red and gold, magenta and purple, lavender and midnight blue. I'm glad neither of us took a photo of it. Some things you want to remember in a more personal way.

Then Izzy turned toward me, rolling halfway onto my chest so she could look at me in the fading light.

"I'm sorry—" she began, but I stopped her with a kiss.

"Please don't say that again," I said. "Stop saying you're sorry."

"No, it's this show and everything. It's wrong."

"Izzy, we talked about this. It's not comfortable, and sure, a lot of it is fake, but not everything. Not the things we know are true."

"I know . . ." She shook her head. "I don't want this to happen, Tristan. I've been trying not to say it too much, but I have to. I don't want you to go. I want you to stay here. On Earth. With me. I want us to be *us*. Like normal people. Like we love each other and want to be together."

I started to reply but this time she stopped me.

"Let me finish, okay?" Her eyes searched mine. I nodded. "I'm saying what I want. Me. Isolde Marie Drake. That's what I want. I'm sixteen and if I had what I really want then we'd be together all through school. We'd go to the same college together. We'd get married, maybe, or at least live together. We'd *be* together. Always and forever."

I said nothing, knowing there was more.

"Sometimes I wonder what our kids would have looked like. Your eyes, my hair. They'd be a little of each of us.

They'd be able to fix anything and they'd be good in school, and they'd have a sense of humor. And they'd love animals. And . . ."

Her words ran down, but I still waited.

"You're going to think I'm crazy, but I sometimes believe that we'll have that life, and that those kids will be born and grow up. Not here, not in *this* world, but in some world. I sometimes think that that other world is the real one and this is a bizarro dimension where everything is just a little bit wrong. That this is the broken version of the world."

The sky was darkening, the colors draining down over the edges of the clouds.

"I know it sounds stupid," she said. "It sounds desperate."

"No," I said, "it doesn't."

She kissed my chest, right over the heart. "Tell me one thing, Tristan," she said softly, "and don't lie, okay? I want you to tell me the truth. Promise?"

"I promise."

"If the Mars thing didn't happen . . . or if your family washed out of the training . . . do you think we'd stay together? Do you think we'd stay in love? Do you think that my bizarro world could ever be real?"

Oh man, that was such a hard question. My heart and my head had different answers. Who knows what would happen? I loved Izzy, no doubt . . . but how many kids who fall in love in school ever stay together? No matter how much they love each other. No matter how much they can't imagine loving anyone else. No matter what. The counselors in the mission gave us statistics and probabilities and all of the math. They explained it all in a big-picture way.

I knew all of that. I understood the logic.

And I'd spent a lot of time wondering if I'd have been a better person, and a kinder one, to simply break up with Izzy months ago. To take her off the hook. To stop hurting her and dragging her through all of this.

But . . .

I touched her cheek and, as gently as I could, steered her lips toward mine.

We kissed for a long, long, long time.

They were very good kisses.

And they gave her my answer better than anything I could have said in words.

Chapter 22

We heard Mindy and her producers calling for us. After a minute Mrs. Drake tapped on the window frame. Izzy and I were wrapped in each other's arms.

"It's time, sweeties," said Mrs. Drake. When I looked at her I could see that she'd been crying. "I'm so sorry."

She backed out of the window and gave us another minute.

We got up slowly, reluctantly, and went inside. Izzy freshened her makeup; I combed my hair. We kissed again at the top of the stairs and then went down to film the Great Good-bye scene.

Mindy staged it on the porch, with the porch light spilling down on us. It was supposed to look as though we were alone and I was saying good-bye like we were at the end of a date. Just the two of us, a private and intimate moment. As if there weren't five thousand people on the street and in the neighbors' gardens and sitting on the roofs across the street, and as if millions of people weren't going to watch it on cable and YouTube and everywhere else.

So, sure, we kissed, and we hugged each other, because to us some of it was real. It was our last moment.

I'll never be sure which one of us started laughing first.

PART TWO

BLACK VOID

Looking at these stars suddenly dwarfed my own troubles and all the gravities of terrestrial life. I thought of their unfathomable distance, and the slow inevitable drift of their movements out of the unknown past into the unknown future.
—H. G. Wells, *The Time Machine*, 1895

Be humble for you are made of earth.
Be noble for you are made of stars.
—Serbian proverb

Chapter 23

We left the next morning. Mom, Dad, and me.

Frick and Frack loaded our stuff into their SUV and we were rolling before the sun even came up. I sat in the corner of the backseat, my head craned around to look at our house as it grew smaller behind us. One of us forgot to turn out the living room light. It looked like people still lived there.

Then we turned the corner and the house was gone. The people who moved in would have pretty interesting stories to tell their friends. *Hey, you know where we live? You know the Harts, those crazy people who went to live on Mars? Yeah, it's their old place.* That'd be a heck of a story topper.

Even though it felt like we were running away, I knew that wasn't the truth.

We were running *toward*.

Chapter 24

At the airport some mission people came and took our suit-cases. Some of the other astronauts had arrived at the same time, including several from other countries who were coming off of a press tour here in America. One of them was Sophie Enfers, a French girl I'd talked to a few times. She was nineteen but would turn twenty three days before launch, so the press never included her in the "four teenage astronauts going into space" thing. I think that was as much her decision as theirs because she was one of those people who always acted older than she was, the kind who always seemed like an adult. So much so that the adults in the program accepted Sophie on her own terms. She was one of "them," not one of "us." Sophie's mother had been one of the finalists for the mission but had withdrawn because of a health issue. Sophie chose to stay in the program as one of several "astronaut colonists," meaning she didn't have a specialty. She knew a little chem-istry, a little engineering, a little of a lot of things, but so did everyone else. I think the main reason she got included was because she was young, smart, and seemed willing to learn anything and try everything. Oh yeah, and she could cook.

During several of the underwater habitat-training sessions she managed to turn our freeze-dried rations into something that humans might want to eat. I was an okay Earth food cook, but when it came to the high-protein pastes and nutrient cakes we had, everything I came up with tasted like it was made from cardboard, school glue, and despair.

Sophie even had her own personal tool kit. A good one too. Professional grade. When I asked her why, she said that she always liked to fix things and maybe I could teach her some of what I knew so she'd be more useful to the mission. I said sure, but it was something we never got around to during training. Maybe on the flight, if she was still interested.

Sophie was also really pretty and she laughed at my jokes. Izzy met her once at a press thing and hated her on the spot. When I asked her why, she said that Sophie kept "looking at" me. I told Izzy that she was nuts, that Sophie was legally an adult and I was sixteen, and she was being ridiculous. And we had a real big fight.

Bottom line is, I liked Sophie as a friend and we were going to be on the same ship together. At the same time, I didn't actually know her all that well. She smiled a lot but there was always something a little sad about her. Maybe it was her eyes. None of those bright smiles ever seemed to reach her eyes. When Izzy smiled her eyes filled with light, but for Sophie Enfers it was more like her eyes filled with shadows. Does that make sense? Maybe I'm being too poetic for my own good.

Sophie saw us and came over. She kissed Mom and Dad on both cheeks and then did the same to me. It's a European thing. When she bent close I could smell soap, sweat, perfume, and chemicals.

"And how are you today, Monsieur Hart?" she asked me, pretending to be formal. It was her thing, and even though she did it all the time it seemed clear that it was some kind of private joke with her. Maybe it was one of the reasons everyone treated her like an adult rather than "another teenager" on the crew.

"I'm good," I said.

"And now it begins, *oui?*"

"Guess so."

She studied me. "Are you perhaps having some doubts?"

"Nope," I said. "None at all."

She nodded and looked around and then up at the beautiful blue sky. It was such a perfect color, with small islands of white clouds. A line of birds sailed above us, their wings and bellies so white it hurt the eye.

"How can we leave all this?" said Sophie. "Surely we must be mad."

Her accent was so thick it took me a moment to understand her. I just nodded.

"I know," I said, and she turned to me.

"I saw you on TV. You and your girlfriend, Iseult," she said, using the old-fashioned variation on Izzy's name. "Such a lovely girl. So pretty and so sad, and as tragic as the Irish princess from the old stories. Do you know those stories, young Tristan?"

"Yeah," I said flatly. "Doomed young love. Got it. That's been in every feature story they've done on us."

"I expect so. Au revoir," she said, then joined Marcel, a friend of hers from Paris. He was one of those moody guys who never smiles. Like, ever. And he always looked annoyed. At everyone and everything. When you talk to him you kind of get the vibe that he thinks you're uncouth, uncivilized, and not housebroken. But Sophie seemed to like him, so there's that.

She walked away with her head down as if she was thinking deep thoughts, hands in the pockets of her jeans, ponytail bobbing. Marcel fell into step beside her, neither of them saying a word. Strange people, both of them, and in different ways. But then, a lot of the people on Mars One were strange. Maybe I was strange too. I mean, look at the decision we all made. Even though there were forty of us going and a couple of hundred thousand people wanting to go, you couldn't call us normal. There were nearly eight billion people who did not apply and if the news services were right, most of them thought we were out of our minds.

Maybe. Jury's out.

Chapter 25

While Mom and Dad signed some papers for the airport people, Frick and Frack escorted me along a line of people who wanted me to sign autographs. They were on the other side of police barricades and monitored by city cops, airport security, mission security, and my two private thugs. If all that security freaked out the people, it didn't show. They yelled, they held signs, they screamed my name like I was a rapper or rock star. It was nuts.

There were some other people there too, scattered through the crowd. They carried signs too, but not with our pictures on them. Not with the Mars One logo or anything like that.

They had signs like, MARS IS DEATH.

And like, MARS IS HELL. YOU WILL BURN THERE.

And, GOD IS ON EARTH—FIND HIM HERE!

And, YOU CANNOT FLEE FROM YOUR SINS.

Frack must have caught my vibe because he and Frick closed in on either side of me, body blocking me from going anywhere.

"They're not Neo-Luddites," said Frack.

"I know, but they—"

Frack cut me off. "Don't bother. And don't pick fights you can't win."

And Frack corrected him, "No—only pick fights you *know* you can win."

Frick thought about that, nodded.

Mom and Dad finished their paperwork and we had to go through speeches from the mission people and some scientists from NASA, SpaceX, and other groups. Then handshakes with all sorts of people, most of whom I didn't know. I heard Mom warn Dad not to crack too many stupid jokes in front of the press. He crossed his heart and held up a hand to God, but his fingers were crossed. Mom looked at him suspiciously and shook her head in exasperation. The vice president was there. This wasn't an American mission, so we didn't rate the actual president. A lot of NASA people were there and even some people from our rival SpaceX. They were very cool. Lots of smiles and good wishes. No one talking trash, no one putting us down.

A few Hollywood superstars were there, and that was cool. Mostly actors who'd been in space movies over the last ten or twenty years. Sandra Bullock, Matthew McConaughey, George Clooney, Matt Damon, Sam Rockwell, Rooney Mara, the whole cast of the last six *Star Wars* movies, and four of the actors from *Star Trek*. Steven Spielberg, J. J. Abrams, and Christopher Nolan were there too. All three of them had Mars movies in the works, so I guess this was as much about

PR for them as it was support for us. That was cool. Maybe they'd kick something into the Hart Foundation.

There were *more* speeches, and it seemed like people were just saying the same things in only slightly different ways. Everyone seemed to want to be recorded saying a catchy sound bite. When all that stuff was done we all went into the terminal building. And yes, we still had to go through security. Some of the reporters went through too, because their networks and news services had paid Mars One for special access to do interviews during our flight.

Those reporters used every possible second to ask us the same questions we'd already answered in a million previous interviews. Not sure how this was going to be different. I mean, we were heading to the Netherlands for the last part of training and mission prep—we weren't leaving for Mars yet. But I guess the twenty-four-hour news cycle needed to be fed. Dad's way of putting it, mind you. So, because it was required of us and because it passed the time, we answered the questions. Sometimes we tried to make the tired old information sound brand-new, but after a while we were all repeating the same answers we'd come to rely on. I guess that's how it works. There's only so much you can say, but saying it again—fresh and live—makes it "new."

They called our flight and we headed out to the boarding gate, showed our tickets, boarded the plane. Frack sat in an otherwise empty row in front of us, Frick sat behind us.

Reporters were all around us. Nobody got much rest, but sometimes the focus wasn't on me and I could tune it all out. I turned to the window and looked out at the clouds. At the green-and-brown land far below. At the blue of the water. And then up at the sky, trying to find that flicker of red way out in the black. It was there, I knew. Waiting.

We flew to Amsterdam, capital of the Netherlands. It was the last place we would all live on this planet.

Chapter 26

I said good-bye to Frick and Frack at the gates of the Mars One Center compound on the outskirts of Amsterdam. Their job was done and the mission's in-house security detail would take over from here. They shook hands with my folks and when Mom and Dad walked in through the gate, the two big bodyguards stood there for a moment, looking at me. Even after all this time I couldn't read their expressions.

"Thanks," I said, "you guys have been great."

Nothing. They stood there just looking at me.

"I . . . guess I'd better go in." I cleared my throat. "Right, then, okay . . . well . . ." I really had nothing, so I held out my hand, not sure if either of them would take it.

Frick did. He shook it with the hard, dry single pump you'd expect. But then he didn't let go. And after a second he used our grip to pull me into a hug.

Frack wrapped his arms around both of us and we stood there, the two of them crushing me between them, in the strangest hug I've ever had. Or ever will have.

Frick released me first, stepped back, and stood there, a

strange expression on his face. Pretty sure he was trying to smile, but it looked like it actually hurt his face muscles. Frack gave me a final squeeze, put his hands on my shoulders, and pushed me to arm's length so he could look me up and down. He shook his head and he smiled too. His looked a little more human and less like a gargoyle trying to grin with stone lips.

"Off the record," said Frack, "when we got this gig we thought you'd be some privileged, snotty-nosed little creep who thought he was all that."

"Um . . . ," I began, but he wasn't finished.

"But you're okay, Tristan. You might actually turn into someone. You got the makings. My guess is that even you don't know what you got. But I think you're going to keep on surprising people."

He released me, clapped me hard on the shoulder, and stepped back. I stared at him and tried to think of some way to respond. But like I said . . . I had nothing. I was too shocked. So I stuck to the basics.

"Thanks."

Frick and Frack nodded.

"Go be amazing, kid," said Frick.

"See you in the history books," said Frack.

And with that they turned and walked away.

I lingered a couple of moments longer, watching them get into their rental car, trying to process what just happened, realizing that you can never really know everything about people. Especially when you don't bother to look very hard.

Frick and Frack. Henry Kang and Angelo Carrieri.

I had a lot of friends that I was leaving behind. More than I thought.

Chapter 27

I stopped halfway to the mission training center and looked back to where the bus and cars were pulling away. Something about that sight grabbed me, made me watch.

My cell phone buzzed and when I looked at it I saw that there was a new text from Izzy. It was a selfie. In wrinkled pajamas, with no makeup and tragic bed hair, her eyes bleary and puffy from crying. But she had on a crooked, ironic little smile.

How can you bear to leave all of this?

It was supposed to be funny. It was Izzy trying to take me off the hook. I touched the screen with my fingertips.

"I love you, Izzy."

Only that wasn't me saying it. I spun around and standing ten feet behind me was a tall kid about my own age. Intense dark eyes filled with a kind of humor I couldn't quite identify. Not actually mean, but on the spiky side of sarcastic. A big smile with a lot of white teeth. Hair shaved to a shadow on his head, skin the color of milk chocolate, and a complexion most girls would kill for. He stood there with his hands in the pockets of loose board shorts. Sandals and a SURF JEFFREYS BAY tank. A necklace made from pieces of coral. A tattoo of the African continent on his left shoulder.

"Luther," I said.

"Tristan," he said. "The second teenage boy ever to step onto Martian soil."

"Second? Yeah, I don't *think* so."

He laughed as if this were all a done deal. "We're creating a meritocracy, boy. The most important member of the team takes the first step, and right now I'm so far out in front you might as well stay on Earth. I'll send you pictures."

"Like I said, we'll see." It wasn't the crushing comeback I'd have preferred. I'm usually pretty good with zingers but for some reason my sarcasm guns misfired around Luther. Not sure why. Maybe it was because he always acted as if he'd already won every contest before we even started. I knew it was a tactic, but it was an annoying and effective one.

Luther Mbede was—as he told me three separate times during our previous training sessions—Zulu. All Zulu. Not a trace of anything else in his blood. It was a point of pride with him. He had a lot of pride in his people, his culture, his heritage. I liked that about him. His runaway ego . . . ? I didn't like that as much.

What was really annoying is that he was probably as good as he said he was. Like both of his parents, Luther was a geologist. He graduated from high school at fifteen and had been taking intense college courses in hydrogeology for the last year. His whole family was part of the water team, which was one of the most important—or maybe *the* most important—science team on the mission. Without water we wouldn't have shielding for radiation, oxygen, water for cooking or drinking or bathing, or pretty much anything. The liquid water the rovers and satellites discovered would probably be too salty for us to use. It could be filtered, but there also didn't seem to be a lot of it—at least as far as we knew. But ice was different, and there was supposed to be a lot of it in the polar caps and in the ground. The Mbedes had to find water ice in large quantities, harvest it, process it, refine it, and store it. They'd work with the chemistry team to break it down to its atomic components—hydrogen and oxygen. And they also had to work with the survey team to locate and evaluate caves so that we could use them for greater protection from the radiation, dust storms, and temperature shifts. A lot was riding on them, but to hear Luther talk, it was all going to be just fine. That's how he always put it. "Just fine." He was confident he was going to be the boy who saved Mars One. Or something like that. He probably already had sketches of the statues future generations should build in his honor.

So, no, we did not rush at each other for a back-slapping hug. I'm not saying we stood there like a couple of Old West gunslingers, but that's how it felt.

"When'd you get in?" I asked.

"Yesterday."

"How is it? They make you jump right into training?"

Luther grinned. "No. I went out last night with some local girls. Had some fun at a dance club."

He didn't say "wish you were there," 'cause we both knew that he was glad I wasn't. Let's face it, Luther knew he was all that. He walked into any room and the girls were all over him.

Why should that matter to me? I loved Izzy, right?

Yeah, well, I think we could both agree that situation was pretty complicated. I loved Izzy and I was positive I was going to love Izzy for a long, long time. But we were going to be on Mars forever. Soooo . . . there was that.

I think Luther was somehow able to follow my thoughts because he gave me the biggest, widest grin I'd ever seen.

"Everyone else here?" I asked.

"Zoé is here but Nirti's got a family thing and she won't be here for a few days." He clapped his hands together and rubbed them briskly as he looked around. "This is going to be fun."

"Sure."

"Of *course* it is. Every historian in the world is sitting there with their fingers over their keyboards ready to write the next chapter of history."

I narrowed my eyes. "Who are you quoting?"

"The latest mission PR packet. But what does it matter? It's true. After all the testing and preliminary rounds and all that, we're *here*, dude. We're in the last phase before we leave. Aren't you excited? I am. I'm ready to jump out of my skin. We're going to conquer Mars."

"Technically," I said, "Mars can't be conquered because of the agreement . . ."

Yes, there is an actual agreement. It's called the Treaty on Principles Governing the Activities of States in the Exploration and Use of Outer Space, including the Moon and Other Celestial Bodies, and the bottom line is that the major nations agreed that everything beyond Earth's orbit belongs to *all* of humanity. No one country can stake a claim. Which sounds great if you don't know anything about human history.

"I'm not talking about an armed invasion, dude," he said, shaking his head. "I'm talking about claiming our place in history. I'm talking about the fact that we're about to really become who we were born to be. A thousand years from now everyone will still know our names. There will be statues of us on Earth and on Mars. They'll name schools after us in our hometowns. They'll give scholarships in our honor. Think about it. The Luther Mbede Scholarship for Advanced Exogeology. The Zoé De Jaeger Award for Excellence in Astrophysics. The Nirti Sikarwar Special Award for Space Medicine."

"Hey, what about me?"

"Oh, sure, there will definitely be coupons for the Tristan Hart School of Air-Conditioning and Heating. Or, at very least, the Tristan Hart Scholarship for Lawn Mower Repair. I'm sure they'll come up with something appropriate for the mentally challenged."

I took a swing at his head. Not trying hard to connect . . . but if I had, would it have been a bad thing?

Luther ducked back, laughing, and then ran for the building with me in hot pursuit. I guess I was laughing too. It was easy to hate Luther, but it was hard not to like him.

We were still a hundred yards from the main entrance to the mission training center when the door burst open and Ecklund, one of the senior flight officers, stepped out, looked around, spotted us, and began to wave his arm frantically.

"Hart, Mbede! Get in here," he bellowed. *"Now!"*

Ecklund didn't sound angry. He sounded very upset. Freaked.

Luther and I exchanged a quick, worried look and then we were running full tilt for the building.

Chapter 28

We crashed through the door together, all shoulders and elbows, and then raced side by side to catch up to Ecklund, who was hurrying into the big mission control room.

Luther shot me a brief worried look. "You think it's the Neo-Luddites? You think they did something?"

"God, I hope not."

Everybody was crowded inside, all turned toward a tall, pale, sad-faced man who looked like he should be running a funeral parlor. Mission Director Jurgen Colpeys. He was the man in charge of everything from training the colonists to overseeing the delivery of the supply payloads. He was also going to Mars with us, and once we launched he'd turn everything over to Ecklund, who'd be staying on Earth. In almost every way that mattered Colpeys was the guy who took all of the science and made it work. He and my mom worked together on a lot of the most important mechanical aspects of the mission. They didn't always get along but they were a lot alike. Usually stiff, unsmiling, unemotional, and impossible to read.

Except now.

As Luther and I skidded to a stop near the outer fringes of the crowd, we could both read the expression on Colpeys's face. Or . . . *expressions.*

Anger, mostly, and a whole lot of it. Some fear, too. And what looked a lot like indignation.

Behind him was the eighty-foot-wide, fifty-foot-tall high-definition view screen, which showed a huge structure of girders, machines, and habitats wrapped in reflective foil, wires, and struts. It all formed a huge wheel and it hung in geostationary orbit 390 miles from Earth. I recognized it. Everyone who'd paid attention to the space race over the last few years knew it. They called it the Shanghai Wheel, and it was a kind of floating factory the Chinese built in space in order to assemble spacecraft for their long-range plan to colonize the moon. Although China had signed the same Outer Space Treaty as everyone else, it didn't mean they were working *with* the rest of the world. Most countries had their own space programs, and there were some multinational groups— official and private. Mars One was a nongovernmental group with volunteers from dozens of countries, and even though we had some Chinese members, they were not there by official sanction. Most of them were Chinese who had citizenship in America, England, the Netherlands, and elsewhere. China officially stood apart and kept its own space program heavily under wraps. They didn't share technology or information and generally didn't even communicate much except in times of a major international emergency—and there weren't a lot of those in the world of space exploration.

We knew some things about what they were doing, though. The Shanghai Wheel had dozens of the ultra-high-tech 3-D printers used to make parts for lunar landers, habitats, and more. We had a launch station, too, though ours had a double hub built around the two transit vehicles. We called ours Lucky Eight because it kind of looked like a big figure 8.

The Shanghai Wheel was really more of a cylinder, and even while they were still building it the Chinese astronauts covered the whole structure with a special kind of Mylar called Kapton. The version they used—at least as far as our scientists had been able to guess—had several loose layers directly over the Wheel to reduce heat buildup while at the same time acting like solar panels to provide extra juice for the machines. NASA was working on something like it, and so were a few private companies, but the Chinese were way out in front of anyone on that kind of tech. Aside from heat management, the Kapton sheeting pretty much hid everything. No one really knew what they were building up there. It was the exact opposite of Mars One, because we sold the TV rights to almost everything we were doing. Before the Chinese blacked out their signal, we'd seen that they were building something, but no one could quite figure out what it was because it was too big to be a lunar lander. The running theory was that they were building an asteroid mining craft.

There was a separate space race going on among industrial nations and private corporations to strip-mine asteroids for everything from titanium to gold, just floating around out there for the taking. The Outer Space Treaty did not prevent either corporations or countries from taking what they could grab. It was crazy, but you couldn't plant a flag to claim ownership of a moon, a planet, or even an asteroid, but you could mine them for raw materials.

Now, the Shanghai Wheel was empty, the Kapton shielding torn away and, it seemed to me, burned. A lot of the girders were twisted out of shape and debris floated away from it toward the pull of Earth's gravity.

"What's going on?" asked Luther loud enough for half the crowd to turn toward us. "Is it *them*?"

Everyone knew whom he meant, but I saw heads shaking. No.

Then what?

Colpeys saw us and signaled to a tech. "Run it again." While the technician began tapping keys, Colpeys looked at the crowd. "For Luther, Tristan, and anyone else just joining us," he said gravely, "the video footage you're about to watch is highly confidential. It is part of a longer video, however this part has not been broadcast to the public and isn't even on the Internet."

I saw a lot of heads nod.

Colpeys nodded too. "The Chinese have been leading the

race to colonize the moon, and we've benefitted from some exchanges of technology and information. But they have generally kept out of the world community of space programs. They are the only space-faring nation that declined to join the International Mars Exploration Working Group because they publically stated that they have no interest in going to Mars. The moon has always been their goal. The Shanghai Wheel was the first factory of its kind put into orbit, and to a great degree we've emulated their design, though our factory was designed to fabricate parts for our mission and to use it as a launch station for the transit vehicles."

The video began to play from the beginning as Colpeys spoke.

"At three thirty-one this morning a malfunctioning Chilean communications satellite collided with the Shanghai Wheel. That impact did considerable damage to the structure and, as you can see, tore away much of the Kapton covering. Luckily there was no loss of life and the three technicians aboard the Wheel have been able to return to Earth via a small supply spacecraft. They splashed down in the South Pacific four hours ago."

"Only three technicians?" asked Tony Chu, Mom's engineering assistant. "I thought they had twenty or thirty people stationed on the Wheel."

The director spread his hands. "The Chinese government issued a statement stating that all three of the current staff have been safely returned to Earth. There was no indication that anyone was left behind or, God forbid, killed during the collision."

Luther spoke up. "Okay, but so what? I mean, it's great that no one was killed, but why is everyone so freaked? The Lucky Eight's nowhere near the Wheel. The debris field isn't going to mess with us."

Colpeys fixed him with a steady, steely stare. "The debris is inconsequential," he said slowly. "What matters is that the Wheel is empty."

"Again," persisted Luther, "so what? I don't mean to be rude but—"

"Watch the video, son."

"*Eish,*" growled Luther impatiently, then rattled off something else in Afrikaans that I'm pretty sure was obscene. He only said it loud enough for me to hear. I'd been trying to learn some of his language, but this came out rapid-fire and all I caught was a reference to something nasty about goats.

As we watched, the image changed to one with a time stamp that stated it was from November of last year. It was taken from something that moved from left to right across the top end of the Wheel, which was an angle I'd never seen. All of the pictures the Chinese had ever shared were of the Wheel seen from different side-on angles, and from the bottom, which looked like the bottom of a tube of Pringles. The top in this video, though, was open, and we could see inside.

"This footage was obtained for us by sympathetic friends inside the American NASA program and is in fact part of a longer and more classified video from a DARPA satellite." DARPA is the Defense Advanced Research Projects Agency, which is America's superscience geek squad who mostly make weapons. It's part of the Department of Defense.

The video image crossed the opening of the Wheel and as it did so the angle allowed us to see deeper into the thing. What at first looked like a big black empty nothing was anything but. There was a machine inside. It wasn't a mining ship. It wasn't a lunar lander either. Or a satellite or anything like that. It was way too big.

I heard Luther gasp. Or maybe it was me. Inside the Shanghai Wheel was a spaceship. A transit vehicle. Almost exactly like ours.

"That footage was taken last November," said Colpeys into the stunned silence. He clicked the button to show the current image of the ruined Shanghai Wheel. "And this was taken this morning."

Now the vast emptiness of it meant something. It was devastating.

We turned to each other in silence, each of us unable to speak. No one was naive enough to ask "where's the ship?" We knew. As far as modern science went there was only one place a ship like that would go.

The Chinese had already sent a ship to Mars.

Chapter 29

Colpeys told us what they knew. It wasn't much. You'd think that with the space race so hot and with so many eyes looking up you couldn't hide the launch of a spaceship. Yeah, you'd be wrong.

You've got to remember this, though: Space is big. Really freaking big. Even the distance between here and the moon is enormous. We're talking 238,000 miles. Now imagine a zone of space around Earth stretching out that far in every direction, and spinning around in that zone are more than twelve hundred active satellites and three thousand outdated dead ones. And half a million bits and pieces of assorted space junk. Could you hide the launch of a transit vehicle that's not much larger than a subway car in all that?

Sure. And we might have never known about it if that satellite hadn't collided with the Wheel.

"Mr. Colpeys," I said, raising my hand to catch his attention, "what's this all mean? Are the Chinese already there?"

He took a long time answering that. Way too long.

"We don't know," he said. "We simply do not know."

"Do we have any estimates of when they left?" Someone

asked a question, and I turned to see Zoé De Jaeger standing ten feet away. Her thick blond hair was twisted into a single braid and pulled around front, and she stood there wrapping the end of it around her fingers with her usual nervous energy.

Colpeys shook his head. "The optimum launch window is November fifteenth, which is our launch date." He paused to pinched the bridge of his nose. "It's possible that they could have left as early as last June eleventh, in which case they would already be on Mars."

"No," I blurted, and everyone shot me annoyed looks for interrupting. My face went hot, but Colpeys gave me a go-ahead nod. I cleared my throat and plunged in. "If they were already on Mars they'd be yelling about it. I mean, really . . . It's Mars. It's not just history, it's politics. It means they won, that they beat everyone else. Why would they keep it quiet?"

Colpeys shook his head. "We simply do not know."

Chapter 30

There was a lot of discussion and a lot of theories, but it was all guesswork. I noticed that Tony Chu was now standing with my mom, their heads together in a private conversation. They didn't look happy. No one did. And no one knew where the Chinese ship was, whether it was actually going to Mars—though where else *would* it go?—or how far into the trip they were.

Or if they made it at all.

There's a running joke that "Space travel is an exact science—except when it's not." There are so many things that can go wrong on a trip like this. Mechanical failure, debris, unexpected foreign objects, human error. Take your pick. And it's not like you can go back to the barn and try again tomorrow. The fact that more people haven't died out there is incredible. We had lots of smart people nitpicking every detail, lots of backup systems—what we called redundancies—and procedures to make it as safe as possible.

So far only robots, orbiters, and rovers had gone to Mars. No people had. People have different needs than empty spacecraft, so there's been a lot of focus on providing the things we'll need for private time and downtime. Sometimes you just need to blob and watch your shows, you know? So, we were all taking as much digital media—books, comics, TV shows, and movies—as we could. We were going to be out there a lot longer than 501 days. Luckily digital media wouldn't add much actual weight, and more could be uploaded later.

Oh, getting back to the unmanned flights—a lot of them had crashed or gone missing, and we still hadn't figured out why. That was very scary, and the result was that Mars One had gone way overboard on safety, efficiency, backups, and telemetry—which is information collected by sensors and sent back to Earth. A lot of experts would be watching all the time.

But those same smart people hadn't figured out what happened to those unmanned probes. Hook that up to the fact that space—like I said before—is *big*. If something happened to the Chinese ship, we might never find them and never know what went wrong.

That was insanely scary for a bunch of people about to blast off to Mars.

Luther and I went over to Zoé, and then the three of us went through the building into the recreation yard out back. We grabbed bottles of water and sat in the shade beneath the leaves of a sweet cherry tree.

"It doesn't mean they're going to *make* it to Mars," said Luther. "We'll get there first, so it's all fine."

Zoé looked less certain. Her family was from right there in Amsterdam. Thick blond hair, ice-blue eyes, built like a gymnast with obvious muscles and rock-climbing calluses on her hands. All four of us kids on the mission were smart and got good grades, but Zoé left us in the dust in terms of sheer smarts. Actually, she left everybody in the dust. Everybody. She completed all of her high school courses by the time she was twelve and earned her PhD at seventeen. Some people can't be accurately measured even with advanced IQ tests, but best guesses put her at around 190. From what I heard, the docs thought they shorted her by thirty or forty points. It ran in the family; both of her parents were math prodigies. Her dad was on a Nobel Prize team for astrophysics and her mom was one of the youngest PhDs from the Netherlands. The only person in her country to get that degree at a younger age was Zoé.

Zoé tried really hard not to make everyone else feel stupid around her, which was nice except that even in a group of geeks, nerds, and scientists, almost everyone *did* feel stupid around her. And I think *she* felt kind of stupid too, because smart as she was, Zoé was totally clueless when it came to how to be a normal kid. Not sure she ever had a chance at that. She wasn't even nerd-girl cool. She called herself a freak and that was what she believed she'd always be. As far as I knew she had never been out on a date and probably hadn't even been kissed.

Ever since Zoé hit puberty—and hit it hard—Luther had been dedicating a lot of his time to helping her come out of her shell. He'd been coming on to her, first in a subtle way, then more and more blatantly. He was about a step away from posting his intentions on a billboard. Either Zoé was actually clueless or she was pretending not to notice because she didn't know how to react.

It was kind of fun to watch. *They* should have had their own reality show. *Luther and Zoé Don't Hook Up*. I'd watch *that* show.

What was really cool and very, very interesting was Zoé's tattoo. She had a string of numbers inked in spirals around her left leg, from hip to anklebone. The numbers were 3.14159265 3589793238462643383279502884197169399375105820974944 59230781640628620899862803482534211706799.

I'm no mathematician but I know the value of pi when I see it. Why she had that done was a mystery she wouldn't explain. On the pretense of having a great interest in tattoos, Luther had tried several times to examine those numbers very closely. Zoé, socially awkward as she was, had managed very nicely to chase him off.

Right now, though, she looked really scared. "I don't want to be *second* to land on Mars," she said. "One of the main reasons my family is going is to be first."

Luther nodded. I didn't.

"I mean," Zoé continued, "everyone knows the names of

Neil Armstrong and Buzz Aldrin because they were the first ones on the moon. How many people can name the next ones to land? Or even say how many Apollo astronauts went to the moon?"

I thought about it. I knew that there had been twelve astronauts who left footprints in the lunar dust. I could name all of them, but now didn't seem like the time to show off.

"You're right," said Luther, shifting his attitude to concede to her point. "If the Chinese get there first then it's going to hurt."

"Exactly!" snapped Zoé. "And if that happens the whole mission could lose a lot of sponsors. And we *need* those sponsors."

"Yeah," I said glumly. The whole sponsorship thing still bugged me, mostly because of *Tristan and Izzy*, and because something as important as this shouldn't have had to go begging for cash. "They only sent one ship, and from the size of the Wheel it couldn't have been anywhere near as big as ours. It's probably more like the four-seater ship we were going to use originally, or maybe a little bigger."

Zoé swiveled around to give me an acid look. "So?"

"So even if we're second we still get to establish the first real colony. We have families. We have . . . well . . . *us.*"

"There's that," agreed Luther. He tended to jump back and forth between agreeing with the girl he liked and siding with whoever was saying something optimistic.

But Zoé gave a firm shake of her head. "No. *We* have to be first."

I opened my mouth to argue with her, to try and hit her with the Big Picture answer that the mission PR people used in a lot of their interviews—that the bottom line was colonizing Mars so that the human race had somewhere to go and somewhere to grow. That was on the tip of my tongue, but what I said was, "Zoé's right. It's got to be us."

"Okay," said Luther. "I hear you, but *why*? I'm playing devil's advocate here. Why us and not anybody else? The Chinese—if they built a ship sooner, if they solved the science quicker than us, then why not them? What have you got against the Chinese?"

"I don't have anything against the Chinese," I said. "It's not about where they're from, what country or politics or any of that stuff."

Zoé was nodding as I spoke.

"Then what?" insisted Luther.

I glanced at Zoé, then up at the dark blue of the afternoon sky, and then at Luther.

"I don't know," I said. "If there's still a chance . . . any chance, then it's got to be us."

It wasn't a good answer. It made no sense.

But we all nodded. Even Luther.

It had to be us.

Chapter 31

Herc texted me that night.

Herc: *Did u see this crap?*

He sent me a link to a Yahoo News article about a post from the Neo-Luddites' freak squad. In big red letters on a white background it said . . .

FIRST TO FLY, FIRST TO DIE

BETRAY THE TRUST—PAY THE PRICE

The graphic they put with it was a spaceship blowing up. Photoshopped, but they made their point.

Herc: *Did those freaks blow it up? [animated explosion emoji]*

Me: *No.*

Herc: *U sure . . . ?*

Me: *No. I don't think so.*

Herc: *Y not?*

Me: *They're saying it was an accident. Rogue satellite.*

Herc: *Even so. Watch ur butt.*

Me: *Yeah.*

I didn't get much sleep that night.

Chapter 32

Over breakfast with my folks I told them about the link Herc sent me. The extremist Neo-Luddites were still claiming they destroyed the Chinese ship. I expected Dad to make a joke, but instead he looked troubled and angry.

"What's *wrong* with those people?" he muttered, and then he snatched up his tablet and swiped over to the comics page.

Mom waggled her fingers for me to hand her my phone. She clicked the link and read the article. She looked delicate because she was about a size nothing, but she was made of airline cable and could bench-press one or both of the Dakotas. I got some of my strength from her. Neither of us looked anywhere near as strong as we were. Or as fast.

The big difference between us, apart from gender and age, was that I smiled a lot and she almost never did. Right then she was actively frowning at the article, and then she made a small disgusted sound and slid the phone across the table so fast I had to lunge to catch it before it flew off. She had some choice words about the news story, and then she caught me grinning and pointed a finger at me. "You repeat one word of that and I will disassemble more than your laptop."

"You never disassembled my laptop."

Without looking up from the comics, Dad said, "You missed that, did you?"

I ran to my room, and sure, I actually did repeat some of what she said. And meant every word too. But I kept my voice down. She'd taken it apart and put the pieces in a bag that sat on my desk. The note on it read:

YOU HAVE HOMEWORK

XOXOXO

I stalked back into the kitchen and slumped down in my chair. Maybe there was a hint of a smile on Mom's face. Dad, on the other hand, was shaking with the kind of laughter that's so deep you can't make a sound. The tablet was gripped tightly in his hands and his eyes were squeezed shut.

"I hate you both," I said.

"I talked her out of burying the mother board in my zucchini beds," said Dad when he could talk.

"I still hate you."

He coughed, thought about it, nodded. "Fair enough."

Mom gave me a sweet smile, the kind you'd expect from mothers who did not just disassemble your personal property. "Another pancake, Tristan?"

We didn't talk about the laptop. What would be the point? She'd never put it back together. Not in a million years. That was on me if I ever wanted to use it again. So instead I tapped the screen on my phone.

"What about this?" I asked. "You think they did something to the Chinese? Do you think someone blew them all up?"

Mom's mouth tightened and she cut a microglance at Dad.

"There have been some rumors about them stepping up their game," she said slowly. "People think the extremist Neo-Luddites went away, but they're like termites. You can smoke them out or fumigate the nest, but there are always more."

"Wow. That's optimistic," I said.

She shot me a look. "You can be a realist or you can stick your head up your own—"

"Jean," said my dad, still not looking up.

Mom sighed and drummed her fingers on the tabletop. "Okay, Tristan, you tell me. Do *you* think they blew up the Chinese ship?"

"No," I said at once, surprising myself by how fast that answer came.

"Okay. Why not?"

"Because we'd know."

She nodded as if pleased with my comment. "Why would *we* know? Support your opinion."

"The Chinese went nuts when the Neo-Luddites hit their plant last year. They were all over the news yelling about it."

"Yup," agreed Dad.

Mom nodded. "Which means . . . ?"

"Which means they would yell even louder if those freaks blew up their spaceship."

"Transit vehicle," she corrected.

"Spaceship," Dad said quietly, eyes fixed on the document on his tablet. Mom ignored him. She made a finger-twirling motion for me to continue.

I thought about it. "If anyone was taking that post seriously it would be the only story on the Internet."

"Good," she said. And that's where she left it. "What about that other pancake?"

Chapter 33

The mission people gave us no chance to get any more stressed about the Chinese ship or about the Neo-Luddite Internet posts.

Most of the remaining team members arrived at the training center two hours after my family. Only Nirti's family was still in India. The rest of us, though, kicked into high gear. The mission administration had one last chance to evaluate us working through simulations of everything from getting in and out of space suits to team-member rescue operations to assembling equipment under various harsh though simulated conditions. We wore biometric monitors so the medical team could make sure we were all in tip-top condition. It was rough, but as Colpeys pointed out, "You'll have plenty of time to relax on the trip."

So, once we got there everything moved fast. If my life were a movie this would be the montage part, complete with jump cuts and inspirational music heavy on the power chords.

We weren't raw recruits or strangers. Sure, we didn't know each other as well as we would once we were in the black, but we'd all trained together. So what we did was go into our own heads and tighten our games. They hit me with a lot of mechanical problems to solve, most of which had been designed by my mom; the woman who carried me, gave birth to me, nurtured me, and was clearly trying to drive me insane. She put my laptop, my external drives filled with my music and shows, and all of my pictures of Izzy in an airlock, and then set a small incendiary device in with it. The airlock mechanism was damaged—she did that, too—and she gave me a set of pocket tools and a timer. I had to wear a bulky EMU, or extravehicular mobility suit, which is a big, marshmallow-looking space getup while I repaired the mechanism to save all my stuff. And, get this, she reduced the amount of oxygen in my suit to match the timer on the burner. I mean, sure, she was right there and wouldn't let me die, but she was all in when it came to all of my stuff being destroyed.

I started to yell at her, but she tapped my faceplate and pushed the button to start the clock.

"I rigged the timer so it can only be shut off from inside the airlock," she told me. "Love you, honey."

She was *smiling*, too. I was so glad we had a therapist on the mission.

The days were like that. And the trainers woke us up in the middle of the night for "emergencies." Fake fires, fake collisions, hull breach simulations, and all of that stuff. They'd take us in small groups up on a big McDonnell Douglas C-9 transport jet, which flew high enough for gravity to drop way down. Then, while we were floating around like balloons, they'd give us challenges like changing in and out of pressure suits, collecting all the scattered tools from a kit designed for EVAs, making us work together to retrieve and assemble the components to a radio they'd tossed at us. That was fun, and the teams raced each other. Luther almost always came out on top for anything that involved coordination, but if it was a mechanical test I won. Every time. I even beat my mom's best time on the radio reassembly, which got me an actual smile from her.

She got her revenge, though. After we went one three-day endurance period with no sleep at all Mom gave me another of her special challenges. She locked herself in a scale model of the engine room and turned the valve to gradually flood the room with CO_2. I had to get her out even though I was dead on my feet and could barely spell my own name. The damage she'd done to the door-locking system was crazy. I had to remove a piece, measure and fabricate a new one, install it, and open the door. Dad tried to stand there and watch but he got so fritzed out that he started yelling at me and at Mom. That didn't help.

Did I get her out?

What do you think?

Chapter 34

I talked to Izzy every day.

"How's school?" I asked.

"Okay," she said.

Every day.

"How's training?" she asked.

"Okay," I said.

Every single day.

Sometimes we'd have these long silences on the phone where we didn't know what to say. Conversations between people who care about each other need optimism. You expect to see that person again. You expect to share something with them. But with us . . . where were our conversations supposed to go?

I'd been fishing around for comparisons to help me figure out what to say to her. Maybe this was like friends on the last day of school who want to stay in touch after they go to college or move away. But each of them knows down deep in their hearts that they won't, or if they do they know that their friendship isn't going to be the same. I had really close friends in grade school who I never talked to anymore. We went to different middle schools and different high schools. Our common ground kept getting smaller until there was nowhere for us to stand together.

I know that's part of life, but it's sad. And it's sad in a way I don't know how to define.

Maybe it's like someone saying good-bye to someone they love who's going off to fight a war in another country. Like during the wars in Afghanistan and Iraq. People had to say good-bye, and most of them kept in touch, but some of those soldiers died. And some came back as different people from the ones who went away. They came back as strangers.

I'd never be coming back and everything about my life from here on was going to make me a stranger to Izzy. And everything she did back home was going to make her a stranger to me.

We could feel that starting already.

Sometimes the silence on the phone was because neither of us wanted to say "I love you," which was what we always said when we hung up. When "I love you" becomes the same thing as "good-bye," how do you force those words out of your mouth?

Chapter 35

I spent a lot of time in the fitness center, training on the ARED, the Advanced Resistive Exercise Device, which was how we were going to keep fit in space and on Mars. It's a really cool machine that uses piston-driven vacuum cylinders to create resistance and has a flywheel system to simulate free-weight exercises in normal g. We had to become familiar with it on Earth and get as fit as possible, then use the machines every day to maintain muscle tone and bone density. Our ARED system would be installed on a section of the transit vehicle called the "wheel," which was a ring that spun in order to provide limited gravity. Only for that part of the ship, though. The wheel was there to train us for Martian gravity, to help with our fitness, and to use in case anyone on board needed surgery—'cause you do not want to do surgery in micro-g.

In microgravity astronauts lose 1 to 2 percent of their bone and muscle mass per month. Some of the astronauts who stayed for months on the ISS lost mass permanently and were never able to get back to normal. That's dangerous, and for those of us who were going to be in spaceships for seven months, it could be fatal. And it didn't get much better for people planning to live the rest of our lives on a planet with a third of Earth's gravity. If we couldn't counter those negative effects, then leaving Earth would kill us in less than two years. The ARED was part of our survival.

I was streaming sweat when I got a call from Herc. I looked at my watch and was surprised because it was way early in the morning where he was.

"Hey, man," he said, his voice tight and filled with anger, "something happened."

"What's wrong? Are you okay?"

"It's not me," he said. "It's Izzy. Whoa, wait, it's not like it sounds. She's okay, she's fine. It's just something weird happened."

He told me. It was weird. And by the time he was finished I was angry too.

The Drake family had all been in bed sleeping when they heard the downstairs front window shatter. They ran downstairs with Mr. Drake leading the way with a baseball bat. There was glass everywhere and a big rock lying on the carpet. Through the smashed window they could see long streamers of red and white fluttering in the branches of the tree by the curb. They went outside to find that the house, bushes, porch, and tree had been covered with streamers. And a big stick had been driven into the ground with a poster stapled to it.

EARTH IS OUR MOTHER

EARTH IS LIFE

MARS IS FOR THE DEAD

There was no one on the street except for neighbors who'd come out to investigate the noise. None of them had seen anyone, of course. No one saw anything.

But we all knew.

Especially when the other reports came in. This didn't just happen with Izzy. There were other kinds of vandalism outside the houses and apartments of mission members all over the globe. Not everyone's family or friends got targeted because not everyone on the mission *had* family or friends. So between the forty of us going there was a total of thirty-one incidents of what the media called "protest."

Protest? Really? I can think of better words. Not printable words, but better.

The fact that this wasn't just directed at Izzy didn't make me feel any better. Actually it scared me ten times worse because it showed how well-coordinated this stuff was. Thirty-one incidents, all done around the same time, all pulled off so quickly and smoothly that no one was spotted, no one was arrested.

I made a call to Frack and told him about it. He and Frick were back in Wisconsin. I asked him if he could maybe check on Izzy and her folks. He laughed, which was something he almost never did.

"What's funny?" I asked.

"Where do you think we are right now?" he said.

Chapter 36

I called Izzy about fifty times to see if she was okay. She had her best friends with her now and they were keeping her sane and keeping everyone else away. That was good. Not that there were armed hordes of Neo-Luddites showing up everywhere. Actually there was no sign of any at all, even in the crowds outside Izzy's house during the taping of her segments for our show. Protestors, sure, but no one with a red scarf. What did that mean? They were lying low or in disguise? How could anyone even know?

The anger and frustration I felt was pretty intense. I wished I could be with Izzy because she was scared. Sure, Frick and Frack were now working for the Drake family, but even so it soured the whole day for me and I decided to try and turn in early. Maybe nicer things were happening in dreamland.

Sleep was just starting to pull me down when I heard my Mom arguing with someone. I sat up and listened. The thing is, they weren't shouting, so it wasn't volume that woke me. It was the fake whispering people do when they're mad and they think they're keeping it all dialed down, but they're not. You hear couples do that when they're fighting in public. I kicked off my blanket and got out of bed, crept to the door, and leaned close to listen.

". . . being unreasonable, Jean," said a male voice. Not Dad. Director Colpeys, I thought. "There is absolutely no reason to believe that the Neo-Luddites have anything at all to do with the mechanical faults. Not at the launch site and certainly not up on the Lucky Eight. It's preposterous."

"Don't give me that crap. I want to go up and see for myself."

"We need you down here."

"Chu can finish the prep down here. Everything's set and checked to *my* standards here. I need to go up and see if someone's messed with my ships."

Colpeys didn't correct her about the ships not being hers.

"Oh, come on . . . how could anyone have even gotten *up* there? Certainly not the Neo-Luddites."

Mom fired back, "They could have done something to the machinery before it was launched. That's why I want to do a thorough inspection."

"You're talking about adding four full days to the liftoff. We're already at the edge of the launch window as it is. You're overreacting and you're being unreasonable."

"Unreasonable?" snapped Mom in as cold and sharp a voice as I'd ever heard her use. "How about I pull the plug on the whole damn launch? Would you like that, Jurgen?"

It really surprised me. Mom was having it out with Colpeys.

"Jean, you're being overcautious," said the director. "Johannsen and his people have been over the structure and it is absolutely sound."

"Oh really?" Mom growled, her voice colder and sharper still. "I read those reports. Did you read the same ones I did? Because I seem to recall seeing a notation about the exterior auxiliary docking hatch locking system on the *Huginn*. It was within one-point-six-six of failing the stress test."

"But it did *not* fail that test, Jean," insisted Colpeys. "You know as well as I do how wide a margin of error we built into our diagnostics. By anyone else's standards one-point-six-six would be a joke, so far outside of the possibility of failure that even NASA would—"

"Don't you presume to tell *me* about acceptable safety standards, Jurgen. We've had this discussion before and you know where I stand. If NASA has a lower standard, that's on NASA. This is my mission and I don't think a one-point-six-six margin is anywhere near acceptable. It's not like we can pull into a service station and get it fixed."

I heard the sound of a long, heavy sigh. "For God's sake, Jean, we're talking about the docking hatch. The *auxiliary* hatch. We're never even going to use it. Never. It's a redundant system for a process that plays no part in our mission. The docking mechanisms were meant to be used on the Lucky Eight and if we needed to dock the ships in stationary orbit. They were never intended for docking while traveling at these speeds. And the *Huginn* and the *Muninn* will not be docking at all during the transit. It would be an absurd waste of time and money to do what you're suggesting. Delays would cost us a million dollars a day, not to mention the PR backlash and loss of confidence in the overall mission."

Mom said, "Listen to me and try to get this through your head. I'm the chief toolpush on this mission. When it comes to all hardware issues I have the final say, and I'm telling you right here and now, Jurgen, that if you push me on this I'll scrub the launch. You can try again in twenty-six months, but the Hart family won't be on board and I will make damn sure everyone knows *why* the mission was scrubbed. I'll hang you with it."

"Jean . . . please . . ."

I could hear equal parts fury and exasperation in Colpeys's voice, but my mom was relentless.

"You know where I'm coming from, Jurgen," she said. "I was scheduled for the Olympus Space Station mission. I had to withdraw because I got pregnant. I didn't go and instead they sent Mike Bellamy, and good as he was he didn't mind cutting corners to catch a deadline. He wouldn't have minded a one-point-six-six error. He'd be on your side right now, maybe even have *my* job, but he can't. And why? Because he didn't triple-check everything and then check it again. When that bad wiring faulted and triggered the explosive bolt on the escape hatch, he burned up along with every single person on that station. They all died, Jurgen. Seventeen people. The worst tragedy in the history of space travel. Worse than the *Challenger* disaster."

"Look, Jean, I know you blame yourself for not being on that mission, but—"

"Don't," snapped my mom in a low and very dangerous voice. "You think we're having this conversation because I'm on a guilt trip? Really? How about crediting me with a little professionalism. My concern is for *this* mission."

"Look, Jean, I didn't mean to—"

"No, you listen to me," Mom fired back. "I'm going up to recheck everything on that transit vehicle and I swear to you, if I find a single screw or wire that isn't one hundred percent, I'll bury Mars One and you along with it. Look into my eyes and tell me if I'm joking. No? Good, now get out."

I was frozen to the spot as I listened to Colpeys mumble some kind of apology. Then I heard the front door close. Hard. My guess, it was Mom who slammed it behind him rather than Colpeys yanking it shut.

A heavy silence seemed to fill the world on the other side of my bedroom door. I debated going out and seeing if Mom was okay. I didn't. Nor did she come into my room to say good night.

Chapter 37

We spent the next day in the pool doing equipment drills, undertaking emergency EMU repairs, practicing EVA—extravehicular activity—techniques, and a lot of other things. It was stuff we'd done before, but they had a couple of NASA experts there as part of some kind of cooperation deal. I'm not sure of the details, but the NASA people were clearly looking for things they could criticize. It's not like they wanted us to fail and they certainly didn't want us to get hurt, but I hadn't met too many of them that thought we were going to succeed. They gave us glassy smiles.

But we surprised them.

Mars One may not have been an official government agency, but Lansdorp and his people hired the best of the best. They trained our butts off. Everyone on the mission now had skills way beyond expectations. Mars One wanted everyone cross-trained in as many things as possible. When a 911 call is fifty-four million miles away, you have to have mad skills.

After the space suit drills, the trainers said that we could put on our regular swimsuits and relax in the lap pool. It was the first time we could just chill out. Before I changed into my trunks I stood in the shower for a while. Space suits make you sweat and after a day in one you smell like an armadillo's armpit. Luther was in the next stall, singing some South African rap. I couldn't help but move under the spray along with the beat. It was a good song. Then we put on our suits and grabbed towels and headed into the pool area. We saw Zoé come out of the girls' locker room and then it was an instant race to see who could be the first into the water. Luther won but I cannonballed down next to him.

Then for a long time it was the three of us, floating there, not saying much.

Feeling weightless.

I closed my eyes and imagined we were in the ship, deep in the black, millions of miles away from Earth. After a while I peeked and saw that the others had their eyes closed too. Drifting, dreaming in the weightlessness. Maybe practicing not being here anymore.

I let my eyelids drift shut again, and the black pulled me back and wrapped itself around me.

Chapter 38

It was 8:20 at night in Amsterdam, which made it 1:20 in the afternoon back in Madison. I went into my bathroom and closed the door and called Izzy. I knew she'd be in class, but I also knew that the teacher would let her take my call.

"Tristan!" she cried. "Gimme a sec."

She muffled the phone but I could kind of hear her tell someone—the teacher, I guessed—who it was.

A few seconds later Izzy spoke again, her voice hushed and warm and familiar. It also sounded a lot less stressed than I expected. She was still coming back from the shock of the Neo-Luddite thing at her house. "I'm out in the hall," she said. "Is everything okay?"

"Yeah," I said, and very nearly told her about what had happened between my mom and Mr. Colpeys. I'd told Izzy about the Olympus Station disaster a long time ago, and once I laid everything out to her she said that maybe Mom's anger was tied to guilt. She hadn't been there to make sure everything was in top shape and blamed herself. It was a sad thought because it wasn't her fault at all, but guilt's a funny thing. We keep taking it on as if it's ours even when it's not.

And, I have to admit that I had a flicker of it too. After all, Mom didn't go because she was pregnant with me. If I could feel guilt like that, what Mom was going through must have been a hundred times worse.

What I didn't tell Izzy was the *other* thing that was making me feel guilty—that I was kind of praying Mom would find something wrong. Something so bad the whole mission would have to be scrubbed. Even though I really did want to go, there was that nasty little part of me that wanted an out.

It wasn't something I could ever tell Izzy. If I told her the truth then she'd also start hoping and praying that the mission would never get off the ground. *Wanting* that would hurt, and it would hurt worse if we still left. Sometimes I'm not a total clueless moron.

"I just wanted to hear your voice," I said. "Wanted to make sure you were okay."

"Oh," she said, then, "Are you sure . . . ? Your voice sounds funny."

"No, really, I'm good." I hated to lie to her, and I knew I wasn't very good at it. If she hadn't been at school she'd probably have grilled me and gotten it out of me. I was glad I called her at the wrong time. "They've been working us really hard and I'm really out of it. Heading to bed, but I wanted to hear your voice and tell you I love you."

There was the kind of pause that let me know she was evaluating what I just said.

"I love you, too," she said slowly. Almost putting it out there as a question, or as an invitation for me to say something else.

"Talk with you soon," I told her.

And hung up.

Chapter 39

Dinner was weird on the day after Mom's fight with Colpeys. Dad was all chatty, telling us about the mutant species of superbarley he'd developed, which was growing like crazy on the ISS and in trays on the transit vehicles. It was going to be *the* most important crop on Mars. He went on and on about it, apparently unconcerned that I only grunted and Mom didn't say a word. Not one word, all through breakfast.

When Mom finished and got up and left, all the air seemed to go out of Dad. He exhaled slowly and sat back in his chair.

"Mom okay?" I asked.

After a few seconds of him staring into the middle of nowhere, he looked at me. "Your mom is the single most stubborn woman on this or any other world," he said. "It's actually one of the reasons I love her." He reached over, patted my arm, got up, and left.

"What the actual hell was that about?" I asked the empty room. Nobody materialized out of thin air to fill in all the blanks. But let's face it, I probably already knew.

The lumpy gray science project in my bowl that was supposed to be high-nutrition stew sat there and dared me to eat another bite. I couldn't do it, though. So I bailed and went to the gym and had spent three grueling hours on the ARED, trying to work up a decent sweat, when the door opened and Luther strolled in. He took one look at my face and shook his head.

"Jeez. You look like someone kicked you in the nethers, boy," said Luther.

I only grunted at him. Luther pulled over a stool and sat down to watch. He'd brought in a pair of protein shakes and set mine on the floor. It looked like bile. He sipped his and tried not to wince. The protein shakes were packed with vitamins, nutrients, and calories, but they tasted like camel vomit.

I groaned my way through another set of dead lifts. My thighs were on fire and there were angry fireflies dancing in the air in front of me. Luther sat and watched me, his earbuds in, head bobbing to the beat of whatever he was listening to. South African stuff, probably Kwaito, which is a slow-tempo house beat style where the singer shouts out the words rather than raps. I was still getting used to it. Right then, though, the only sounds were the noises I couldn't help but make while I lifted what felt like a Mack truck for the zillionth time.

When I finished the last rep I paused, then did five more. That was a thing with me. Doing a set was okay, but that was hitting a goal. I liked exceeding goals. It set a standard for myself. Go the extra mile.

The last three reps were, I was absolutely positive, going

to rupture something very important in my extreme lower abdomen. Screw it. I doubted I'd ever have sex once we blasted off. Even if the science guys figured out how we could safely reproduce I'd be the crippled virgin who died alone and sad on Mars.

But I eased the weight back into place, released the wing bar . . . and collapsed down against the back wall of the cramped gym. My heart was a machine gun and it felt like I was breathing fire. I flopped a hand out and Luther bent and put the protein drink against my palm. I drank half of it. It still tasted like camel vomit. But it was wet and cold camel vomit.

Luther stood up and inspected the fittings on the flywheel and resistance pistons. He frowned. "Did they rebuild this? I've never seen this stuff before." He grabbed the bar and lifted one-handed. It didn't budge and he gave a grunt of surprise. He tried it again with two hands and it rose, but he had to put some muscle into it. He let it sink back. "Holy smokes, this is set all wrong. Who messed this up? It's broken."

"No it's . . . not messed up . . . ," I puffed. "I modified it."

He shot me a look. "You did this?"

"Yeah . . . it wasn't enough . . . so I fixed it."

Luther shook his head, air toasted me with his cup, and sat back down. "They teach that in shop class at the slow school?"

"Bite me, rock boy."

"'Rock boy'? That's the best you can do?"

I flipped him the bird. "It's been a long morning. I'll come up with a crushing reply when I'm hydrated."

We drank. He said, "You want to tell me why you look like someone stole your puppy?"

I pulled myself up to a sitting position against the wall, my knees up to my chin, sweat running in lines down my calves.

"You really want to hear this?" I asked.

He shrugged. "Why not?"

Luther wasn't Herc, and maybe he wasn't even a friend, but I told him anyway. Or, some of it. Not about the mechanical problem. Instead I told him about Izzy. He already knew about the window, the sign, and the streamers at the Drake house. That was all over the news. No, what I told him about were the conversations I'd been having with Izzy. About how they made me feel. Luther nodded a few times but didn't interrupt. When I was done he thought about it for a moment, then nodded.

"Did you ever watch the videos of the first candidates?" he asked. "The interviews they did to ask them why they were going?"

"I watched a lot of them. We all did."

"Remember the one with the kind of nerdy kid who said that he'd never been kissed and didn't expect to ever have sex? Remember him?"

I did. He was still in the program, though not on the first wave. "What about him?"

Instead of answering, Luther asked, "Remember the doctor from Mozambique, the one who said that it would be okay if he died on Mars because there was too much hate and pain down here?"

"That's not exactly what he said."

"Close enough. He said he wanted to see a better world than this one."

I took another sip, gagged, and pointed at him with the cup. "You getting somewhere or just talking?"

He started to say something, then stopped. He looked momentarily confused, and then he smiled. "Maybe I don't know what I'm trying to say."

"Yeah, well, that's kind of my point," I said. "No one's ever had this kind of conversation before, so we got nothing to go on."

Luther's smile lingered for a bit, but it changed. Less of a happy-go-lucky smile. More ironic. We sipped our raw sewage drinks and said nothing. I was pretty sure Luther was going somewhere with what he'd said, but it felt like one of those conversations that maybe we weren't ready for yet.

Chapter 40

I guess I should explain about why I didn't dig Luther all that much. There was this *thing* going on between us. He started it. Or, I think he started. Pretty sure he did.

Anyway . . . it was all about this meritocracy thing. Someone was going to be picked to be the first person to step down from the landing vehicle and put the first human foot on Mars. At government-funded programs like NASA the obvious choice would be the mission commander, but with Mars One it was different. They wanted it to be completely fair; they wanted to make sure that everyone who volunteered had an equal chance of being chosen to be the one to take that step. Officially we'd been told it would be a lottery, with a name selected randomly by computer, but Luther had somehow convinced himself that the selection was really going to be based on merit, on an evaluation of what we did on the mission.

I tried to convince him he was nuts. I mean, how would someone like, say, Sophie, who was mostly our cook on the flight, shine brighter than someone like my mom, who was the chief engineer? But Luther just smiled and said I was being naive. I thought he was nuts, but he really seemed to believe it, and everything he did was a competition. He tried too hard to be the best at training, games, evaluations, performance, citizenship, blah-blah-blah. . . . He was also doing a pretty good job of making sure I looked like a loser.

They say competition is healthy.

We were doing a mini–fitness marathon last year. He and I competed against each other because we were the only two boys. The adults were put in teams and the girls were their own team for strength events and short-distance running. For the first four rounds of the one-hundred-meter races, Luther and I were even. I won two, he won two, and neither of us showed any real superiority. Something like half a second differences. But in the tiebreaker, we were tearing down the track at the training center in Brussels. Luther was half a step ahead when suddenly I felt like an extra lung opened up and I could feel new energy flooding in. I turned the dials all the way up and was starting to pull even with him when he seemed to stumble a bit and his elbow jerked up as he fought for balance. The point of his elbow caught me dead center in the deltoid. Not hard, but enough to send me sideways for one full step. I corrected and poured it on, but by then the finish line was right there and Luther motored across it a quarter second before I did.

I didn't say anything at the time because I thought it was an accident.

Until it happened again.

Next time was an underwater safety drill and there was a malfunction on my air regulator that made me have to surface halfway through a timed drill. Luther wound up with the winning time for the exercise and I was disqualified.

Stuff like that.

Could I prove that Luther messed with my gear? Of course not. He, Sophie, Nirti, and two other mission people were all there at the time. I couldn't even prove *anyone* messed with it. Accidents do happen. If I could have pinned it on Luther I'd have beaten him into his component molecules. Or maybe told Colpeys and gotten him and his family cut from the program and the history books.

I thought about it too. Boy, did I think about it.

Suspicion isn't proof, though

But that was the point at which Luther and I began to treat each other like enemies.

No.

That's the wrong word. Too strong, and "rivals" is maybe too weak. For my part it was a trust issue. I guess I never really trusted him after that.

Chapter 41

Mom left three days later.

Not the program . . . she left the planet to head up to do her review of the mechanical issues on the transit vehicles. Colpeys apparently took her threats and demands seriously. He did, however, finesse the schedule for other things so that the launch date would be pushed back only two days instead of four.

Mom could pretty much take each of those transit vehicles apart, down to the last nut and screw, and then put them back together again. Perfectly. She was the absolute queen of type-A detail-oriented control freaks. If she were going to check your homework, you'd better not have fudged the math or forgotten to dot an *i*. Been there, done that, have the psychological scars. Believe me, you didn't ever want her to give you a long, unsmiling stare and then tell you that she was "disappointed in you." Much better to be devoured by piranhas, and it would hurt less.

In orbit the assembly crews had everything bolted together up at the Lucky Eight, including the fuel stages. Don't get me wrong, those guys were top engineers, and they'd all logged a lot of hours working on the ISS, on satellites, setting up the mining rigs, repairing the Hubble and other telescopes . . . but Mom didn't trust anyone else. Not completely. She took her handpicked technical crew up there to make sure every rivet, weld, seam, and connection was triple-checked and perfect by *her* standards. Like I said, God help anyone who made even the smallest mistake.

The day before Mom left, Nirti Sikarwar arrived. Not counting Sophie, Nirti was the fourth teen on our mission and the last person to join the colony training team here in Amsterdam. She'd been mourning her grandmother, who'd been very sick for a long time. The funeral was two days ago, but when she found me in the gym she gave me a huge smile and a hug. We sat and talked for hours.

She told me about her grandmother, who'd been a pediatric surgeon for forty-two years and then a teacher at a medical college in India. Then we talked about my mom and what she was going into orbit to do.

It was a good, long talk. About people, and about heroes. About sacrifice and commitment. I told her about the Hart Foundation and she told me about the Sikarwar College Fund she'd started to give girls from poor families a chance to go to college.

"Isn't it weird that we're making the world a better place by leaving it?" she said. It was intended as a joke, but neither of us laughed. It's not that the conversation depressed me or anything.

Kind of the opposite.

I gave her another hug and drifted off to find my folks.

I had only one more chance to be alone with Mom before her flight to the launch center. It was in the hall leading to the back door where her car was waiting.

"You'll be careful up there, right?" I asked, mostly because I didn't know what else to say.

I caught the tiniest flicker of an expression that looked like annoyance. Maybe I was reading it wrong.

"Of course I'll be careful, Tristan," she said. "I've done this before, you know."

That was true enough—Mom had logged more hours in space than anyone but the two pilots. Which didn't matter a bit to me.

"I know, but—"

She cut me off. "Tristan, you're sixteen, not six. Please try and act it."

Ouch.

"No," I insisted, "I'm not being a needy little kid."

"Then what?"

"Um . . ."

She straightened. "Ah. You've been surfing the Internet again, reading those conspiracy stories about the Neo-Luddites."

"It's not all theories. They were saying on the news that the Neo-Luddite extremists have been making threats again."

"*Specific* threats or the usual vague stuff?" asked Mom.

"Um . . . vague. But scary."

"Don't dwell on it," she said. "After what happened to Izzy's house and everywhere else they've really stepped up the security, and a lot of law enforcement agencies around the world are working on this. Your job is the mission. We all need you to become the best possible mechanical engineer. Which means it's on you to get better than me and to reach that level at a younger age than I did. We've had this conversation too many times. Pay attention to your studies. I left you some, um, *problems* to solve back in our apartment. Concentrate on that and your mission training and leave the politics to the people who enjoy that kind of crap."

Then Mom smiled—half-cold, half-loving—hugged me for two seconds, kissed my cheek, turned, and left. As she went through the door she said, over her shoulder, "I'll see you soon."

And she was gone, just like that.

I tried really hard not to let her words hit me like I was six. Though, maybe sixteen wasn't as old as she thought it was. While I stood there I hated her, loved her, needed her, and never wanted to see her again. All in equal amounts.

Two things occurred to me, though. The first was that she changed the subject rather than actually make a statement about the Neo-Luddites. And the other thing was that she didn't meet my eyes when she did that.

Chapter 42

When I got back to our apartment I found out what Mom meant when she said she'd left me some problems to solve. I don't know how she did it in the time she had after I left for that morning's classes and training, but she'd taken everything apart.

The TV, the music system—complete with speakers—the shower nozzle, my bed, and even the toilet. I almost sat down on the living room floor and cried.

Instead . . .

I burst out laughing.

I rebuilt the sound system first, put Izzy's playlist on, and cranked it up loud enough to sterilize a yak, stripped down to boxers and tank top, and set to work putting everything back together again.

Oh, and I increased the spray on the shower and reset the color values on the TV. Extra mile, baby. Maybe I wouldn't win the Hogwarts House Cup from Luther for being the best at everything, but I was at least going to make myself comfortable.

Chapter 43

Dad and I sat in the mission control room and watched Mom blast off.

During the long wait before the countdown we talked like it was any other day. "You see the game last night?" he asked.

"Which game?"

"Any game."

"No."

He sighed. "Me neither."

That's the kind of conversation we had. No jokes that made either of us laugh. No topics that drew our interest enough to make time pass. And nothing at all about Mom. It was weird because we were both clearly avoiding talking about the obvious, but it was obvious that neither of us wanted to start the conversation we should have been having.

When the countdown started, Dad took my hand the way he did when I was little. He needed to. I needed to hold on to him, too. We sat there watching the dual image of the exterior view of the rocket and the interior-cockpit live stream of the technical crew aboard the transit rocket, all of them in their color-coded space suits. With each tick of the clock, each number counted down audibly by the mission control officer, Dad and I clutched each other harder.

"We have liftoff," said the controller, and that froze us there, holding hands as if our combined strength could hoist the rocket up and fling it safely into orbit.

The command vehicle sat on one of the Falcon rockets leased from SpaceX. This was a pressurized capsule and payload hull resting atop a reusable rocket that needed to reach a minimum orbital speed of at least 9,300 meters per second in order to beat the pull of gravity and aerodynamic drag. To lift all of that mass that high and that fast the rocket burned a lot of very flammable fuel. Which meant Mom was sitting on top of a big bomb.

If things went bad.

If things went the right way, the rocket was a well-designed and well-constructed machine that would carry her safely into orbit.

The fact is that "we do this all the time" is a comfort all the time except when you're sitting there watching one of those big sticks of dynamite take your mother away from you.

Dad squeezed my hand, I squeezed his, and both of us wore these stupid grins that probably looked like happy smiles to anyone with the IQ or insight of a garden slug. We watched as the huge first stage burned through its fuel. Then there was that moment when the controller's voice said, very clinically and dry, "Detaching first stage."

The launch stage dropped away as the second stage fired. I knew there was nothing left in the first stage, but it was somehow weird and scary to see it suddenly stall and then fall back to Earth. Then the big parachutes deployed and the dead fall jerked to a stop and the empty rocket began drifting down. It descended slowly out of shot, falling onto someone else's screens over at SpaceX. It was their rocket; they'd recover and reuse it.

My eyes were glued on the second stage, watching it push up and up and up. The image switched from ground-based cameras to a satellite keyed to track it. So instead of it moving away from our point of view, it was suddenly coming toward us. The atmosphere thinned around the ship as it rose and then it crossed that line of sixty-two miles from the surface. It's not an official marker, but most people say that's where Earth's atmosphere ends and space begins. It's the point at which you can say that you've left the planet.

The ship kept going, though. No longer up but "out."

Then, almost as if this was just a normal day at work, the controller said, "Orbit achieved."

Dad held my hand for another two seconds, then let it go and rubbed both his palms on his thighs to dry off the sweat.

"Well," he said, "that was fun."

"Yeah," I said.

We sat there for a few minutes, staring at nothing. Finally Dad turned to me. "You, um, want to do something? Grab lunch? Talk? Whatever . . . ?"

I shook my head. He looked relieved, I think. I know I was. Dad stood up, stretched, patted me on the shoulder, and left the room. I watched him go. He was as tall as me but not as muscular. Wiry and thin. A happy man who was having an unhappy day.

I sat there for a long time, alone with my thoughts.

Chapter 44

Halfway back to my room, Herc texted me.

Herc: *Dude, ur mom is a total badass.*

Me: *I'll tell her.*

Herc: *U okay about her going?*

Me: *Sure.*

Herc: *Liar*

I walked back to my quarters. Everyone I met along the way stopped to shake my hand. Mission support team, mission public-relations crew, other colonists. Anyone with a pulse. As if I'd been the one riding the rocket instead of Mom.

Izzy texted me.

Izzy: *You okay?*

I didn't lie to her.

Me: *No. Scared.*

Izzy: *That's normal.*

Me: *I guess.*

Izzy: *Call me later?*

Me: *Yes.*

Izzy: *I love you.*

Me: *I love you.*

I wasn't living with Dad at the moment. A few days ago they moved me into a tiny room with Luther. It was a little bigger than what each of us would have on the *Huginn*. In flight we'd have private pods, but for now they put us in a glorified closet. Partly it was a bonding thing, and also because they figured it would help us get used to confined spaces. It was nice to have the room to myself. Luther wasn't back yet.

So I crawled into my bunk and watched the mission feed on my phone, wondering how many kids around the world would be doing something like this when the big rockets went up. Watching us on their phones or on their tablets. Maybe wondering what we were feeling and trying to understand why we were going. Or maybe thinking about going, too. To Mars, to the moon, to one of the space stations. This new space race wasn't slowing down. I saw one scientist from NASA on TV saying that it was likely for there to be a million people living in space by the end of the century. Maybe that was true, but if so there was still a lot of science to figure out. I mean, most people—even a lot of the NASA people— thought that everyone on Mars One was going to die in the first year or two. Any one of ten thousand mechanical failures could kill us. We could die on landing. We could run out of food or oxygen if we couldn't produce it on the planet. We could all get cancer from the high radiation. There were all sorts of medical dangers, not to mention the ones we didn't know about because nobody had ever done what we were doing. Or we could discover that there are bacteria and viruses on Mars—which everyone thought was likely—and maybe that could kill us.

I know, gloomy thoughts.

And I realized I was kind of slipping down into a depression. Luther, Nirti, and Zoé had a lot of laughs, and some of the instructors and trainers were hilarious. We watched a lot of comedy, too. Stand-up specials and movies. The Mars One project was filled with laughter. So, I know I've been making it sound worse than it was. That's on me. Or maybe that *is* me. It was scary, too, because I needed to break out of that before I let them strap me into a chair on that rocket.

Sucked.

The smart thing to do would have been to go to the mission psychologist and open up, but I knew I wouldn't do that. No way. The second smartest thing would have been to talk to Dad, but he was really busy and had his own stuff to deal with, what with Mom gone. He hadn't cracked a single joke since she went up.

Who then? Herc? He'd go straight to the family lawyer, who would go to the mission director. Luther? It was tempting. Could we talk about that, though? I wasn't sure enough to risk it. I knew that Luther wanted to go to Mars more than anything. He was already writing his story for the history books. I am not joking, I'd seen the Word file.

I spent a lot of time inside my own head, working it out.

Understand, I *did* want to go. This was who I was and being part of this mission made me feel like I mattered, like I was really going to play a part in something special. Most of the time all I needed to do was look at the big picture and I felt good about all of my choices, even the hard ones. But is anyone 100 percent committed to anything, ever? Is there anyone who can absolutely swear that there isn't—and never was—some doubt? Some worry that, despite the decisions you've already thought through and the promises made, that it's still a bad call?

I knew that if I went to the mission shrinks they'd scrub me and my folks. They didn't want us to have *any* doubt. Was I the only one who felt like this? Or did every single person on this mission have moments like this? I had to believe they did.

Funny, but thinking that made me feel a little better about it.

Chapter 45

The last days burned off.

I didn't crash—emotionally or psychologically. I didn't bail and I didn't tell anyone what I was feeling. Instead I threw myself into the training and let that keep me steady.

It would have been really nice if I could have fixed my own head as easily as I could repair a damaged starboard solar alpha rotary joint or a malfunctioning intake valve on an oxygenator.

Sure, and after that I'd cure the common cold and solve world hunger.

Izzy and Herc kept calling and texting. They were worried about me. Or maybe they just wanted to keep in touch while it was still easy. Soon it would be radio, and then long-distance satellite communication with a time lag. Even using the latest Laser Communications Relay System—LCRS—there was going to be a delay in any conversation.

Mindy set up interviews with me almost every day. The closer we got to launch the higher the ratings rose for *Tristan and Izzy*. And for the other shows. There were twenty-seven reality shows running right now. Nuts.

We also had a whole slew of mini–press conferences with corporate sponsors. These were companies that were absolutely throwing money at Mars One in exchange for us taking their products to the red planet. I'm not joking. Coke, Nike, Apple, McDonald's, and about a hundred more were paying huge bank for endorsements. That meant at some point one or another of us on the mission would take a selfie or stand for a photo holding a bottle or a can or something. Think about that. Here's me in my clunky white EMU space suit standing on the soil of another world holding up a pair of Nike's new Mars Runners or a tub of KFC. Sure, the fried chicken tub, Coke cans, and other products would be empty and the running shoes would be useless up there, but these corporations were not afraid of writing checks with a lot of zeroes on them. Mars One needed the bucks, so we all agreed to smile our way through the press conferences, film promos on Earth and on the trip, and do stand-ups on Martian soil.

Was the whole world nuts? You betcha, and we were taking that brand of crazy all the way across space.

Chapter 46

Zoé and I were working in a half-million-gallon deep pool, practicing buddy rescue techniques in our space suits, when we got the first update about the Chinese ship. Luther came and jumped feet-first into the pool to tell us to come up. We did, and by the time the crane lifted us out of the water and onto the side of the pool, Nirti had the big wall-mounted TV monitor tuned to the mission channel. Director Colpeys was on camera, looking grim and depressed as always. Or maybe a little grimmer and more depressed. Hard to tell with him.

"—Chinese government today officially confirmed that they have launched a ship to Mars carrying a crew of twenty-two astronaut-colonists," he said gravely, and my heart sank. "That ship, *Red Dragon*, was assembled inside the Shanghai Wheel but then rendezvoused with a launch platform in deep orbit, two hundred thousand kilometers from Earth. The existence of this platform was known to the governments of a few countries, including the United States and Russia, but that information was not shared with Mars One until today, following this morning's statement by the president of the People's Republic of China. The *Red Dragon* was launched this morning."

"Wait," gasped Luther, "*what*? I thought . . ."

Zoé grabbed Luther's arm. "*This morning!* That's great. We still have a chance."

"How?" I asked. "We don't leave for days . . ."

"Speed," she said. "Ever since we found out about the Chinese ship I've been reading all about their technology. Everything I could find. They have great ships, but their rockets aren't in the same league as the new-design SpaceX rockets that will launch our transit vehicles. Our rockets can achieve greater speed, and our launch window is better. So, we might even catch up."

Zoé rattled a bunch of numbers for fuel tables, launch angles, weight-to-thrust calculations, variables, and more.

Nirti cut me a knowing look. She'd told me in confidence that Zoé had an amazing recall. True total recall, what's called a photographic memory, isn't a real thing. Zoé had hyperthymesia, which is a fancy word for a highly detailed autobiographical memory. That means she could remember every detail of her entire life. She also had an eidetic memory, which means that she had a much greater capacity to remember images, sounds, or objects with perfect clarity. Put those things together with off-the-charts IQ and you had a teenage supercomputer. If she spit out a fact, you could bet on it being accurate.

"Yeah, but ten days," insisted Luther. "That's a lot of time."

"The fastest Chinese rocket ever tested," said Zoé, "reached seventeen thousand five hundred miles per hour. The rockets we're using on the transit vehicles tested out at thirty-two thousand miles per hour, and that was still in the combined field of Earth and lunar gravity. If we fire them again midway we could theoretically reach thirty-nine thousand miles an hour. Possibly more depending on length of burn. They've worked those calculations out a couple of times. That's more than fast enough to catch up to the *Red Dragon*."

"It would also cut down the travel time by a couple of months," said Luther, nodding.

"Never going to happen," I said. They all gave me sharp looks.

"And why not?" demanded Nirti.

"Because even though they did the math we didn't run the tests."

"So what?"

"So," said Zoé, stepping in on my side, "it would change every part of the mission: we'd have to launch at a different angle and redo all of the navigational calculations."

Nirti made a face. "Again . . . so?"

"And it would mean we'd burn up our reserve fuel," she said, and I nodded.

"Who cares?" asked Luther. "We're not coming back."

"No, but we don't know everything about what's out there," I said. "If there's a problem, if one of the ships fires incorrectly or they have a mechanical fault, if we get hit by a micrometeoroid . . . jeez, there's a million things that could go wrong. If we don't approach Mars exactly right and have to do last-minute course corrections in order to slow enough for a safe landing," I said, shaking my head. "If we were going to burn through the extra fuel just to catch the Chinese then we'd be gambling too much. My mom would never allow it."

Luther grinned. "Your mom? She's just a used-car mechanic. She doesn't know jack about—"

I grabbed a fistful of Luther's shirt and jerked him forward so that we were nose to nose. "That's my mother you're talking about, asshole."

Luther tried to slap my hand away and shove me back but I had the leverage. Zoé grabbed Luther and tried to pull him away from me, and Nirti put her hands on my wrist. I ignored them and shook Luther as hard as I could and then thrust him backward with such force that he lost his balance and fell. The people closest to us stepped back, looking annoyed as if this was typical kids horsing around. No one seemed to notice or care that we were scuffling. Or maybe the thought of us fighting never entered their minds.

It entered mine, though; I can tell you that. And from the way Luther came up off the deck, fists balled, I knew it was on his mind too. His dark eyes seemed to flash with real heat and he stepped to me, but I was right there, ready to bring it.

Nirti stepped between us and jammed her tiny palms flat against our chests like a boxing referee.

"*Stop it,*" she snarled. "Right. Now."

Chapter 47

The night before the launch we had a huge ceremony. We were all in Mars One jumpsuits, our names embroidered in white on red-and-white cloth. Thirty-nine of us sitting in two rows on a stage. Only Mom was missing.

Five thousand seats were stacked on risers so that the audience made a huge half circle around the stage. There was a band down front, special sections for the press, and reserved seating for invited guests: heads and deputy heads of state, dignitaries, and, of course, movie stars. There was one section of seats reserved for the CEOs of the TV networks that owned the reality shows, and some Hollywood producers who were planning to make movies about us. There was a big screen behind our chairs to project the image of whoever was at the podium, and it seemed like every person who had the power of human speech needed to be photographed saying something. I zoned out. My cell was on mute but it vibrated in my pocket constantly. Sneaking it out and hiding it in my hand took some ninja skills. But I managed.

Herc: *You look like ur falling asleep.*

Me: *I AM.*

Herc: *WAKE UP WAKE UP WAKE UP WAKE UP!!!*

Me: *Bite me, puny earthling.*

More speeches.

Izzy: *R u ok?*

Me: *Bored.*

Izzy: *How can u be bored? Ur going to Mars.*

Me: *Not soon enough.*

No reply from her for a long time. And I'm sorry to say it took me a while to realize how stupid and insensitive my text was. I felt like inviting Luther to take a really good punch at my face.

Finally the keynote speaker came up to the podium. It was Dr. Ilse Aukes, a physicist who had worked with the founders of Mars One to develop the technology that had turned dreams into a reality. Dr. Aukes was a small, silver-haired woman with an enormous intellect. After she went through all of the greetings and compliments and all the thank-yous, Dr. Aukes talked about the mission. This was the point at which I sat up and listened.

"The questions I have been asked many thousands of times since signing onto Mars One back in 2012 are . . . why? Why go to Mars? Why now? Why at all? Why send people? Why not continue to send robots? What's the point?"

I watched the audience; some of them were nodding at those questions. Even some of the sponsors. Dr. Aukes had a science nerd's nervous smile. I liked her. We all did.

"Why go?" she asked the audience and, via satellite and cable, the world. "Why indeed. If we could go back in time and ask that question of the first humans to migrate out of Africa or the Aboriginal people who settled in Australia fifty thousand years ago, perhaps their answers—could we but understand the language—would be the same as mine. As *ours*. New land, new things to see, new places to live, new opportunities to be free. And . . . on a more mundane and less heroic level, the chance to build commerce. The Phoenicians traded throughout the Mediterranean three and a half thousand years ago. It is possible some of them made it as far as Central America. The Greek explorer Pytheas of Marseille was the first to circumnavigate Great Britain and explore Germany twenty-three hundred years ago. I expect there are those among his peers and critics who thought he was mad, that he would fall off the edge of the world. We all know that he did not. Pytheas was one of many visionaries who wanted to see farther than was possible from where he stood. He had to go and prove that his theories were correct. We also have the diaries and records of explorers like Christopher Columbus and Captain Cook. And there is strong evidence that the Chinese reached Chile in 1407. I could go on and on. Exploration is part of the human experience, and a need to discover is key to who we are, how we've grown, and why we've survived."

More nods from the crowd; they were interested now.

"We love this planet. Our home. Our mother. We love her, but we have abused her, neglected her, damaged her, and now we are crowding her. While some of our colleagues in the sciences and in world government are working to repair and reverse the damage done to this world, others of us have thought to look beyond. To new worlds. To new places where mankind can live and grow and thrive. We know that we cannot live for extended periods of time in zero gravity. And the moon is not a world we can make habitable. It has no atmosphere and the gravity is only one-sixth of Earth's. For those and many other reasons it is not the future home of mankind. A way station, to be sure. A research lab, no doubt. But we will never till the fields of Luna."

For some reason more applause broke out.

"Why go to Mars?" asked Dr. Aukes. "We go because it alone, of all the reachable places we know, offers the best potential for human life. We must and will go there. This has been my dream, and it's become the shared dream of the fine men and women who share this stage with me, and of those hundreds training now for the next ships. And the next. And the next. Our robotic probes and rovers have proven to us that Mars was once warm and wet. Eleven years ago we found the first proof of liquid water, and we know without doubt that there is water ice there, and in abundance. Perhaps we will even find life there. Microbes in the groundwater, or bacteria."

Much more applause and Dr. Aukes waited for it to die down. "Why go to Mars? We go so that we understand more about our own world. The changing climate is our greatest threat, and we know that Mars has undergone catastrophic change. By examining it, by studying it, perhaps we will unlock secrets that may contribute to the saving of Earth. That is not a pipe dream—that is geophysical science. It is planetary science. After all, it was studying the atmospheric dynamics of Venus that led us to a true understanding of the threat of global warming by greenhouse gases. Mars is the world most like Earth and it is a book waiting to be read." She paused and looked around. "Why go to Mars? We go for the challenge. Oh yes. We humans thrive on challenge, and without it we falter and fail. There is a saying in America that necessity is the mother of invention. We, as the dominant species on this world, are in need, and we must pioneer new areas of science and deepen our understanding in all areas of knowledge."

Sophie Enfers was seated right behind me and leaned forward to whisper in my ear. "Look at them. They're eating this up."

I nodded because she was dead right. Dr. Aukes had the crowd in the palm of her hand. If there was anyone out there who had doubts, she was winning them over. Sophie gave my shoulder a squeeze and sat back. I cut a look over my shoulder and saw that her friend Marcel was sitting with her. He gave me the same kind of dirty look he always did. I ignored it, though I was glad he wasn't going on the *Huginn*.

"Why go to Mars?" said Dr. Aukes, her voice rising in pitch and power. "Because never in the history of humankind has so great an undertaking been attempted by a group so diverse in ethnicity, cultural background, sexual orientation, and political affiliation. For once—*for once*—a group stands together, not as members of their countries, but as representatives of the grand and wonderful collective called the human race. We send them as pioneers and explorers, yes, but first and foremost they are our ambassadors. Of conscience, of goodwill, of humanity at its best. You ask me why go to Mars? And I say that we—emphatically *we*—must."

The crowd went nuts.

Chapter 48

After the speech there was a party. A huge spread of food for the guests. Unfortunately the mission specialists and astronauts were not allowed to eat any of the fancy catered food. We drank vitamin water and ate small protein bars and tried our best to look like we enjoyed them. Luther, I think, did. Either he was a great liar or he was adapting faster than me to the realities of life in space. Fine dining was one of the many things we were leaving behind.

Sophie Enfers caught up to me afterward and we stood talking for a few minutes.

"Hey, Sophie," I said as she joined me, and I nodded to Marcel, who was standing apart from the rest of the crowd, as if not wanting to become dirty by touching the unwashed. He saw my nod but instead of responding like a normal person he gave me a flat, cold, and completely hostile stare, like I was something he noticed on the ground and was glad he hadn't stepped in. He's a real sweetheart. "You better watch out. I don't think your boyfriend digs me all that much."

She turned to consider Marcel, shrugged, and smiled at

me. "Don't worry about Marcel. He's like that with everyone. And . . . he's not my boyfriend."

Her accent was really thick but I was used to it by then and could understand her.

"He looks pissed," I said.

"He always looks like that. Just ignore him." She said it almost loud enough for Marcel to hear.

"Maybe he's mad 'cause you guys will be on different ships."

"Perhaps."

"You could have put in a request to be on the same ship, you know."

Sophie shook her head. "No, this will work out much better for everyone, trust me."

"Um, okay."

She touched my arm. "By the way, you haven't forgotten that you promised to teach me how to do some basic repairs, have you? Once we're in flight, I mean."

"Huh? Oh, sure. No problem. Anytime."

Lansdorp entered the room, his arm interlaced with Dr. Aukes's, and there was another round of applause. Then the physicist was swarmed by reporters.

"That was some speech, *non*?" Sophie said.

"Yeah," I agreed, "Dr. Aukes is a rock star."

"She could sell coal to the devil," she said, nodding.

"She's not trying to con anyone," I said, rising to what

sounded like a challenge in her tone. "She really believes in what we're doing. She knows it's the right thing."

She studied me. "The right thing for whom?"

"Weren't you listening to what she said? For us. For humanity. You know, that whole pushing the limits of science, finding new places for people to live, all of that . . ."

"Couldn't all the billions being spent on space exploration—not just with Mars One but with SpaceX and NASA and every other space program—be put to better use here on Earth? There are billions living at or below the poverty line. There are droughts and famines. There is a need for advanced science. Imagine what could be done with a few hundred billion. New kinds of agriculture, improved water purification systems, repairs to rail, road, dams, and shipyards. Literacy programs and education . . ."

Her voice trailed off and she cleared her throat.

"If you feel like that, Sophie," I said, "why are you going at all?"

I gave her a moment to come up with an answer. While she'd ranted her cheeks had flushed red and odd lights began burning in her eyes. "I'm going because *we* are going."

"Sorry . . . you lost me. What?"

She adjusted one of the fastenings on her suit. "These rockets are going to Mars. You and I and all of the others. That is happening. That is certain. Why am I going? Because I'm needed. I believe that I have been called to go. Destiny is not an abstraction. Besides . . . I have skills that are crucial to this mission."

She was mostly a cook, not a mission specialist, but I thought it'd be the wrong time to point that out.

"Everyone's bringing game," I said, "but everyone else seems to think Mars One is a good idea."

"Do they?"

"Sure."

"Do you?"

"What's that supposed to mean?" I demanded.

"Iseult," said Sophie. "I've been watching your show. *Tristan and Izzy.* I've seen the pain in your eyes when that witch of a host asks you questions about leaving your pretty girl behind. I saw the episode where she ambushed you with old friends. That hurt you."

"Of course it hurt . . ."

"No," she said, shushing me gently. "If you were one hundred percent committed to this mission and to all that it implies—leaving your friends, leaving a future, denying yourself the chance to start a family, probably living a shorter life, the possibility of diseases and medical conditions unique to space travel, the uncertainty of what we'll find, the risk of never really being happy . . . should I go on?"

I had to grit my teeth as I said, "I know the risks."

"I have no doubt. I saw that in your eyes during every episode of that show. It's there in the carefully worded love letters to Iseult . . . the ones the producers probably asked you to write. I wonder what is in the letters no one but your girl reads. Do you tell her your true feelings? Or do you keep all of that bottled up because it would sour the great sacrifice you are making?"

"You don't have a right to say that to me."

"We will be a community of inmates on a metal ship, Tristan. It will be like living inside a confessional. Do you think any of our secrets will remain hidden? Or should?"

"I don't have secrets," I lied.

She laughed. Soft and low. "You are a terrible liar, Monsieur Hart."

With that she walked away and joined a conversation group, kissed cheeks, shook hands, laughed. From then on she and Marcel were never more than a few feet apart. But every once in a while I caught her looking back at me.

Chapter 49

Feeling weird and uncomfortable after that bizarro conversation with Sophie, I coasted the edges of the party. But I wasn't really into it now. So I used every second I could to text Izzy and Herc—sending them celebrity pictures and trying to be normal with them.

Normal was another thing we were leaving behind. Though, I guess I already had.

Then Izzy sent me a text that really hit me hard.

Izzy: *Tristan . . . will you forget me?*

I immediately texted back that I wouldn't. Ever. Never ever. Her answer was a knife that went deep and turned slowly.

Izzy: *You probably should.*

Before I could compose an answer a shadow fell across the cell phone screen and I looked up to see Nirti standing there. She was looking at me, not trying to peek at the screen, but from the expression on her face I think she might have read what Izzy wrote.

"Are you okay?" she asked.

I made myself grin. "Um . . . sure. Never better. Going to Mars tomorrow."

When she wandered off I texted Izzy back, my thumbs flying over the little keys.

Me: *Nothing in the universe could make me forget you.*

There was no response.

Me: *I love you.*

Nothing.

Me: *Love you forever.*

No matter how hard you stare at a cell phone and will it to show a text, sometimes it simply refuses. Sometimes the world is that cruel.

The crowd swirled around me and I felt like a toy boat bobbing in the current. People talked to me and I tuned out as much of it as I could. Eventually I washed up against the wall farthest from the action. After a while Luther, Zoé, and Nirti drifted to stand with me, and for a long time we said nothing, just stood and watched. We all said the right things when someone from the media shoved a mic at us, and we smiled pretty because we'd been schooled on how to give good interviews. But we weren't there. Not really. All four of us were already on board the rocket. Or maybe we were already deep in the black and heading to our new red home.

Nirti told Luther and me to behave ourselves, and we did.

At one point Luther punched me on the shoulder and ticked his head toward the door to the restrooms.

"I don't need to pee," I growled.

"Yes you do," said Zoé. Nirti nodded. And then I got it.

I followed them through the door, down the hall, past the men's and women's rooms, and out the service door to a storage yard closed in by a chain-link fence. We waited until the door closed and then everyone let out a sigh. We sat on packing cases, watching the sun set on the far side of the launch site. The four massive rockets were silhouetted against the red sky.

"The pillars of heaven," murmured Nirti.

"What?" I asked, and she pointed to the ships.

"They look like they're pillars holding up the sky."

We all looked and nodded. Even Zoé, who didn't much believe in heaven or anything. My guess was that she was mentally doing mass-versus-thrust calculations. That was how she relaxed.

The western sky was still streaked with red when the first stars ignited overhead, and Luther began naming them. Zoé corrected him twice. And Nirti gave us the Hindu names of the constellations they belonged to. Luther, not to be outdone, gave the Zulu names. I gave them names from old science-fiction stuff. Gallifrey, Arrakis, Skaro, Mongo, Tatooine. Zoé started looking those up on her cell, apparently unnerved that I knew something she didn't. She didn't watch old movies or read fiction. At all. When she found the entries she punched me. Not hard.

The very last of the sunlight gleamed so intensely on the ships that they seemed to catch fire.

Not the most encouraging image the night before takeoff.

Nirti must have felt it too, because her small brown hand slipped into mine and squeezed. She wasn't coming on to me. She was hanging on.

Was it fear? Doubt? Excitement? All of that?

Yes.

That's exactly what it was.

Chapter 50

Launch day.

Even though we'd been planning this forever and it was the only thing I'd been able to think about, I couldn't believe it was about to happen.

Our ride into orbit would be aboard a reusable Falcon heavy-payload rocket, one of four that would rise in sequence from the launch site. My dad and I were in the second rocket. Luther and his folks were in number one, Nirti's family was in three, and Zoé in four. It wasn't actually intended that way. Seating was based on random computer selection.

We had to wear the latest generation of bright orange space suits called ACES (Advanced Crew Escape Suit), which included suit, boots, gloves, a helmet, and a bunch of emergency gear shoved into pockets. This was what we'd wear during our ascent into space. Space programs began using these types of suits after the space shuttle *Challenger* tore itself to pieces back in 1986. They were designed to keep people alive in the event of what they called a "survivable bailout" from an unsafe or failing spacecraft. This meant that we might—and "might" is an iffy word—stay alive if the rocket were to fall into water. If it actually blew up, we'd be dust. If it crashed to the ground, we'd be roadkill. Basically, the suits were nasty. They were heavy and hot, but what we wore underneath was a lot worse—because we had to wear frigging diapers. Okay, they called them Maximum Absorbency Garments, or MAGs, but they were diapers. You can't unzip and take a leak while you're on a rocket. Can't drop trou and dump your cargo either, if you get my drift. They made us wear space-age Pampers. If you're going into outer space you leave your personal dignity back home along with your sense of privacy.

Over the MAGs we wore long underwear made somewhere in Switzerland by, I can only assume, people who hated the thought of astronauts being comfortable. Add to that thick socks, and we were baking. But over all that we wore a liquid-cooling garment, so you had sweaty heat and a cooling system. It was a wonder storms didn't form inside the space suit.

We went through ten zillion kinds of system checks and equipment checks and suit telemetry checks and prelaunch prep checks. After a while it felt like we were doing the same thing, checking the same stuff over and over again. And we were passengers. We weren't flying anything. Personally, I thought some of it was actually fake—but it gave us something to do because sitting on a rocket and waiting for it to launch or blow up can kind of work the nerves. Trust me on this.

The pilots were not part of our mission—they worked for SpaceX and they came with the lease on the four reusable rockets. Chauffeurs to take us off world. Our pilots were as unsmiling as Frick and Frack. Total professionals who could hit the hold button on their emotions while they did their job. Like Mom, I guess, though she left that button pressed most of the time.

The twenty colonists on my ship were seated in rows of five, all of us facing the same wall of screens, watching the live feeds from ten different cameras. Four of the screens showed the interiors of the passenger cabins. I could see myself there, second row back, middle seat. Another four screens showed the exterior of our ship as it sat on launch pad. The ninth camera showed a satellite view of the four rockets in a row, each separated by half a mile, like a picket fence in a giant's yard. And the last camera showed another satellite view, but this was facing out rather than down, and there, snugged into the hoops that formed the Lucky Eight, were the two transit vehicles, the *Huginn* and the *Muninn*. The two largest spacecraft ever built. No one had ever even attempted to construct ships capable of carrying a crew like ours. Plus supplies, crew's quarters, a gym, a galley, and other chambers, all built like cells in a beehive. Every inch of space had been planned for multiple uses, and every possible comfort was provided— but "comfort" in space travel didn't mean the same thing as it did on Earth. Comfort was a tiny screened-in cubbyhole so you could take a zero-gravity poop. Comfort was a VR helmet so you could step off the ship and back onto Earth while you worked out. Comfort was a common room built without a thought about gravity. All twenty people on each ship could crowd into that room and sit on the walls, floor, ceiling, all at once, or they could float around between everyone else.

The mission specialist, a woman with a hard mouth but kind eyes, came into the crew capsule to do a safety check. She made sure all of the right wires, tubes, cables, and feeds were attached to each of us. Some of those would monitor our vitals during the flight. I can only imagine what my pulse was in those last minutes before final countdown. I'm pretty sure that my blood pressure could have launched all four ships.

"You okay?" asked Dad.

"Oh, sure," I said. "Why wouldn't I be?"

He frowned. "I'm serious, Tristan. You're flushed."

"Prelaunch jitters," I said. "It's all good."

He studied me for a moment longer, the frown still etched around his mouth, and then he patted my knee and turned away to watch the screens. Then the voice of the mission controller at the launch center filled the air around us—through speakers on the wall and the earbuds we all wore.

"We are cleared for launch."

Oh my God, I thought.

The mission specialist left the crew chamber and sealed the door. On the screen the countdown began. The voices of the pilot and copilot were as calm as if they were two guys talking sports over coffee at Starbucks, but they were running through the last prelaunch steps.

Then the voice from the launch center spoke again.

"We are T-minus ten."

This was it.

"Nine."

I thought of Herc and all the great things he could and would do with the Hart Foundation.

"Eight."

I thought of my friends at school. Kids I grew up with and kids I'd just met.

"Seven."

I thought of our house. The yard outside, my room, my dad's botany lab in the garage, the machine shop and engineering workspace my mom and I shared in the basement. My old bicycle. The cat, goldfish, and box turtle we'd had to bury in the backyard over the years. The boxes of Halloween and Christmas decorations in the closet. The marks of my height penciled against the kitchen door frame. All of it gone. Not even history, because another family would change everything about that house. They were only memories now, and it hurt me to think that they would fade and vanish the farther I got from that place.

"Six."

I thought of all the people who were watching this. The

thousands standing or sitting on the grass on the hills outside. What were they thinking? How many of them wished us well? How many—like those freaks in the Neo-Luddites—hoped that we'd blow up on liftoff? How many thought we were wrong, or crazy?

"Five."

I thought of the millions who were seeing the countdown on computers and tablets, on TV and on their phones. Millions, maybe billions. What Sophie had said came back to me. These ships cost billions and there were starving kids, people scrambling for a cup of polluted water from a dying well, farmers who were being foreclosed on because they couldn't afford to buy seed. All of that was true. All of that maybe mattered more than what we were doing. No, not maybe. Definitely. And yet I believed in what Dr. Aukes said, in what we all knew was true. And, who knows, maybe in leaving Earth we'd see it differently. It's all about how you look at it. Perspective changes everything; it lets you see more and maybe put a higher value on things than you might otherwise do. It was a great lesson. We, those of us on these ships, were about to get a huge perspective check.

"Four."

I thought of where we were going. Mars, the red planet. Named after a god of war. Would it be a place of peace? Would the different nations of Earth manage to colonize it and live together on that new world without bringing hate and prejudice and war with them? Was that even possible?

"Three."

I thought about the world we were about to leave. Earth. Birthplace of the entire human race. Everything that's ever been, everything that defines us as human, as civilized, as people was born there. Every single thing.

"Two."

I thought of the things we were leaving behind. Too many to count. Maybe too many to risk thinking about. So many precious, important things that we would never see again.

"One."

I thought about Izzy. My beautiful Izzy. Smart and gorgeous and funny and sweet and sexy and kind and . . .

"We have ignition."

PART THREE

RED PLANET

I had the ambition to not only go farther than man had gone
before, but to go as far as it was possible to go.
—Captain Cook

Every cubic inch of space is a miracle.
—Walt Whitman

The whole launch thing? It's not what you'd expect. And it's not like they show it in the movies. We had the same cold sweats Mom must have had when she was sitting on a highly explosive rocket. But really, once you're strapped in you have to sit there for a couple of hours. It actually gets boring. The other kids were on the other rockets. Dad seemed to have zoned out and was off in his own head, probably thinking about seeing Mom again. Sometimes it's easy to forget that one's parents are an actual couple, with all of the emotions, drama, needs, and eccentricities that go with that. Realizing that made me feel a different kind of kinship with Dad. A guy-to-guy thing. At the same time I didn't want to disturb what was going on in his head.

The other adults around me were talking to each other, except for those who'd dozed off. Seriously. The ones who'd been out in space a few times thought this part of it was like watching paint dry, so they nodded off.

It seemed to take forever and it gave me way too much time to think of all the things that could go wrong in this kind of thing. Being a mechanical engineer was not a plus in such moments because my whole life had been about focusing on what could go wrong.

Waiting for ignition was the long part but the actual time from when we lifted off until we reached orbit was only eight and a half minutes.

That's it.

We shot away from the ground by burning 1.6 million pounds of solid fuel in two minutes.

What keeps you entertained is the gravitation force. G-force. During the launch we hit 3.5 g. That's three and a half times the gravitational pull of Earth. That kind of force slams you back and tries to pull all the flesh from your bones as the rocket continues to accelerate. It gets harder to breathe with each second until you think you can't do it.

Nine minutes in you're cruising at an orbital velocity of 17,500 miles an hour. That's twenty-three times the speed of sound.

Which was about when my heart started beating again. At least that's how it felt. Not sure I breathed much on the way up either.

Chapter 52

"Mind some company?"

I looked up to see Nirti hovering there. In microgravity you don't have the sound of footsteps to warn you. Like me she'd changed out of the bulky space suit and into a thinner pressure suit designed for maximum mobility that also helped with blood pressure, respiration, and other functions. They were very useful, we'd been told, for newbies in space. Every time you go up it takes some getting used to. And soon the weird parts of micro-g would be normal for us and we'd switch to wearing sweatpants and T-shirts. Right now, though, the snug fit of the pressure suit was comforting.

"Sure," I said, nodding to the cramped space beside me. "Have a seat. Or whatever."

"You sure?"

"Absolutely."

She used the little knobbed handholds that covered most of the walls, ceiling, and floor to steer herself into the nook where I was crammed. It was one of several "contemplating ports," which was a fancy way of saying "window." The ports were comfortable enough for one person to sit but tight when

Nirti squirmed in beside me. We had to hold on to the same no-float straps to keep us in place.

Outside the window was Earth. It filled two-thirds of the port and looked amazing. Mostly blue, with patches of green and brown and swirls of white. Half of the world was in darkness and we could see the glitter of millions of lights.

Neither of us spoke for a long time. Maybe half an hour. We were both caught up in what was happening to us. To where we *were*. We sat together and watched Earth turn. We saw it through the struts and cables that formed part of the Lucky Eight. Astronauts in space suits moved around like slow snowmen. I understood most of what they were doing because it was stuff my mom did, which means she'd taught me a lot about it. I could do an EVA in a full EMU to fix nearly anything on the ship. I spent five weeks working with her team to disassemble and reassemble a full-scale mockup of the front part of a transit vehicle. I could make basic repairs in my sleep. And I almost said all this to Nirti. As a way of breaking the silence, or to make small talk, or to impress her.

I didn't, though. It was Nirti who finally broke the silence. She reached out and tapped the triple-pane glass.

"Look," she said.

"What?" I asked, distracted, looking more inward than out.

"Isn't that your mom?"

I snapped back to focus and looked where she was pointing. One of the astronauts working outside was smaller than the others, moved less clumsily, and had red trim on her white space suit. I couldn't see her face through the gold visor, but Nirti was right.

"Mom . . . ," I said, placing my fingers on the glass.

I could feel Nirti looking at me, but she didn't say anything. It was another long time before we spoke again.

Chapter 53

It's not like we didn't get to have some fun. All four of us, in EMUs, doing EVA drills. Sounds like work? Sure, but we were a couple hundred miles above the planet, in space suits, in *space*. You want to try and tell me that's not a rush?

It wasn't all fun, though. We had a real nail-biter of an exercise. Something happened that could have ended the whole mission.

It started with the four of us—Luther, Nirti, Zoé, and I—working with an old NASA geezer Fast Jack Turner and his grandson. It was the last chance to test us and make sure we had, as Fast Jack constantly said, "the Right Stuff." That's a reference to an old movie about the early days of the space program. He made us watch it for homework, though mostly I think it was so we would get his joke.

Anyway, we were working our way along the inner rim of the B-launch corridor, which was the fancy name for the slot where the *Muninn* was sitting. The *Huginn* was in the A-launcher. The NASA guy was drilling us on buddy-coupling, an exercise where two astronauts hook onto one tether instead of having separate lines. It was part of the worst-case-scenario exercises Fast Jack liked to run.

"We're not even going to have to *do* an EVA," complained Zoé. "Not until we reach Mars, and that has gravity."

"He will," said Fast Jack, pointing at me as we all floated in a cluster with Earth spinning below us. "If I know Jean Hart, she'll have young Tristan crawling all over the *Huginn* like a tick on a swollen vein."

"Eww," said Nirti.

"He's not joking," I said. "Mom loves inspections. That way she knows everything's working right."

Luther snorted something. Through the helmet radios it sounded like feedback.

"Okay, campers," said the old man, "here's the drill. Luther, you and Nirti are going to go up there and hook on. Zoé, you and the mechanic stay on deck until I give the go order, and then you make your way up there at top speed. You do *not* go into free fall. You don't unhook until you've hooked onto the next section of the structure, *capiche*?"

"Sure," I said, and the others nodded.

"I can't *hear* you," roared Fast Jack. "Did you hear me or are all of your radios malfunctioning?"

"Yes, sir," we yelled.

"Good. Now I'll be timing you, and my grandson will be chasing you up. First person he tags cleans the crew toilets on the Lucky Eight."

"Oh, gross," said Zoé.

"You don't like it, don't get caught," said Fast Jack. "Simple as that."

His grandson, Little Jack—who was roughly the size of Mount Rushmore—said nothing. Not really sure if I ever heard him speak a single word. One of those guys who looked like a bridge troll but had less personality. He could spacewalk like nobody's business, though. Bulk doesn't matter much in microgravity, but raw strength does. And experience. He'd grown up in the space program and he had an incredible role model to follow.

Luther and Nirti began to climb, mindful to follow all of the safety precautions. As soon as they were at the top of the wheel, Fast Jack tapped Nirti and me on the arms.

"Clock starts now. Haul it, kids!"

We hauled it.

But we were barely halfway to the top when we heard the old astronaut say to his grandson, "Sic 'em."

Nirti turned to look down, but I grabbed her shoulder. "Don't. It'll slow you down. Climb!"

Actually, looking back would also scare her. Even though this was a drill, Little Jack looked like a space monster. I'd seen him do this drill with some of the adults. He pounced, and—unlike us—he sometimes did it without a tether. It was an insane risk. I think he might have been a little crazy.

"Move," I growled as Nirti and I went up. From a distance it probably looked like the world's slowest chase because everything looks slower in space. Not really how it felt, though. Everything felt speeded up.

I reached up for the next bar in the structure, hooked on with one hand, unhooked with the other, push-pulling myself up. Repeated. Over and over again. Climbing fast, sometimes pulling Nirti to help her keep up. She was tiny and didn't have my reach. Couple of times I pretty much threw her upward.

I didn't look back. I knew Little Jack was gaining.

There's no sound in space but there is inside a space suit. Huffing and gasping, the rasp of my own breath, and, I swear, the hammering of my heart. Nirti's grunts of effort and cries of alarm. This didn't feel like a drill. It felt like an actual chase.

Through the internal suit noise I could hear Zoé over the radio calling encouragement and Luther laughing at us, telling us how slow we were. Telling us we were going to be cleaning toilets all the way to Mars. He promised to eat as many beans and red peppers as he could find.

Then it was there. The top bar, right above me. One last hook, one last pull.

And I heard Nirti scream.

I spun around, expecting to see her floating away, her line unhooked, so I was reaching for my hook, ready to do something stupid.

But she hadn't fallen off the Lucky Eight.

Little Jack had caught her.

Zoé slid down past me and hooked on next to Nirti, trying to put herself between the smaller girl and the big astronaut. Luther kept laughing. Then Little Jack leaned back and pointed up at him.

"You're next," he said.

That didn't stop Luther from laughing. Not for a second. He even reached down to pull Little Jack up to the top bar.

"Any time you're ready," said Luther, and even though I couldn't see his face through the faceplate, I could *feel* that nasty, stupid grin of his. "Or do you want to rest up for a bit?"

Little Jack didn't answer. Instead he pointed the way he'd come. Way down at the bottom of the wheel, Fast Jack waited.

Luther laughed again and, without waiting for Zoé, flung himself over the edge. Little Jack let them get more than halfway down before he went after them. Damn he was fast. You'd think there was gravity pulling him, that's how quickly he moved, slapping at the poles to steer his body, ignoring all the hooks, moving like a shark going after a bleeding swimmer. It was scary.

He reached for Luther, and missed. But he caught Zoé.

The timer on the inside of my helmet gave me the numbers. He'd caught Zoé fast, but he'd nabbed Nirti faster. Luther's time reaching the bottom was three seconds faster than my time coming up.

Luther never stopped laughing.

Chapter 54

Later that night I found Nirti in the head, her feet braced to give her leverage, a rag wrapped around her mouth and nose, scrubbing at the fittings on the toilets. Don't ask how in the universe a bunch of astronauts can make a zero-gravity toilet that messy, but it was toxic. I guess most of the mess was our people and some random technical fault. They weren't as skilled at pooping and peeing without gravity, and the air-suction sanitation system never worked as well in practice as it did when they trained us on it. Ask anyone.

This nasty-ass job was usually assigned to the least trained members of the team, called "general techs" as opposed to "mission specialists." We had a couple of them on each ship, but when someone screwed up and earned a "penalty" job, the GTs were allowed to go off shift. Nirti was doing penalty work because of what happened outside.

Nirti's eyes were red, maybe from the smell or maybe from the humiliation of it. She'd been at it for over an hour. She glanced sharply at me.

"Did you come to make fun of me too?" she demanded in a voice that was maybe one degree above absolute zero.

"What?"

"Luther was already here. He used the stall next to me while I was working. It's disgusting."

A glob of tear had begun forming around her eye but she was wearing soiled gloves.

"Close your eyes," I said.

She was angry but she did it, and I gently wiped the globule away. It floated past me and into the corridor. Then, before she had a chance to open her eyes I took the scrub brush out of her hand.

"What are you doing?" she snapped.

I smiled and used my shoulder to nudge her out of the way, then I jammed one foot against the door frame and began working, picking up where she left off. I didn't say a word.

Neither did she. Instead she opened the next stall, grabbed another brush from the rack, and set to work.

Luther came by half an hour later, but if he had to use the can again, he changed his mind and held it in. He hovered there, watching Nirti and me work. He was there for maybe two whole minutes before he vanished, silent as a ghost.

Chapter 55

You know what felt weird? Not having a cell phone anymore. We left ours behind on Earth because they didn't work up here. But . . . we had tablets that connected with satellites, so we could use things like Skype, Spreecast, and Google Hangouts. We signed away most of our privacy when we joined Mars One. The corporate sponsors and cable TV networks could access our communications devices. So could the Mars One security team. Not everything, mind you, because even astronauts need *some* privacy. I missed being able to text Herc and Izzy.

But I had something else weighing on me. We'd been at Lucky Eight for almost two days, but Mom hadn't tried to find me. Or find Dad. Kind of sucked. I could see her floating around, and I heard about her from the assembly and mission support staff. That was it.

"It makes sense," said Zoé when I mentioned it to her. "In a way."

"In what way exactly?" I asked, instantly irritated.

She flushed and recoiled a little at my tone, but when she realized I was frustrated at the situation and not angry with her, she explained. "Once the launch starts you and your folks are going to be together all the time. You won't be able to get away from them even if you need space. She's logical so she'll know that. She'll know that she can take this time to concentrate one hundred percent on making sure all the technical elements are perfect. She's in a very specific mind-set right now, and she doesn't want to risk breaking."

"Not even to see her son?" asked Nirti, appalled.

"Especially that," said Zoé. "But it's not as cruel as it sounds. Right now her entire world is the safety and integrity of the machines that are going to keep everyone—including her son—safe and alive. Any time she takes away from that makes her doubt that safety. It would eat at her. This way she can feel confident about the transit vehicles and all of their systems. If you look at it that way, what she's doing is right."

"It's cold," said Nirti, shaking her head.

"It's who she is," said Zoé. "She's not being cruel; she's being herself."

Chapter 56

Night before the launch.

Luther was on the bunk below me. "Hey, lawn mower repairman . . . you awake?"

"Ugh. I am now. What's your problem?" I was strapped into my bunk to keep from floating away in microgravity, and I'd finally dozed off. Getting to sleep had been tough enough and I wasn't sure I'd be able to do it again. Sleeping in space was weird. The beds were really shelves with sleeping bags attached to them. Each bag had armholes, so you stuck your arms through and reached outside to tighten the Velcro straps. We looked like bug cocoons. And you had to strap your head to the pillow, which was even less comfortable than it sounds. The pillows were only pieces of foam. If you didn't pull your arms back inside the bag they'd just float around. I woke up once and saw something about to hit me and freaked, but it was my own drifting hand.

"I can't sleep," complained Luther.

"Oh, that's a shame. No . . . wait, I don't give a crap."

"Can *you* sleep?"

"Not with you whining like a sissy."

I heard him undo one of the Velcro straps and then he punched the bottom of my bunk. Not to hurt, just to make a point. I was thinking of something nasty to say, sorting through some of Herc's best insults, when Luther asked a question.

"Are you scared, Tristan?"

I almost responded with an insult. Almost.

Didn't, though.

"No," I said.

A pause. "Want to come down and—I don't know—talk . . . ?"

I thought about it.

"Tris . . . ?" called Luther.

"Yeah, okay." I hit the release on the sleep straps, wormed my way out of my cocoon, grabbed the rail, and pulled myself over, pushing downward so that I floated like a ghost in front of him. Up to that moment I kept thinking he was joking, that this was a setup, asking me if I was scared so he could make fun of me.

But I was wrong. The lights were on low but not out. We weren't experienced enough with micro-g to risk blackout conditions, even for sleep. I could see that Luther really was scared and for the first time since I'd known him—which was three years now.

I said, "Yeah, I'm scared too."

We looked at each other for a while. He nodded, and so did I.

"Move over, rock boy," I said, and when he did I pulled

myself in and wrapped one of the straps around my arm, anchoring myself to the foot of his bed. He scrunched into the corner by the pillow. It was the middle of the night. We were launching from the Lucky Eight tomorrow.

"We should be trying to get some sleep," he said.

"Why exactly? We're not flying the ship. We're not part of the command crew."

He nodded. "Right. We're luggage."

"Yup."

Outside we could hear people moving, the clank of metal, the crackle of radio chatter.

"You say good-bye to your girlfriend?" asked Luther.

"About a hundred times."

"You say good-bye for good?"

"No," I said.

"Wow."

I sighed. "I know."

If I expected Luther to slam me for not breaking it off with Izzy, I guessed wrong. "It must be nice," he said softly.

"What?"

"To have someone," he said. "To be in love."

I cut him a look. "You're going to be on a spaceship with two girls for seven months, dude. Odds are pretty good."

He shook his head.

"Oh, come on, man." I laughed. "Zoé? She knows you like her."

"Zoé thinks all I want is to get into her pants."

"Well, to be fair—"

"It's not like that," he said, and I could hear something different in his voice. He was trying to be real. "I dig her. All of her, you know?"

"You ever tell her that?"

Luther looked down at his hands.

"Oh, come on," I said. "You've had girlfriends before. How'd you handle it?"

He took a long time getting an answer out. "I've been out a couple of times. But . . . the mission, the training, getting ready . . . It's not easy having a real conversation."

"Girls freaking fall all over you," I said. "You have whole websites of girls saying they'd marry you. You could get laid every single day if you wanted to."

Again I expected him to make a joke, but once more he surprised me. "You think that's real? You think that actually means anything? Nah, Tristan, it's all nuts. It's fantasy." He shook his head. "It wouldn't be what you have with Izzy."

"Maybe not," I admitted. "But it would be easier to walk away from."

He laughed and shook his head. Then he cut me a look. "What's going on with that French girl, Sophie? She seems to like you."

"I keep telling you, she's just a friend."

Luther looked at me, then shrugged, giving it up for now.

I thought he was totally off base about Sophie. She wasn't into me at all. No, I think what it was—and maybe it was something Luther wasn't capable of understanding—was that Sophie was lonely and just wanted a friend. Someone she could talk to. I'm easy to talk to, and maybe because I was so obviously—and, I guess, *famously*—in love with Izzy, that was as much of a comfortable buffer zone as our age difference. No, Sophie was maybe a little sad and a little scared. A friend. A neighbor. Besides, she wanted me to teach her how to fix things so she'd be more useful to the mission. That was all.

Luther didn't immediately let it go, though. "You're going to have to stop being in love with Izzy sometime, you know. It's drama now and the whole world watches your show, but it's just a show. More now than ever. Definitely once we leave. I mean . . . even you're smart enough to understand that, right?"

"I understand it," I said, the words coming out low and jagged. "Besides, even if I was single and interested, she already has a boyfriend."

He snorted. "Who? You mean that stiff Marcel? He's not her boyfriend."

"How do you know?" I asked.

"Marcel's gay, Tristan."

"Really? How do you know *that*?"

"Nirti told me."

"How would she know?"

He stared at me. "You really are not bright, are you?"

I think I said something clever like, "Oh."

We didn't say much more to each other. Eventually Luther and I fell asleep, both of us sitting—hovering—inside our nest of straps. I wonder what he dreamed about.

I dreamed of Izzy, but as the dream went on I realized that I wasn't able to see her face. It became more and more blurred, and after I woke up it took me a long time to remember what she looked like.

That scared me more than the fact that our ships were launching today.

Chapter 57

Launch day.

Last speeches. Special news coverage on every channel. Mindy's network did a marathon of every episode of *Tristan and Izzy*.

They gave us one hour to say all of our last good-byes. I called Herc and we talked about everything except the launch. He told me about a list of charities he was building for the Hart Foundation. Spice had really stepped up and was finding a whole bunch of small organizations that didn't have the money to do the mass-mailing cash appeal stuff. Herc said he was also thinking about doing some kind of competition. His working title for it was Have a Heart, but we both thought that was corny, and because it wasn't the spelling of my name, people might not get the joke. The idea was cool, though: launch a competition for Madison schools to come up with programs to help people in need.

"If it flies," he said, his voice filled with excitement, "we could have some nice prizes, do some PR on the web, maybe even get some kind of mention on your show. That would be easy if Izzy was down, and I'll talk to her about it tomorrow. Spice said that we should talk to the lawyer about getting it set up through the school board."

It made me feel great that Herc was seriously into running the Hart Foundation. He was loud, crazy, always goofy, and had the biggest heart of anyone I knew. My dad once said that Herc acted like "an affable idiot" because he was embarrassed to let people see who he really was. Dad should know.

After I was done talking with Herc I called Izzy and spent forty minutes with her. And . . . yeah, mostly we talked about nothing. Not about the launch. Not about Mars or Madison or much of anything. She told me that the cops never were able to get anywhere with the smashed window. We talked about her car and the fact that she named it Kermit because it was the same color as the Muppet. We talked about some of the best memories we had. The ones that made us laugh, the ones that made us hot, the ones that made us want to cry.

After one long pause, Izzy said, "We have to stop saying good-bye."

I laughed because it was almost the same thing Nirti said the night before we left Amsterdam, but the laugh died right away when I saw the pain in her eyes. She wasn't making a joke.

"I'm sorry," I said quickly.

She shook her head. "Tristan, we have to stop saying good-bye because you're already gone."

There was more, but that was what she'd wanted to say, and I was free to interpret that any way I could.

None of my interpretations made me happy.

Chapter 58

They told us to get some sleep but then woke us up a few hours later. I had only just managed to drift off—pun intended—when the alarm went off. I still hadn't made the adjustment of no real day or night. Sleep wasn't going to be a "night" thing anymore. You slept when they told you it was time for sleep. A personal nighttime, completely subjective. And this time there simply wasn't enough of it. Can't say I felt very good. I woke with a jerk and felt like I was standing on the edge of a cliff, arms pinwheeling, fighting to keep from falling. My brain slipped gears for a couple of seconds and I didn't know where I was.

Then I remembered exactly where I was. And what was about to happen. My hands shook as I got dressed and there was a sick feeling in the pit of my stomach. We left all of our stuff behind. The sheets—well, cotton envelopes, really— pillows, clothes . . . that was all temporary stuff. Our actual gear was already aboard the ships. We got into pressure suits and went out into the hall.

Mom and Dad were there, floating, waiting.

For a moment I thought Mom was going to ignore me,

but as soon as she saw me she kicked off from the opposite wall, grabbed me, and hugged me so hard I thought my ribs would snap. She kissed my face a dozen times. Fifty times. And smoothed my hair.

It made me feel like I was six years old. It made me want to cry.

But we all laughed instead. Not sure why. The three of us, with Dad closing in for the group hug as we floated in micro-g.

Mom put her lips right against my ear and whispered.

"Let's go to Mars," she said.

Chapter 59

We'd practiced this part so many times it was like doing another run-through. We gathered in a big corridor for a short prayer from the mission interfaith chaplain, and then we shook hands all around. The *Huginn* crew and the *Muninn* crew. Handshakes, hugs, some kisses, a few jokes, good wishes. We wouldn't see the other crew for seven months except on video.

I watched Marcel and Sophie. They hugged for a long, long time. Maybe Luther and Nirti were right and Marcel was gay, but that hug had a heck of a lot of emotion in it. He kissed her cheeks and her hand for long while. Then it was time for all of us to go.

So we went.

I followed Mom and Dad through the airlock, into the *Huginn*. The ship was bright. Everything was white or off-white or eggshell white. Some kind of white. A few things weren't. Trim, handles, signs. But mostly it was white.

We gathered in the biggest part of the ship, the common room. It had a technical name, Central Colony Habitat Large Area Room. We all called it the common room. There were chairs lining the walls, each with straps. Nirti was in the seat to my left, my parents in the two seats to my right. Well, at least Dad was. Mom buckled us into place, then went around and checked everyone else. She was not the safety officer for the mission, but the safety officer was scared of her, so he didn't make a scene when she double-checked his work. When everyone—*including* the safety officer—was strapped in, Mom launched herself across the common room, caught a handhold, swung around like a monkey, landed in her chair, and had the buckles clicked into place as if this were what she'd done every day for her whole life.

Nirti leaned close. "Your mom is going to be a hard act to follow."

"Tell me about it."

Nirti's smile was very pretty, her eyes filled with intelligence and laughter.

"Are you okay, Tris?" she asked.

"Yeah," I said. "Just another day in the Mars One program. Why? Is anything going on I should know about?"

"Idiot," she said, shaking her head. She gave my hand a squeeze. Her hand was small and warm and sweaty with fear. I held on to it.

Mom reached over and I thought she was going to hold my other hand, but instead she pressed something into my palm. It was a small high-capacity data stick. When I looked up she leaned close and said, "This has all of my inspection notes. I want you to review it and be ready to answer any question I have."

"Um, can it wait until after, you know, we take off?"

Her smile was there and gone. "You'll have plenty of time later today," she said. "But read it today. Not tomorrow."

Dad, listening, closed his eyes and began humming an old hippie song. "California Dreamin'," I think

"Sure," I told Mom, and thought to myself, *I am the son of freaks.*

Mom turned away and nodded to Garcia, the safety officer, who called in that the crew was secure. Garcia also switched the audio and video feeds from the command capsule to the big screens on the walls. We all saw the pilot and copilot in one half of the screen and the Lucky Eight with the noses of both ships in the loops on the other half. Then a smaller window popped up, overlapping both screens. Bas Lansdorp's face smiled at us.

"On behalf of everyone at Mars One," he said, "and everyone on Earth, we wish you Godspeed."

There was the sound of applause behind him. I knew he was on a podium down on Earth, surrounded by half a million people.

Then his image was replaced by ours. One by one the face of each of the colonists filled the screen, with our names and countries of origin below us. They showed the crew of the

Muninn first. I knew every face, every name, and almost every story about them. Some of them were friends. Others would become friends, I hoped. All of them were family, I guess.

Marcel's face was there. Even in his official project photo he was scowling. Maybe he'd be happier in the black, or down on the red planet.

Then they began showing the faces of the *Huginn* crew.

Luther and his parents. Sophie Enfers. Zoé and her family. Nirti and hers. Garcia. As each picture flashed on the screen I looked around to find the real person sitting in a padded chair. We smiled at each other. Sophie gave me a smile and a nod and her eyes lingered on mine for a few seconds. Then she closed her eyes and leaned back into her seat. For just a moment I wondered if maybe Luther was right and Sophie had a thing for me. I mean, sure, guys my age think about females of just about *any* age, that's biology, that's a given. I even had a weird ten-second fantasy about Mindy, but I came to my senses and threw up in my mouth a little. But Sophie . . . ? He had to be wrong.

Besides, I loved Izzy and that was that.

On the screen I saw Mom and Dad. Me. All the way to Director Colpeys. His photo vanished and was replaced by a live image of him. He was in the command capsule with the pilots. His face was a little sweaty and his eyes were so bright it looked like he had a fever. His face was as grave as someone giving a eulogy at a funeral. He cleared his throat and said the words that would become part of history.

"What we do now," he said slowly and heavily, "we do not for each of us but for all of us. What we do now we do not for one country but for all the nations and all the peoples of Earth. In the name of mankind and for the betterment of all, we go forth with a mission of hope for all of us." He turned to the pilot, and the shot widened to include the whole cockpit. "Let's go to Mars."

The engines rumbled, sending trembles through the ship and all the way down to my bones. On the screen we watched the *Muninn* explode out from the socket of the Lucky Eight like a bullet leaving a gun. Beside me Mom and Dad reached for each other's hands.

Like the *Huginn*, the *Muninn* was massive. Even without engines the size of grain silos, the ship was huge, a white spike of light. And yet in seconds it seemed to dwindle to nothing except for the glow of the constant rocket burn.

That was actually scary. Maybe the scariest thing of all. I heard Nirti gasp and when I looked at her it was clear she was thinking—*feeling*—the same thing. The big black swallowed that ship and everyone aboard her just like that.

And we were still close to Earth.

There were millions and millions of miles to go. Farther away, deeper into space.

I started to say, "It's all going to be fine."

But the moment I opened my mouth the *Huginn*'s rockets fired. We were slammed back into our seats by the massive g-force. We blasted out of the Lucky Eight and vanished into the big, big, big empty black.

Chapter 60

The g-force lasted for only a few seconds. After that it got weirdly still all of a sudden. That's because the ship, everything on board, and all of us were traveling through space at exactly the same speed. Sounds weird. It felt like nothing.

Out here there was so little gravity that it was like floating in really salty seawater. Except it was dry. I know, that sounds stupid, but it's the closest thing I can imagine. We did some training in the Dead Sea in Israel, and it was like this.

A drop of water wouldn't fall. It floated there in front of you, looking almost like a little planet.

The downsides to micro-g are crazy. First, when all that body fluid rises to your head you get a headache. A killer headache. The mission docs wanted us to pee as much as we could because the body wants to compensate by getting rid of about a liter of extra fluid. So in the name of science and good health we took turns whizzing.

About half the crew got sick to their stomachs. There's a whole different kind of seasickness you can get in space travel. I dodged it, but it put Zoé, Tony Chu, my dad, and a bunch of others in a bad way.

Mom taught us a good trick for helping the nausea go away. She said it was because of the loss of "up" and "down." The eye keeps trying to settle on up and down and those eye movements trigger all sorts of chemical and neurological responses in the body. So as she put it: "Lose the 'up.'" She said to focus on whatever direction we needed to go instead of trying to stick with normal up and down. It worked, too.

Once Luther felt better he and I began racing through the hab, the corridors, and around the common room, pushing off from walls, spinning in the air, pulling ourselves along the handholds on the wall faster and faster.

Until people started yelling at us.

Oh, and here's another downside that's also kind of an upside. With the fluids going all wonky in your body, it affects your taste buds. I sneaked aboard some of the chocolate the kids at school sent me, but out here it tasted like socks. Bummer. The up part of that was the camel-vomit-tasting food they served on the ship tasted like socks, too. Which was a little better. Trust me.

Sophie was going to be doing most of the food prep on our ship, but I need to explain that she wouldn't be doing much actual cooking. Most of the food was already prepared. She would cook on Mars, though. Not sure how or what. A lot of that depended on how well the supplies made it on the unmanned missions and how effective my dad was. Mostly Sophie took thermo-stabilized packets of food, added water, stuck it in a microwave, and passed it out. Mind you, we could do that ourselves, but everyone needed a job to fight the tedium of the long flight. Besides, she added a little spice here and there and somehow made it taste okay. Even so, it wasn't like she was laboring all day long in the galley. I thought she'd be bored, but she was always smiling. She wore earbuds all the time. Not sure what she was listening to, but it seemed to keep her happy.

I thought about all this while I floated slowly back and forth along the wall that most of the crew still thought of as the ceiling. That would change, but for now it was a quiet place. Everyone was busy with something. Luther was still doing marathon bathroom runs. Zoé was just starting to get space sick and was turning different shades of gray, green, and purple. My mom was checking everything. She did that a lot. Dad was in his greenhouse making sure that all of his dirt and seeds survived the launch. Nirti was with her folks.

And suddenly I realized something that I already knew but never really understood.

This was it.

The actual *it*. We were in space, traveling away from Earth at incredible speeds. I pulled myself over to one of the portholes, grabbed a strap to stabilize myself, and hung there watching Earth get smaller and smaller. Watched it get farther and farther away. I became intensely aware that I was not being pulled toward Earth anymore. Not really. Sure, we'd be within Earth's gravitational pull for a while, but the planet wasn't trying to drag me back. Or take me back.

It let me go. The whole world let me go.

Izzy let me go.

And . . . now I was gone. I placed my hand flat against the glass. My palm covered the blue planet completely. As if it was not there at all.

Chapter 61

The communications specialist, Lehman, floated up and tapped me on the shoulder. It woke me up and I was immediately surprised that I'd fallen asleep. I sputtered and thrashed for a second, but Lehman put a steadying hand on my shoulder.

"Take it easy, Tristan," he said. He was one of those people who didn't have much of a sense of humor, but there were no spikes, either. Nice in a vanilla kind of way. You always knew where you were with him.

"What is it?" I demanded, still not back in my own head. "What's wrong?"

He smiled. "Nothing's wrong. It's showtime."

It took me a few seconds to process that, then, "Oh," I said.

"Oh," he agreed. "Time to get real."

That was what he always said. Get real as in get ready to do a segment of the ongoing reality show that would be part of our daily lives for as long as the network kept writing checks.

I knew we were each supposed to do a segment to share our launch-day experiences, but somehow during the whole launch thing I forgot. And I really didn't want to, even though this was actually something that still connected me to everyone back home. The reality show people wanted us to go, but they didn't want us to go away.

"Okay," I said.

He nodded and kicked off from the wall with an easy grace that I envied. Lehman hadn't spent any more time up here than I had, but he seemed to have taken to micro-g as if it was more natural to him than walking on Earth. Weird.

And it made me want to practice some to try and match that. If I put some time in on it I could be miles ahead of Luther by the time he was done throwing up the entire lining of his stomach.

I pulled myself into one of the private niches we called "com-pods." They were soundproof and just about the only place on the ship other than our sleep pods and the toilets where anyone could actually be alone. It was a bit like sitting inside a big eggshell. Same shape, same color. There was an ultra-high-def screen, built-in microphones, and a keyboard for typing messages that could be sent to the production team, posted as an information crawl, or sent as private messages.

Because all of this bleeding-edge communications equipment was paid for by corporate sponsors, and the biggest check writers were the reality shows. We each signed contracts to appear in the interview booths at least once a day. The sessions were like the ones on the reality shows on Earth. They asked you questions to get you started, but really you were supposed to talk out loud as if you were keeping a diary. Once I sealed the com-pod and logged in, the logo for the network popped onto the screen and a second later there was Mindy. All fiery red hair and bright white teeth. I flinched when I saw what was behind her. She was broadcasting live from the Drakes' living room.

"Aaaand a big hello to space traveler Tristan Hart from everyone back here on planet Earth!" she said. I heard applause from inside the house but offscreen, and a rumble of muted noise that told me there were people outside. Mindy probably had big screens set up so the crowds on the street could see.

I wanted to resent her for it. Instead I smiled and yelled, "Hello, earthlings!"

The crowd went nuts.

Chapter 62

So yeah, I actually had fun.

Mindy had my teachers there, some kids from school, Herc, and of course Izzy. Everyone laughed a lot, all of us cried a little. But it did not suck.

At one point when Izzy was on, I gave her a little nod and pretended to scratch my chest. Really I was touching my heart and she knew it. She touched the button of her blouse that was over the same spot. She also raised one eyebrow and I gave her a tiny nod.

Talk later. In private.

When the session was done the last image was Mindy, standing right in front of the couch so that she blocked Izzy. So it was just her filling the screen with her too-white teeth and hair extensions.

She said something that was probably corny and scripted, but I didn't even listen. Izzy leaned out to peer around Mindy. Herc leaned out to do the same on her other side. Photo-bombing. Nice.

The screen went dark.

I sat in the com-pod for ten minutes, feet braced against

the wall to push me back into the seat. That position made it feel like there was gravity. A cheap thrill for space travelers.

"I love you, Izzy," I told the blank screen.

Swear to God I could hear her say the same thing.

One second later the alarm bells began ringing all over the ship.

Chapter 63

The amplified voice of Director Colpeys came punching through the alarm bell. "All crew members please report to the common room. This is an emergency meeting."

Everyone scrambled. We all went . . . well, not running. Floating? Flying? Whatevering. I did a ceiling crawl so fast I didn't even grab the handholds. More like slapped them to keep me moving. I nearly collided with Luther, who was coming out of one of the toilets. His face was the color of a rotting eggplant, but even sick as he was he leaped up to follow me.

"What is it?" he called.

"Don't know," I said.

We reached the common room and flung ourselves inside. Most of the others were already there. Zoé and Nirti were hanging together, holding hands, looking scared. I spotted Mom hovering near Colpeys, with Dad hanging back. Sophie Enfers was hovering by one of the microwaves. She saw me and nodded. Everyone was talking, chattering, asking questions, filling the common room with noise.

The alarm cut off and Colpeys held up a hand and had to

shout to be heard. "Please!" he cried. "Please, everyone settle down. There is no cause for alarm. There is no danger."

Luther looked pissed for having been dragged out of the bathroom. "Then why the alarms?"

His dad, who looked exactly the way Luther will probably look in twenty-five years, shushed him, but Colpeys made an apologetic face.

"Sorry," he said, looking embarrassed, "the crew notification alarm volume setting was too high. We'll adjust that in the future."

The crowd fell quiet and there were as many hostile looks as confused ones.

"What *is* happening?" asked Mr. Mbede in a more civilized tone than his son had used. "Is there a problem of some kind?"

"No," said Colpeys, "not with the ships or the crews. Everything is in the green."

"Then what?" asked my mom.

Colpeys cleared his throat. "It's the *Red Dragon*."

And the common room went dead silent. Colpeys was sweating. Lines of it ran down his face. "We have received an update from our friends at NASA and I'm afraid the news is going to hit us all very hard."

Your stomach can't sink in micro-g, but it can try real hard. Everyone was still, staring, scared by what was coming.

"We have confirmed that the ship launched from the Shanghai Wheel was not, in fact, a transit vehicle." He looked around, meeting our eyes. "We have verification from China that it is an unmanned support vessel whose primary payload includes a rover and a satellite."

Luther said, "What—?"

Mom frowned at Colpeys. "Did you say 'unmanned'?"

"Yes," said Colpeys in a voice that seemed ready to crack. "This morning, a few hours after our launch, the president of China announced that the *Red Dragon* is the *second* ship they've sent to Mars. The first, known as the *Golden Dragon*, was launched from their deep-space platform twenty-two months ago. The launch was not noticed on Earth because it was accomplished during a fifty-eight-minute gap in satellite surveillance. No one was looking, and that is what the Chinese wanted."

The silence was absolutely crushing. There wasn't enough air to breathe and all the lights were too bright. I heard someone start crying and turned to see Zoé bury her face against her mother's chest. Other people were crying too. My eyes were dry and they felt like they were welded open.

Colpeys cleared his throat again. "However . . . there's more and it's not good. The Chinese admitted that they lost all contact with *Golden Dragon* months ago. No radio signals, no telemetry. All the Chinese know for certain is that the ship reached Mars and is in orbit."

"How true is the orbit?" asked Tony Chu.

"It's good. They're orbiting four hundred and sixty miles from the surface."

"Isn't that a little high?"

"It's, ah . . . unusual."

"Does that mean they've landed?" asked Luther.

Colpeys shook his head. "That has yet to be determined." Before we could barrage him with more questions he held up a hand. "There's more, so let me bring you up to speed with what I know. Coordinates for the proposed *Golden Dragon* landing site have now been shared with NASA and other agencies, and satellites are being retasked in an attempt to find the crew. However, Mars is a big planet. If they landed anywhere but on their designated down-point, then that will make locating them very difficult. Even if all of them are alive and well—and we pray this is so—it would still be a small settlement. Although their ship appears to be intact, neither the Chinese nor NASA has a good angle on it to determine if it is damaged or what kind of damage might be present."

"Why haven't they said anything before this?" asked Nirti. "How come we're just finding out about this now?"

Colpeys looked pained. "The Chinese government has a history of secrecy that has often been a hindrance to its own better interests. It is an ongoing policy for the People's Republic to resist admitting failure or defeat. Had they been more open, there is no doubt that NASA, the Russians, and other agencies—public and private—might have been able to help. Now they are at a worst-case-scenario moment. Because of the inevitability of our arrival on Mars, they have decided to break their self-imposed silence." He gave us a small, sad smile. "It speaks to the integrity of the larger space exploration community that no one is publicly chastising them. Instead, everyone is stepping up to offer whatever assistance is possible."

"What can *we* do?" asked Luther.

"That remains to be seen," said Colpeys.

"What can anyone do?" asked Sophie.

"Well, a lot of things are possible," said the director, "but quite frankly no one has any answers at the moment. The *Red Dragon* payload includes a rover that will be deployed to try and find the lander, or debris, on the surface. They're also bringing a new generation of survey satellite that will be put in orbit to help hunt for evidence."

"Why didn't the Chinese send a rescue team?" asked someone.

"They're prepping one," said Colpeys, "but they didn't have one ready to go and as you all know that takes a great deal of timing and planning. They did have the unmanned ship prepped for the rover and satellite delivery already, so that's what was launched."

"They're looking for bodies not survivors," said Tony.

"Let's hope not. The Chinese are making every effort to try to find the *Golden Dragon*'s lander and its crew."

I saw Mom mouth the word *try*.

"How many people were on the ship?" asked Dad.

Colpeys floated to the big screen on the wall and touched a button. Images began filling the screen. One by one smaller windows appeared, each with a photograph of a smiling face. Twenty-two of them, all Chinese. Most of them were adults, but there were three teenagers among them. Two boys and a girl. Luther and I looked at each other, and for a moment his face lost its cocky smile. The three kids were about our own age. The boys were Cheng and Da. The girl was named Ting. Someone told me later that Ting means "enduring." God, I hoped that was true for her.

The twenty-two faces looked at us, and I could almost imagine them whispering *our* names. Calling us. Asking us to come find them in all that cold darkness.

"*Nooit,*" murmured Luther. Afrikaans for "no way."

Mr. De Jaeger spoke up. "Jurgen, is there more to this? Is there something else you're not telling us?"

It was clear from the way his mouth twitched that Colpeys didn't want to keep dropping bombs on us, but Zoé's dad had called him out. He took a breath. "Although, as I said, we, um, don't have all of the information we need, NASA believes that the Chinese colony landing capsule may still be attached to the transit vehicle."

We all stared at him in shocked horror.

Colpeys licked his lips. "If that is true, then the crew is still aboard the *Golden Dragon*. However, all attempts to reach the crew have been unsuccessful."

"I don't understand," said Nirti. "Why would they stay on their ship all this time? They wouldn't have enough supplies for everyone for this many months. Wouldn't the Chinese have sent the bulk of their supplies by unmanned rocket, just like we did?"

"Yes," Colpeys said gravely. "A supply rocket was sent two years before the crew left, so the recent flight is technically the third mission. That first rocket's payload included a habitat, food, and other supplies. However, that will only matter if the crew made it down to the surface. But . . . if they are still alive and aboard the ship, then, ah . . . their food would have run out four months ago."

"God almighty," I heard someone say. Maybe it was me. Maybe it was all of us.

"Even if they went to half or third rations?"

"I'm afraid so. That estimate is based on bare-minimum rations. As with our own program, the Chinese have admitted that they sent two supply rockets prior to the *Red Dragon*'s launch. All of the food and supplies their colony would need are down on the planet."

We stared at him, then at each other. What Colpeys didn't say—what he didn't need to say—was that even if the Chinese colonists were alive on their ship, we could never get there in time to save them. Not one chance in ten trillion.

If they were still somehow alive, then by the time we got to Mars, their ship would be a tomb. A steel coffin in a decaying orbit. Once we landed we'd always be watching the sky, waiting for that day when the *Golden Dragon* fell into the atmosphere and burned up. Damn.

Sophie came up beside me. "Space hates us all," she said quietly. Almost more to herself than to me. When I turned to her, she shook her head and wouldn't meet my eyes.

"What happened to them?" asked Zoé, her voice hollow and hushed. I glanced up but all Colpeys could do was shake his head.

"The Chinese space administration does not know," he said. "We don't know either. Nobody knows. NASA is retasking two of its satellites to try to get a closer look at the ship. Until we have clear pictures, all we can do is guess. And pray for the lives of the colonists on that ship. We must pray that they have found some way to survive."

He meant it too, I'll give him that. It was clear he wanted them to be okay. I'd like to think all of us aboard the *Huginn* and the *Muninn* felt the same way.

But there were so many things wrong with this picture. I mean, why was the capsule still there? Why hadn't the Chinese crew gone down to the surface? If the capsule was damaged, why hadn't they called it in to their own people? What had happened to the ship? And what had happened to the crew? Twenty-two people were out there. Three of them were kids my own age. Maybe dead. Maybe starving to death.

This was our first day in space.

Chapter 64

Zoé and Luther were still too space sick to get together, and Nirti was so upset about the Chinese ship that she stayed with her parents for most of the next few days. We talked for a few seconds, though, and she looked haunted and wrecked, but also guilty.

"I wanted us to be there first," she said hollowly. "I wanted us to beat the Chinese ship and get to Mars first, but not like this. Not because all those other people died."

"I know," I said. We hugged like people do at a funeral and she went off to find her parents.

The news about the *Golden Dragon* was hitting us all really hard, but Nirti had the biggest heart of any of us. She wasn't processing it very well.

I kept thinking about that girl, Ting. She was about to turn fifteen when their flight left, which meant she was a little older than me now. According to the data we got from news reports, she was the only child of a woman who was the *Golden Dragon*'s chief mechanical engineer.

I know. Another toolpush's kid. I don't much believe in fate or coincidences, but that was kind of hard to dismiss.

Ting was like me. A mechanic, a kid on a spaceship, a voluntary exile from Earth.

One of the reality show producers contacted Colpeys and asked for each of us to give our reactions to this new development. It made me so mad. It made me want to scream obscenities at the camera.

If it bleeds, it leads.

Yeah, yeah, whatever.

We all did the interviews. Even gray-faced Luther, though his was pretty short. When I watched it later, I saw that they edited his segment so it looked like he was really emotionally torn up about the Chinese. You couldn't tell that his glassy eyes and tears were really because he desperately needed to get back to the toilet. Even with everything that was going on, I laughed my ass off.

When it came to my interview, I kept it simple. "They have a smart crew of well-trained people on board," I said. "Whatever's going on, they'll figure it out. No doubt at all."

It was all crap, though. We knew they didn't have enough supplies. But sometimes lying is easier than telling the truth.

Lansdorp made a statement too. He said that the resources of Mars One were at the disposal of the Chinese government and that the crews of both of our colony ships were ready and willing to help the astronauts aboard the *Golden Dragon* in any way we could. Maybe that was lip service, but no one on our ships took it that way. Even if the Chinese were already on

Mars and had beat us onto that page of history, they were still people.

It was Dad who put it the best way. "Of *course* we'll help them. We've all left so much behind. Surely we can discard politics along the way. This isn't one space program proving itself by rescuing some other country's failed attempt. This isn't Europe, Africa, and America riding to the rescue of the Chinese. It's not about any of that. It's about people helping people. It's about basic humanity. Everyone who sets foot on Mars will be a Martian. We have to think like that or we're going to accomplish nothing out there."

The producers used that as the last segment, and the credits rolled after a long moment of the camera focusing on my dad's face.

Chapter 65

Mom didn't give me much of a chance to drown in my own moods. She took me with her to inspect the ship—inside and out.

My first EVA on a moving spaceship was a whole lot different from goofing around on the Lucky Eight.

It meant putting on the big white spacesuits. Even in micro-g they were bulky and awkward. Not heavy anymore because of new developments in materials and microminiaturization of equipment, but weird and clumsy. That also meant putting on the MAG diaper and long johns and all that junk. The cotton comfort gloves were nice, though. They keep the outer gloves from chafing at the points where you have to apply pressure.

What most people don't know is that the suits aren't tight. There's room inside to wiggle around and stay as comfortable as possible. There's also a slight lag time when you move, because your hand or foot has to make contact with the inside of the suit and then push it. You get used to that.

The suits are white to reflect heat, and yes, there is heat out there. The sun's shining all the time and there's no atmosphere to stop it and no nighttime to cool things down. I know, that's different from what you've probably read. The real science geeks out there will yell "2.7 K" anytime anyone asks how cold it is. I know, I've heard them. And sure, in the deepest part of outer space, way beyond the heat of any sun, the ambient temperature is 2.7 degrees above absolute zero on the Kelvin scale. But . . . we weren't in that kind of space. We were in the solar system. The "solar" part means that we were in the neighborhood of a sun, and it was always shining. The bright side of the moon—the part that gets hit by the sun—gets as hot as 248 degrees Fahrenheit. Mind you, flip over to the dark side and it gets nippy. Down around minus 338. Brrr.

So out where we were, a few hundred thousand miles from Earth, the real danger wasn't freezing . . . it was the vacuum. So far, no one had ever been chucked out of an airlock, so we didn't really know what it was like to be "spaced." No one was lining up to find out, either. I mean, we were crazy but we weren't stupid. The mission doctors told us that the first thing that would happen would be that our eardrums would rupture because they couldn't hold back the pressure. Then everything with moisture in it would swell . . . and that includes the brain. So basically you'd be in screaming pain before you suffocated from lack of air.

But you wouldn't freeze. Not sure that's a win, though.

Spacecraft are built to withstand the buildup of heat caused by sunlight. Our suits did that too. And there was even a little bling because the sun visor had some real gold in it.

Our EVA wasn't anything critical. Nothing was falling off the ship. I think Mom was trying to shake me out of the mood I'd been in since hearing about the *Golden Dragon*. We were tethered to the ship, which was still moving at thirty-two thousand miles an hour. You'd think that we'd get whipped off and left behind, but that's not how it works. Remember, we were also traveling at that speed. It's a hard thought to grasp. Harder still when you're out there with only a cable and some metal hooks between your spaceship and dying in the void. They can't stop and rescue you. If you're gone, you're gone.

So the first thing I did with Mom was go over every inch of the airlocks, the hooks, and the handholds, and then double-check the compartments built into the exterior of the ship. That was where we stored extra tools and some emergency equipment. The *Huginn* was small inside, but outside it seemed enormous.

"Take your time and get everything right," said Mom, her voice crackling over the radio. We had several different channels, including one that connected us with the reality show. Later during this space walk we'd use that for the entertainment of everyone at home sitting on couches with pizza and cold bottles of Dr Pepper. Right now, though, we were on the "specialist" channel, which allowed the team leader to select who was in on the conversation. According to the screen display on the upper left of the inside of my visor, there were only two lights, indicating that it was just the two of us. Private conversation, Hart family style.

"This is going to take forever," I said.

"Are you in a particular hurry to be anywhere?" she asked.

"I guess not."

"Good. Now open the panel and check the manual override."

We were outside the secondary airlock. There was a keypad for entry, and in the event that failed, there was a big hydraulic lever behind a white panel. I took out my screwdriver, attached the magnetic end to the first of four bolts, and unscrewed them. The bolts were attached to lengths of high-test airline cable so they wouldn't float away. Once the bolts were off I turned the handle set into the panel, felt the bolts release, and then lifted the panel cover off and let it swing on its small safety cable. The lever inside had two arms and a crossbar.

"Tell me what you see," said Mom.

I didn't touch the handle, but I leaned close to examine everything. It was all very clean and neat. However there were two thin strips of red electrician's tape wound once around the center of the handle. I knew that tape. I saw it in my dreams. It was a kind of signature and it made a statement.

"You inspected this," I said.

"Of course," said Mom. "And . . . ?"

"You repaired it?"

"Are you asking or telling?"

"Telling. You repaired the handle." I turned to her. "Is this why you came up early?"

"It's one of the reasons, Tristan," she said. "Can you tell me what I did, and why?"

I didn't even have to take a second look. I knew my mom's work. "You either found a mechanical fault or you thought there might be one, and you replaced the handle mechanism."

"How can you tell?"

"It's clean. Everything's clean."

"Spaceship parts are supposed to be clean. It increases efficiency and safety."

"Sure," I said, "but there's space program clean and there's Hart clean."

She laughed, pleased. "That's something you learned very well, Tristan. It'll save lives one of these days."

"So which was it? Did you find an actual fault or—?"

"No. But the stress tests on this mechanism were too close to the yellow zone for me."

"Heard that," I said. We worked for a while and then Mom stopped, paused for a moment, then reached out to touch my shoulder. "Tristan, do you know why I didn't come to meet you and your dad when you arrived on the Lucky Eight?"

"Yeah, I think I do," I said.

"If you were me, what would you have done?"

I thought about it as I closed the panel and tightened the four bolts. She didn't push me for an answer. Finally I said, "Look, I know how you are when you're working. It's all about the work and you don't let anyone or anything break your concentration. I get it. If you want to know what I would have done in your place, taking into account all the weight that's riding on getting it done right . . . then, sure, I'd have done the same thing. Maybe I'd have left a voice mail message or something, but maybe not. I wasn't in that situation so I can't really say."

She made a small sound. Not an actual word. I tightened the last screw, getting it exactly right, then stowed my screwdriver and inspected my work. Doing what she did. Focusing on the practical stuff before I shifted gears into the emotional. Maybe it was that moment, out there on the skin of the *Huginn*, deep in the black, when I got it. Got her. It was nothing she said.

I turned to her. "A lot of people think you're cold," I said. "You know that, right? They think you like machines more than people. Or that you only care about being right and you don't give a crap about what people think or feel. But I know that's not true. It's completely backward. You wouldn't do all the stuff you do, or do it in the way you do, if it wasn't all about people. About keeping them—*us*—safe. About keeping everything working so they don't get hurt or get scared. I know about what happened on the Olympus Space Station. You don't ever talk about it, but I know."

She stared at me, unable to speak.

"I love you so much for who you are and what you do," I said. "I always have and I always will."

We didn't hug. We were in big space suits floating in outer space. And . . . we're Harts. It wasn't a hugging moment. Instead Mom reached out a gloved hand, and I took it. A single squeeze, held for two full seconds.

"I love you, too," she said.

We floated at thirty-two thousand miles an hour for a few seconds. There was no way in any world we'd have had this real a conversation on the ship, face-to-face, without space suits and helmets and opaque visors between us. Not Mom and me.

She shoved a wrench into my hand.

"Stop daydreaming, Tristan," she said. "We still have a full ship to inspect."

Which is what we did.

Chapter 66

Izzy . . . I wish you could see the stars.

I've been concentrating so much on the mission and my own crap that I forgot to tell you about the stars.

On Earth we can see a few hundred of them most nights, and a few thousand if it's really clear and there's no moon. But out here?

God.

It's like floating inside a black bag filled with diamonds. You can't begin to imagine how many there are and how beautiful they look. Stars and planets, and whole galaxies, spinning out there in the bottomless black. Glittering. Shining. Endless. Perfect.

Some people come out here and they feel small, overwhelmed, dwarfed by it all. They get so insecure they cry.

Some people look at the stars and they get frustrated because we'll never reach them.

When we look at stars we don't even see them as they are. We see them as they were when the beam of light started out on its way across the black. The light from Proxima Centauri is more than four years old when it reaches us. Some of those stars are really galaxies more than ten billion light-years away. Some of those stars we see don't even exist anymore. And there are new ones whose light hasn't reached us yet.

I'm not going to lie and say that I understand all the science about relativity or light speed or even distance, but I get the gist. All we'll ever have of those stars are their light, their beauty. All those mysteries will burn out there forever.

Izzy . . . I wish you could see the stars from up here. I wish you could see how beautiful they are.

I wish you were coming with me.

I wish.

I wish.

Chapter 67

Days went by. We had no new information on the *Golden Dragon*. Not a word. I kept pulling up the news stories to look at pictures of the *Golden Dragon* and its crew. Looking into the eyes of Ting gave me a weird feeling. Maybe it was ESP or maybe I was a little nuts, but I swear that every once in a while the eyes in that picture changed.

"You're still alive," I said one night as I looked at her picture. "Aren't you?"

She was an engineer and mechanic, just like me. It didn't matter that we were separated by language, culture, politics, and millions of miles of distance. It wasn't as weird as it sounds. I didn't have a crush on her, nothing like that. And it's hard to explain. We were both the same, and I wanted her to be alive.

Every day Mom kept me busy with inspections and repairs—which were really not repairs but mostly taking pieces of equipment apart to clean and inspect them, and then putting them back together again. Her logic was this: If you know a mechanism all the way down to the smallest spring or screw, then when something *does* go wrong you'll be able to assess and diagnose with greater efficiency. Most people might find that kind of stuff boring, but it kept me from going insane.

I hung out with Nirti a lot, and without the others around—Zoé and Luther were still fighting space sickness—I got to know her better. Luther was right; she's gay. She kind of had a crush on Zoé, but Zoé is straight. So there were all sorts of frustrations built into our new life. Besides, like I told Herc, sex wasn't on the Mars One overall colony game plan. Not for the first few waves of colonists. Unless they figured out all the problems about having babies out here, I'd be forever known as the Virgin of Mars. Sigh.

There were huge parts of every day that weren't structured. Free time.

The highlight of every day was Izzy. We were getting to the point in the trip where conversation had small lags. That would increase every day, until it would be easier to record messages rather than have conversations.

For as long as it lasted, though, I wanted to see my girl. To talk to her.

"Tristan!" Izzy said, and her smile was incredible. It lit her up.

"Hey," I said. You couldn't see that smile and not return it. It was that kind of smile.

She was in her room, at her desk. I could see her bed and bookshelves behind her. The wall of framed photos.

My face was in too many of those pictures, and there was a new one, a big picture of Izzy and me at the Madison High Reach for the Stars Fall Carnival. It must have been a candid photo because I don't remember it being taken, and I guessed that it had been taken by one of Mindy's people. It was professionally framed in dark red wood, but I knew Izzy hadn't put it there. It was way too cheesy for something she would have picked. We were laughing, with my arm around her, both of us looking up at something. It looked like one of those placeholder photos they put in picture frames at the store. Look at the happy, carefree people. Izzy glanced at me, saw me looking past her, and turned to follow the line of my gaze. When she turned back her smile had become something else. Still happy, but in on the joke because she knew I understood what it was. She didn't have to say it.

"How are you doing?" I asked Izzy.

"I'm good," she said after a few seconds' delay. "Driving is a little nerve-racking. They're going to do a whole episode of the show about me getting my permit, taking lessons with Dad, then with Mom after she 'fired' Dad from teaching me because of that parking lot thing. And then they've been following me all over. Driving to the mall, driving with Herc and Spice to the movies, driving to school. Everywhere."

"Sounds like tons of fun. Riveting television."

"There's some good stuff," she insisted.

"Like what? You kill anyone? Run over any old ladies? Stray dogs? Squirrels?"

"Don't even! I almost hit a bunny who ran off of the Murphys' lawn. Poor little thing got so scared she stopped in the middle of the street. Okay, so the guy behind me nearly hit me, but what was I supposed to do? Run it over?"

"Did the other car rear-end you?"

"Huh? Oh, no. He just got mad and yelled and then got into a screaming match with the camera guy. It was sooooo embarrassing because everyone heard it and started coming out of their houses and . . ."

There was more. A lot more. Izzy told me every single part of that day. I listened to it all but heard maybe half of it. Finally she wound down. Maybe she ran out of things to say, or maybe she realized that she was just rattling on about stuff that didn't really matter, not even to her.

I cut in, "Did you see the thing about the *Golden Dragon*?"

Izzy stopped and looked at me for a moment, then nodded. "It's terrible."

"Maybe," I said. "They might still be okay."

From her expression it was clear she didn't agree. After a moment she said, "There are kids on that ship."

"I know."

"It's so scary," she said. "How can you even deal with it?"

I shrugged. "We just deal."

That stalled the conversation for a moment, so I shifted

gears and started talking about how Mom disassembled my sleeping pod and left all the pieces floating and a note taped to the wall that said, "Fix it."

In other words, I babbled. She found more stuff to talk about. Shoes she bought. Her homework. Her dog's new collar.

Stuff.

Just stuff.

Then our small talk seemed to run down. We had a few seconds of silence. Each of us looking at the other, the connection distorted by the time delay.

Finally Izzy said, "You know . . . we're not going to be able to talk like this much longer. The delays and all."

"I know."

"We'll have to start recording messages instead."

"Yeah."

Izzy stared into my eyes with an intensity that I could feel across hundreds of thousands of miles.

"I'd better go," she told me. "I love you."

"I love you, too," I said, but before the words were out the screen went dark. She'd already signed off. My words fell into the black and there was no one out there to hear them.

Chapter 68

First thing to know is that they tried—they really did try—to make us comfortable. As much as science would allow. You see, the trick is to balance payload weight with fuel. Because they didn't have to launch the *Huginn* from Earth and push all that mass through the atmosphere, they were able to build the ship big. From nose to tail it was 222 meters long. There was a command capsule up front and a collar around it from which dozens of different antennae stuck out into the black. Then there was a bunch of storage pods and computer banks. There were massive water tanks to provide drinking water as well as cooling water for the electronics, as well as tanks of other chemicals including liquid nitrogen, liquid hydrogen, and more. Then there were specialized control pods packed with instruments of all kinds.

The next part of the ship was the main habitat, which was a huge barrel with a wide central corridor. The hab, as we called it, was split into several sections. The aft-most section (meaning it was at the back) had twenty bunks built into the walls, each about four feet deep, seven feet long, and five feet high. You could sit up on your bunk but if you wanted to stand—or float at full length—you had to leave the bunk. In our bunks, though, we had cabinets for personal stuff, a full medical kit, a mission computer built into the wall, and a place to store our personal tablets. In front of the sleeping section was the common room, which we called—wait for it—the common room. Behind the hab was the wheel, the thing that gave that part of the ship artificial gravity. Aft of the wheel was the galley—with its rows of cold storage, and microwave ovens—then the fitness center, more storage, more of the specialized pods, a machine shop, the big 3-D printers, more bulk storage, and my dad's botany lab and hydroponic garden.

In order to make the transit habitat as comfortable as possible, Mars One needed to spend a lot of money. What helped was that everything, everywhere you look on that boat, had a product logo on it. The seats were IKEA, the computers were Apple, the microwaves were Breville, the freezers were West-inghouse. Every reusable cup had a company brand on it. Every food pouch had a name. And our clothes had a bunch of different names. We were taking human consumerism to Mars, which was how my dad said it. He was right. He wore a John Deere cap when he did his interviews.

The only area that was off-limits for us was the command module, which was empty and locked.

I spent as much time as I could in one of the pods talking with Herc, of course. Sometimes just goofing off but a lot of the time talking about the Hart Foundation. Herc had a lot of ideas and sometimes he just went on and on and on about details and plans.

What I'm not getting to—which I should—are the pod sessions with Izzy.

It was way past the time when I should have just cut things off with Izzy. Made a clean break. But I didn't.

Chapter 69

Space was boring.

We had been out there for four months. What have I got to say about everything that had been happening since we left?

Nothing.

Nothing worth saying, nothing worth hearing.

Space was insanely, god-awful, I-want-to-stab-myself-in-the-brain boring.

Oh my God oh my God *it was so boring.*

Chapter 70

If this were a thrilling big-budget summer blockbuster movie then we'd have encountered an alien spaceship or been hit by a meteoroid or there would have been a rebellion aboard. There would have been hijinks, teen-appropriate adventures, young love, PG-13 passion. There would have been messy violence. Something dramatic.

None of that happened.

The thing is, though, everything done in every single step of preparation for space travel is designed to remove all possibilities of drama. Mind you, the launch itself was pretty dramatic. Big engines, lots of fire and smoke, and all of the travel was in front of us. Any drama *after* we left, though, would have meant that someone screwed up. The fact that we were flying through space getting bored meant that everyone did their job the right way.

Again, if this were a movie, there would be a line of text on the screen saying something like "FOUR MONTHS LATER." After which would be more drama. Landing and unforeseen problems, Martian dust storms, all that.

This is the part of the trip they skip over in movies.

I grew a mustache. Nirti said it looked like a diseased cat-erpillar, so I shaved it off.

Luther grew a goatee. It looked really great and made him look twenty. Everyone dug it. I seriously hated that guy.

We all had birthdays out there. I was taller (thanks to microgravity) so I kept telling myself I looked older. The mustache was part of that plan. Oh well.

We had the world's most boring Thanksgiving. Me and my folks. It's an American holiday, so . . . the whole ship didn't stop to celebrate.

Christmas and Hanukkah were different. They showed *A Christmas Carol*—in Dutch with English subtitles. Mr. De Jaeger told this really nasty story about Krampus, which is the anti–Santa Claus. He comes around when you've been bad and does horrible things to naughty children. Zoé laughed at the story, and so did Colpeys and some of the others from the Netherlands, Norway, and Germany. It creeped everyone else out.

After that we sang carols and some Hanukkah songs for the one person on board who was Jewish. We did not swap presents. I mean . . . seriously, how could we? Really tough to run to the local Walmart for last-minute stocking stuffers, and not even Amazon delivered all the way out there.

Tony Chu put on a fake beard that was made from insula-tion and told jokes we all pretended were funny.

Overall it was really kind of sad. I didn't think we were

going to have a *Martian Family Christmas Special* anytime soon.

What turned it around, though—and really turned a knife in all of us—were the Christmas messages sent from home. Thousands of people in Amsterdam gathered in a town square, everyone holding candles, and sang Christmas songs. They did the same thing in Madison. Izzy and Herc and Spice were there, dressed in wool hats and scarves and earmuffs, their breath puffing white in the cold air.

It was supposed to be them sending love all that way. But . . . after it was over I was more depressed than I've ever been. I spent all Christmas Day in my bunk. Didn't read or watch anything. Just listened to Izzy's playlist. All one hundred songs. No one bothered me. I think the only people on board who weren't bummed out were those who had no family or any real friends back home.

Then there was New Year's.

The year 2027 came in with a big shared meal, and it was a surprise. Lots of stuff they froze for this event but didn't tell us. Real meat loaf, real vegetables, real mashed potatoes with gravy. That actually got weird. First thing was that we had to keep the food from floating away. When you wanted a bite you had to fish around in a bag with a fork. The upside was that it was great to have that kind of meal, and I know the mission folks meant well, but I think we all had the wrong reaction to it. We'd never have a meal like that again. It was going to make our regular food taste a lot worse for a long time, even with Sophie working her magic. Some of the crew saved portions for later, to make it last. Some skipped the meal altogether. I ate it all but after a while the Earth food began tasting weird to me. It bummed me out.

One of the TV networks back home sent us a ten-hour-long comedy and music special. None of us knew they were making it. All these top pop, country, and hip-hop artists singing for us, on stages all over the world. People sent best wishes, prayers, and shout-outs. And Director Colpeys and Mom rigged a countdown that played through both ships so that all forty of us could yell "Happy New Year" at the same time.

That was kind of cool. That was fun.

I got New Year's kisses from Nirti—sisterly; Zoé—awkward; my mom—motherly; a couple other women—strange; and Sophie. That was a little weird. I mean, I'd become really good friends with Sophie. We talked a lot. She was sweet and pretty and very smart. She knew a lot about history and philosophy. Even knew some science.

When she kissed me a little after midnight, it was about two seconds too long and I backed off. She looked at me, a little confused and maybe surprised at what she'd just done.

"Oh God," she said, "I'm sorry."

"No," I said, "it's cool."

It wasn't, though. Sophie knew about Izzy, and even if I was going to eventually *formally* break up with my girlfriend, I hadn't done it yet.

The holidays passed, the ships flew on. Or "hurtled," I guess. Regardless, time passed and except for the fact that we had an official "night," it was hard to tell one hour from another, one day from another. No highlights, no drama.

The way it's supposed to be in space.

The way it was probably going to be for the rest of the trip. We were all beginning to buzz with excitement. We all wanted to stop traveling and actually arrive. To stop being passengers and start being explorers of the unknown.

Mars . . . here we come.

Chapter 71

Izzy and I couldn't really talk in real time anymore. Not for months. It was all taped messages. So it was only an exchange of video files, some of which were chapters in a really stilted and frustrating conversation. Others were impulse videos. Izzy sent a lot of them. Even more than I did. The first ones she sent were short. Stuff like:

"I miss you sooooo much. I love you."

Then things changed.

About two months ago her messages got suddenly longer. She'd sit there and stare at the camera and talk. Just talk. About her life, about stuff that happened in school, about Herc and Spice—who were a serious item now. About her parents. About the segments she was taping for *Tristan and Izzy.*

But there was something strange about those videos and it took me a long, long time to figure it out. When I did, I crawled into my bunk and cried.

She was trying to fill time.

Izzy wasn't talking to me; she was info-dumping because she didn't really have anything to say. Nothing. Not really.

She was having new experiences and so was I and there was absolutely nothing in common. Not even the same sky, the same air, or the same gravity. Nothing.

The videos still came in a couple of times a week, but they were like clockwork. She uploaded clips from the kids at school, but they were getting stale too. And let's face it, I wasn't exactly holding up my end of the conversation. One day I realized that I'd spent twenty-two minutes explaining how I stripped space-particle-collector assembly down to parts, cleaned it, and put it back together. Wow, how exciting is that? I could imagine Izzy sitting through it, eyes glazing as I went into detail about how tricky it was to disassemble it without upsetting the calibrations. She'd hear how truly excited I was about it, too, and she'd wonder who I was.

And who was I?

When had Tristan the high school kid and boyfriend of the world's prettiest and most wonderful girl become *only* Tristan the space mechanic who could only talk about machines and not actually relate to anything else? Where in all this emptiness was the line, and when did I cross it without even knowing?

That was the last time I recorded anything about repairs or maintenance. When you hit one of those moments of self-awareness you're supposed to stop, reassess, and find a better way to move forward.

Which I did.

The problem with that was it left me almost nothing to say to Izzy.

Herc and I could still talk, but that was starting to get a little strange too. He told me about the movies and TV he watched, and what was happening in the comics we both liked. Batman was still moody and antisocial. Spider-Man still had girl troubles. And we talked about the Hart Foundation, but most of that was us just commenting on what he'd already sent in long e-mails. We were talking about stuff, but we weren't really talking. Herc didn't call as often as he used to. He had Spice, had schoolwork, and was reading tons of books about financial investments, nonprofit administration, and charitable trusts.

And I found that although I sent him e-mails and video files, I wasn't *talking* to Herc much. Not about what I was really feeling. There were things I could only talk about with Nirti. And there were things I could talk about with Sophie, because she was older than me but still young enough to understand what I was going through.

The *Huginn* and the *Muninn* flew on. Farther and farther away.

Or closer and closer.

It all depends on how you look at it.

Chapter 72

Luther and I were in the fitness center taking turns on the ARED. They put the machine in the big wheel, so there was some gravity. It was set to Mars gravity, though. We all had to train in there now because we were almost at the point where we didn't have enough fuel or supplies to turn around and go back.

The ARED was getting harder, though, because we were both thinner, our muscles less dense. My bones ached a lot and I knew it was because micro-g was weakening them. The docs and the exercise equipment helped slow that, but it was a factor all the time. A fact of life.

I'd rebuilt the ARED twice so far to maximize its effect on us. Mom and Colpeys were so impressed that they filed a request with the manufacturers back on Earth to get them to sign off on a permanent redesign, and to cut me in on any profits. More money I couldn't spend. More cash for the Hart Foundation.

Luther was running on a Martian-g treadmill while I did sets of squats. He tapped the keys to increase his pace. The environmental systems would reclaim excess moisture from our sweat, purify it, and put it back in the tanks. Disgusting but practical. He was smiling.

"What are you smiling about?" I asked.

Luther laughed. He was running pretty fast now. Because there was gravity in here his sweat sluiced down his bare chest. "I've taken up mathematics," he said.

"Math—?"

"I've been calculating the value of pi."

I paused midlift and looked at him. His grin was pure evil. I said, "Oh."

"'Oh' is right," he replied, his grin getting wider. Like the Joker in the Batman comics, and every bit as spiteful.

"Congratulations," I said without enthusiasm. "And you're a real champ for bragging about it."

"Thought you might want to know," said Luther.

"No, I don't."

He laughed as he ran. Five minutes later he said, "So . . . you and Sophie. You hitting that?"

"Jeez, you're really disgusting," I said as I lifted.

He grinned. "So that's a yes or a no?"

"It's a no, so stop asking. It's always going to be a no."

"Missed opportunity," he said.

I growled low in my throat as I tried to lift the whole weight of the ship. Sophie and I were just friends and that was the absolute truth. After that one weird thing on New Year's Sophie had been totally cool and we'd both left that stuff behind us. We had spent some time together, but only for me to start teaching her how to do repairs. I helped her disassemble and then rebuild one of her microwaves. Like that. Just crewmate stuff.

Suddenly Nirti appeared in the doorway looking scared. "Tristan!" she cried. "Your mom needs you right now."

"What's wrong—?"

"It's the *Muninn*!"

Chapter 73

I wasted no time getting out of the gym and away from the low-grav pull of the wheel. As soon as I felt the gravity fall away I kicked myself into a free fly down the center of the main corridor, grabbed a handle to swing a right, and monkey pulled myself to the open door of my mom's workshop. She was there with Tony.

Mom was busy typing something but Tony turned to me before I could ask and said, "It's the water purification systems aboard the *Muninn*. They failed completely and spewed a lot of raw sewage into one of the tanks of drinking water."

"Oh no!"

"Yeah, well, it's even worse than that, Tris," said Tony. "One of the pipes on the wastewater purification unit burst into the hab and all of that sludge went tumbling around in micro-g. It's a freaking mess over there. The rupture must have started in the middle of the night."

"But . . . how?"

"We don't know yet."

"How can we not know?"

"Don't ask me, kid."

"No, I mean, how'd it get this bad?" I asked. "What about the alarms? What about the automatic shutdowns?"

"Well, that's the million-dollar question, isn't it?" snarled my mom without looking at us. She hammered at some keys and suddenly the face of Inga Holstrom, chief engineer on the *Muninn*, filled the screen. She looked like one of the Valkyries from Norse legend. A gigantic blonde with large hands and a face that always looked like she just sucked a lemon. Pretty good mechanic, though. Mom taught her.

This thing really made no sense. Wastewater and solid waste were piped under pressure from the heads to a reclaiming station. The solid matter was then supposed to be stored in compressed blocks for use as fertilizer on Mars. Poop is full of bacteria . . . Mars, not so much. The urine was cleaned and the purified liquid was returned to the drinking water. Sounds disgusting, and it was. But it was also practical. The waste traveled through long pipes inside the walls. There were shutoff systems all through the process, and also alarms for when even the slightest moisture got into the electronics. Even our backups had backups, and yet aboard the *Muninn* the whole system had faulted out.

So when it comes right down to it, this could not have happened. The fact that it *did* happen had terrified us all.

Tony and I flanked Mom as we studied the data being sent across from the *Muninn*. Inga gave us more information in reply to about a million questions Mom fired at her. I was tense, Tiny looked sick, Inga was scared, and Mom was furious.

We were there for hours helping Inga work the problem. Tony and I threw out any suggestion that came to mind. Mom was open to any idea, any plan, or a possible workaround. Anything. Or maybe that's a space engineer thing. There's no better environment for teamwork than when there is absolutely no chance of anyone else coming to help. Not when we were millions of miles away from home. Not when answers to urgent questions had a long time delay. So we all pitched in and we worked the problem. Colpeys and some of the other scientists aboard offered advice, but none of them were engineers on our level.

At one point, while I was in the head, I heard Mom having another quiet argument with Colpeys. I didn't hear much but I heard Colpeys say, "Jean, I gave you all those extra days so you could make sure we didn't have problems like this."

And Mom hissed at him and said, "I checked every one of those systems myself, Jurgen. Every one. This couldn't happen."

"So why is everyone on the *Muninn* floating around in their own sewage?"

My mother's answer was a low growl.

When Colpeys was gone I came out of the head. Mom cut me a look, realizing that I must have heard the conversation. I didn't say anything and neither did she, but afterward she was even *more* intense. Which I wouldn't have bet was possible. Mom attacked the problem with everything she knew and all of her imagination.

Even so, it took Inga four days to fix the system.

Four very long, very uncomfortable days.

She had to take it apart completely, and that meant closing off most of the *Muninn*'s hab. The rest of the colonists had to capture all the floating drops and lumps of stuff that came out of the broken pipe.

A bunch of people got sick. It became clear that the leak had started small and polluted the drinking water long before the system went critical. Within seventy-two hours half the crew was down with bacterial infections. They burned through half of their stores of antibiotics trying to get ahead of it.

I heard Mom in one of the com-pods talking to Inga. Not actually yelling at her, but close. Mom sounded scared and I think I heard Inga crying. "I understand that you're sick, Inga, but you have to keep at it. What choice do you have? And when you're done with that, I want to hear that you've upped the purification output by forty percent. No, don't tell me you don't know how to do it. Don't you *dare* tell me that. My son could fix that system, for God's sake. You're a professional. Get up and get it done!"

It was harsh but that was Mom. The tougher things got the less she seemed to really care. It was her defense mechanism, but it worked with most people. Would it work with Inga, especially if she was that sick? It was one of those moments when I kind of hated Mom for how she was acting, but at the same time I didn't know what else she could have done.

I fled before Mom came out. Later, when she was calmer, I found her at her desk typing in repair notes on her laptop. She had a real-time chat going with Inga and was walking her through the repair. Inga looked gray and sick and ashamed. I felt so bad for her.

Mom saw me, pointed to the other work space, and said, "Log on and do a workup. I want to know how you'd handle this."

"Handle what? Which part?"

"Focus on the purification system. Go through it and try to figure out how it could fail. I want a list of possibilities. Nothing's too extreme. Give me anything that comes to mind."

I nodded and set to work, half listening to Mom and Inga until the job I was doing became so hard I had to really concentrate. The whole day burned off.

The next day was like that one. And the next.

Finally, after a week of absolute hell, the *Muninn*'s wastewater system was up and running, and the purification was chugging along with a 52 percent bump. Mom compared what Inga did with what I'd come up with. My redesign maxed out at 43 percent. She gave me a long, sour look.

"Do better," she told me. Then she blanked out all of my work and told me to start over.

Moms. Can't live with 'em, can't shoot them out of an airlock.

Chapter 74

The incident on the *Muninn* put everybody aboard our ship on edge for a couple of weeks. Inga had used parts from the backup water purifier to upgrade the main one. If it failed again they'd be screwed. Purifying the polluted water was going to take time because it had to be triple filtered, tested, and filtered again. And like I said, they were now more than halfway through their store of antibiotics.

You see, bacterial infections weren't supposed to be a big thing. Mars probably doesn't have bacteria, and even if it does it wasn't likely to get into our food and water. Everything there would be filtered, and the heavy-duty filtering equipment was already there, sent on the unmanned ships. There were more antibiotics and other medical supplies waiting for us, of course, but they were on the planet. Each ship had enough water for two additional months beyond the journey. Now the *Muninn* was coasting on the edge and they might have to go down to half rations by the time we made it to Mars.

One day over lunch Nirti asked Zoé, "Why can't we just

send some of our water and supplies over to them?"

Zoé stared at her as if she'd asked why we couldn't go outside the ship and sunbathe. "You're joking, right?"

"No. The *Muninn*'s right there!"

"It's not 'right there'; it's two hundred kilometers off the starboard bow." When Nirti looked blank, Zoé took a mustard packet and set it in the air in front of her. Then she placed a ketchup packet to the right side and about a yard away. "The ships are not under power," she explained. "Remember, we're like rocks thrown—"

"At Mars," finished Nirti. "I know. But we *have* engines. And we have retro jets and all that. Couldn't they slow down and let us catch up and then we can send someone over in an EMU with supplies?"

"You don't understand the physics," said Zoé.

"Maybe not as well as you, but I know it's possible."

Zoé said, "Sure, it's possible, but it's incredibly risky. If we slow the *Muninn* there's a risk of interfering with its planned trajectory. A thousandth of a degree off here could make them miss Mars completely. Or they'd have to burn fuel to correct. And to get the ships within EVA distance is very dangerous. There's only a few hundred meters of cable, and whoever's doing the space walk would be taking a terrible risk. No . . . it's too dangerous."

Nirti folded her arms and stared at Zoé. "So what you're

saying is that we're not *smart* enough to figure it out, even if it would mean saving the lives of twenty people? Wow. So much for supergeniuses."

And before Zoé could stop sputtering long enough to come up with a reply, Nirti pushed off and floated away.

Chapter 75

I got a video message from Izzy. It was different from the others she'd been sending recently, and it was the first one in almost a week. I watched it in one of the com-pods, making sure all of the soundproof door seals were in place.

The first thing I saw was her empty bedroom, but I could hear her offscreen, and the camera jiggled so it was clear she was adjusting the angle of her laptop. The only lights were the desk lamp and the glow of the screen. Then Izzy came around and sat down. She wore a pink bathrobe. Something new, probably a Christmas present. No makeup, and her dark hair was damp from the shower. Somehow she looked older. Different. She smiled at the screen, but it wasn't the kind of smile she usually gave. It wasn't the bright everything's-right-in-the-world smile she'd worn during all those recent marathon messages, and it wasn't the smile from before I left. The smile that made the world stop spinning.

It wasn't sad, either.

Just . . . different.

"Tristan," she began, "I'm sorry I haven't written in so long." She paused, shook her head. "It's weird that I call this 'writing to Tristan' when it's just me sitting in front of the camera. Does that make me some kind of old-fashioned girl? Maybe. I don't know. It feels like writing because it's not really live. But then, I guess *we're* not live either. Not really."

She stopped talking and looked down at her hands, which seemed to be wrestling with each other on top of her desk. The digital counter on the lower left of the screen ticked through nearly fifteen seconds before she spoke again. Her eyes came up and she looked directly at me. I knew there was a time lag and there was distance, but I swear that in that moment we were actually seeing each other.

"Tristan," she said in a soft whisper of a voice, "you know that I will always love you. That won't ever change. Not on the level where it matters most. But . . ."

And that was as far as she could get. Tears welled in the corners of her eyes, broke, and ran down her cheeks. She began shaking her head. Very slowly.

Five seconds later she reached out and turned off the video. All I heard were her last four words.

"I . . . can't," she said. "I'm sorry."

And the screen went dark.

Chapter 76

"What's wrong with you?" asked Luther as I pulled myself out of the com-pod. "Have you finally accepted that you'll be the *last* person they let off the ship when we get there?"

I went past him without saying a word. I didn't even tell him to go take an EVA without a suit. Not worth the breath.

My bunk seemed a million miles away. Funny how pain distorts everything, even distance. Back on the Lucky Eight I'd shared a room with Luther, but on the ship I had a sleeping pod all to myself. Funny how something that small could feel huge and lonely.

"Tristan," called a voice and I turned to see Sophie emerging from her bunk. She hadn't put her hair in a ponytail and it drifted around her face like mist. Or like she was a mermaid floating in the water. I almost ignored her, too, but she pulled herself up and over to intercept me. She looked at my face and there was immediate concern in her eyes. "What's wrong, *cher*?"

"Nothing's wrong," I said, but she could see the lie through the cracks in my voice.

"What happened?"

Oh man, I really did not want to talk about this with anyone. Not until I figured out what was going on with that video from Izzy. I wanted to find something to dismantle and rebuild. I wanted to find something broken that I could fix.

Sophie grabbed a handhold to anchor herself and touched my cheek with her other hand. She looked past me, to the com-pods, and nodded. "Is it Iseult?"

"Izzy," I growled. "Her name's Izzy."

Sophie nodded. She took a deep breath and sighed. Then she pulled me to her, wrapping one arm around me while still holding on to the wall.

"Tell me," she said.

I didn't want to. I refused. It was too much and too private.

I told her anyway.

Chapter 77

When I was done going through the whole thing, I felt exhausted, drained, beaten up. Sophie listened without interruption. She held my hand and when I was done she reached out to brush away a tear that clung to the corner of my eye. It floated away and for a long, strange moment we watched it, neither of us speaking.

Finally she said, "Did you only stay together because of the reality show?"

"Yes," I said, then immediately contradicted that. "No. I . . . I don't know."

"You stayed together until the launch even though you knew it would *be* the end. And you've been trying to keep it alive all this time, *non*? Is that safe? For you own hearts, I mean."

"Safe? No. It's not smart, either, and we both know it. It's not practical. Let's face it, could there be a more obvious metaphor for why people break up than a teenage boy literally going millions of miles away to live on another world? But we couldn't let go. I know *I* couldn't. Maybe I can't. Maybe I'm too stupid or immature to do what I know is right."

"You're getting there now," said Sophie. "And I think it's clear Iseault is there a few steps ahead. It happens like that in matters of the heart. I've never heard of it ever happening at the right time for both people. Maybe it has never happened in all of history. But what is very clear is that Iseault has been getting closer to it."

"How come I didn't see it?"

"You probably did, Tristan, but you didn't want to see it. Or admit it to yourself. But you just told me about the videos. Over the last few months her messages have been about nothing, *non*? About minutia? About trivial things? I believe that was Iseault fighting the truth to which she was coming. But she was afraid. There's no doubt, *cher*, that she loves you. Anyone who ever saw you two on your show would know that. Anyone who ever heard you talk about her could see it. But you left. And no amount of love can stretch all this way. It's unreasonable and unrealistic and unfair to expect it to be otherwise."

"I know."

"She is a lovely young woman," said Sophie. "Smart and very pretty. She's also rich and famous, too, which means that the whole world is watching her. Imagine how hard that must be. She is the storybook princess who is supposed to pine for her lost prince. She is supposed to hold true, to *be* true. The world expects her to be every bit as tragic as the Iseult of the poems. And how cruel that is of everyone."

"I know."

"It seems that now the princess has realized that and cannot abide it."

"I know," I said. We sat on the edge of her bunk, held in place by straps, the canvas cover half zipped. Sophie held my hand.

Sophie said, "Iseult is probably drowning."

I turned sharply to her. "What?"

"She is. All that attention, *non*? All of those expectations, and the burden she placed on herself to love you forever? This is too much for anyone to bear, and more than anyone should *try* to bear. Trying to hold on to *Tristan and Izzy* is going to pull her under. She has to let you go or she will drown," said Sophie.

I said nothing.

"If you love her—and I believe you truly do—then you have to let her go. You are a sweet young man, Tristan. Don't let your own heartbreak and loneliness turn you cruel."

I turned to Sophie and wrapped my arms around her and held on to her and tried so hard not to let any of this be true. And all the time I reached desperately for the rope of need and want that tied me to the beautiful girl back on Earth. I did that with one hand, and with the other I fumbled for the knife and began to cut.

Chapter 78

Can a bad day get worse? Sure.

How bad did it get? The water purification system on the *Muninn* failed. *Again*. It was a dangerous malfunction the first time. It was worse this time. Much, *much* worse.

I'd just gotten to sleep and was dreaming that I was back on Earth, with Izzy—of course—and we were both laughing at some joke Herc just cracked. I think I was laughing in my sleep, but then Mom suddenly woke me up by slapping the outside of my bunk. "Get dressed. *Now!*"

I didn't get all the way dressed. She sounded too upset to waste time, so I went sailing through the ship in sweatpants and a T-shirt. Mom was in her shop, with Tony Chu and Colpeys crowded in around her desk. Inga was on the video screen looking really scared.

Mom was yelling at her. "What do you mean, it failed? How could it fail if you fixed it the right way?"

"I don't know," said Inga. She was so defensive that her tone was hostile. Couldn't blame her. It was really hard to be on the receiving end of Mom's anger.

"Inga," said Colpeys calmly, trying to dial it all down, "tell us exactly what happened. What malfunctioned?"

"It was the shutoff valve," said Inga. "It snapped."

"'*Snapped*'?" barked Mom. "How does a brand-new high-grade steel valve snap? It's behind a panel in the wall. What could possible make it break?"

Inga shook her head. "I don't know. The alarms went off and I got there in under a minute. Water was shooting out from around the panel. I opened it to get to the valve assembly and saw that the handle was just floating there. I had to shut the water off at the main."

"Can it be repaired?" asked Colpeys.

"I'll have to install a new valve assembly, but that's not the problem," said Inga. "We have two hundred gallons of drinking water floating around the hab and trapped inside the walls. It's already caused electrical shorts in several systems. We were able to stop it from frying everything in the hab, but there is a lot of damage."

Colpeys's face turned gray. "How much damage?"

Inga's eyes drifted away as if she didn't want to look at us while she gave the bad news. "We're still assessing it, but . . . it's not good. The water shorted out the east wall."

Because there was no up and down anymore, the hab— and the whole ship—was oriented by compass points. The north wall was where "up" used to be. The west wall had the wiring for lights, temperature, some communications, and a few other systems. The east wall of the hab was lined with food freezers and microwaves.

"What did we lose?" asked Mom. Her fists were balled on top of her desk.

Inga shook her head. "Two freezers. The big one and the left-hand one. But the small one and the main day-storage refrigerator are still on line."

"God," began Colpeys, but he shut up when he realized with horror that Inga wasn't finished.

"We lost all of the microwaves."

"All *six*?" gasped Colpeys.

"Yes."

"What's your timetable for repairing them?" demanded the director.

It took Inga so long to answer that I knew it was even worse than I thought. She shook her head.

"I may be able to scavenge the others for parts and get one repaired."

"One . . . ?" said Colpeys in a small, shocked voice.

"How soon?" I asked.

Inga shook her head again. "Once we're done fixing the water system? Two, three days."

Colpeys closed his eyes and sagged back. Mom narrowed hers and leaned forward.

"Forget the microwave. Keep the main freezer shut for

now. It'll retain enough cold to buy you a day. If we have to we can transfer bulk supplies to an airlock and let the big black keep everything cold."

It was a good plan. During an EVA, with nothing protecting you against solar radiation, the heat could get extreme, but inside a metal airlock with no heat being pumped into it, the temperature would drop all the way down. If it got too cold we could make some adjustments.

And I knew we had plenty of food packs and protein drinks that didn't require either refrigeration or cooking. No, that wasn't why Colpeys was freaking out. In the back of the main freezer, locked inside a kind of vault, was blood. Hundreds of pints of it. *Our* blood. Harvested from each person on the mission and stored for long-term used. Plasma, too, and other vital materials that required long-term cold storage. The blood was too fragile to store in an airlock unless the temperature could be adjusted perfectly. That was math we might have to figure out soon. And moving that precious supply was downright dangerous.

We did not have replacements for this stuff. The fact that we had multiple freezers and microwaves on board was a ready-to-go redundancy. Each could get by with two working microwaves—one in a pinch—and one freezer. The others were installed as ready-made replacements. No one foresaw this kind of electrical problem because it pretty much couldn't have happened. I mean . . . it shouldn't have happened. The water leaks? And now the flooding and shorting of the wiring inside the walls? That was so far outside of worst-case scenario as to not be in the playbook at all. If it wasn't happening right now I'd have sworn that it couldn't. There is no way on Earth—or in space—that something like this should have been able to happen. It was supposed to be a design impossibility. Lansdorp and his teams did not cut corners when it came to crew safety. Not one.

So why *was* it happening?

I cut a look at Mom and even started to speak, but she must have tuned in on my line of thought and gave me a tiny headshake. Later, it said.

I nodded.

Mom leaned closer to the screen and began talking very fast. Sometimes she ripped people apart and sometimes she didn't. The deciding factor, I long ago realized, was what was needed in the moment. Inga didn't need a kick in the ass. She needed to know what to do, how best to do it, and that the full resources of her boss were at her immediate disposal. Mom outlined a strategy and even as she spoke Tony Chu was typing it down so that there would be a digital copy they could send. Inga had an assistant and there were other engineers aboard—not as good and not trained by Jean Hart, but able to make basic repairs.

That wasn't the problem. If it was just a matter of fixing the plumbing Inga would have done it and told us later.

Partly it was the fact that so much of their precious water was now floating around the ship. Thousands of globules of it, in all shapes and sizes, that would have be chased down and caught. The rest of the crew could do that, but the water they collected would probably no longer be pure. It would have to be purified again. That was a problem.

But it was a long, long way from the worst problem. There was water inside the walls of the ship, where all of the delicate electronics were. Inga told us about the damage that had already been done, but she left more unsaid. That water, most of it anyway, was still there. It was still capable of doing more damage.

God.

The *Muninn* was in real danger.

The ship and everyone aboard.

Chapter 79

Mom stayed on the video call all day and into the next night. She talked Inga through a dozen different steps to fix the problem, including setting up a new freezer unit to store the blood supplies. After sixteen hours of intense work the entire valve system had been completely overhauled.

Since Inga was burning through a lot of time trying to remove the broken valve stem, I suggested that Inga drill through it, insert two high-grade metal rods, wrap them in duct tape, and turn the stem into a new handle.

It worked.

In situations like these, whenever all problems are equally bad, you have to find solutions without burning away time on theories. There are no do-overs out here. The blood stores were every bit as important as the water. I made a pretty radical suggestion. Tony shook his head, but Mom stared at me for a two count, and then she was back on the video call. It took some outside-the-box figuring, some definitely off-the-books monkeying around with tools, and about a gallon of sweat for Inga to disconnect the entire blood safe and move it—the generator, temperature regulator, and all—to the auxiliary airlock. The key was keeping the generator hooked up the whole time, which meant running a crazy network of wires everywhere. She managed it, though, and didn't lose a single pint of blood or plasma.

Tony gave me a high five that almost sent us both flying against opposite walls. Mom wore one of her thin, calculating smiles.

"You may have just saved everyone on that ship," Mom said. She said that in front of Inga, Colpeys, and Tony Chu.

"I—" I began, but Mom cut me off.

"Now we need to isolate that part of the plumbing system and reroute to another valve. The whole unit has to come out but we need to conserve water. There are thousands of gallons floating around in the hab, and five months' worth of food particles, snot, metal dust, and other particulates in the air. Even if they reclaim all that's lost it'll be impure and the purifier's not going to be able to clean it for weeks. The *Muninn*'s already critically low on pure water."

"And people are still getting sick," said Inga. "We were only just getting ahead of the bacterial infection when this happened."

Mom turned to Tony. "You're on diagnostics. Use our system and the computers and give me five reasonable explanations for why this happened and each one better have a practical solution. Go."

He was out of there like a shot, taking his laptop with him.

Then Mom turned to me. "Tristan, we need to amp up the water purifier. I want a fix for capacity and a minimum ten percent bump in filtration time. Don't come back to me until you have a way for them to scrub their water at a faster rate."

"But—"

"Don't disappoint me, Tristan—" she began, but this time I cut her off.

"No," I said, "I already have that part figured out."

"Don't be ridiculous," Colpeys said. "That filtration system was designed by experts."

Mom's head swiveled around like a praying mantis's and she gave Jurgen a truly icy stare. "And what exactly do you think my son is, Jurgen? You want to see how *you'd* stack up against him in a mechanical challenge? Do you have a solution for this?"

Colpeys opened his mouth but said nothing.

Mom turned back and jabbed me in the chest with a stiffened finger. "Talk."

"We can use the galley," I said. "We may not do much cooking but we have heaters, right? We can rig stills to superheat the water, run it through used O_2 filters, trap the clean steam, and then run that through the purifier. It would only take one pass at that point. Right now we're going to have to run it through the filtration system three or four times to remove all the particulates."

"No," said Colpeys, "you can't refine all of the polluted water that way."

"It doesn't have to be all," I countered. "The main purification system will do most of it, but we could maybe clean a couple of hundred gallons a day. That'll take the strain off the main system. It's not a replacement; it's an addition to the system we already have."

"All that boiling will raise the humidity in the hab."

"Sure, but the water reclaimers will suck it up. Those systems aren't damaged."

Mom swiveled to face Inga. "You get all that?"

"I did," she said. "I'm on it."

She vanished from the screen.

I looked at Colpeys. "Setting up the stills, managing it, collecting the floating water, keeping the whole thing working right, that's going to keep most of the crew busy."

"Day and night," he complained.

"Well, sure," I said, "but that's time they're not sitting around going nuts worrying. And this way everybody gets to be part of how they'll all survive this. I mean . . . that's a win, right?"

"You're saying you can talk them through the procedure?" Colpeys asked me.

"Yes," I said without hesitation.

Colpeys studied me like he'd never seen me before. Then he glanced at my mom. "You were right about him, Jean."

"I know I was," she said.

Colpeys nodded to me. "Do it."

Chapter 80

Inga and her assistant kept working on the plumbing while the rest of the *Muninn*'s crew set up the stills. I came up with an improvement while they were doing it and told them to move the stills to the wheel and up the wheel's rate of spin to full, which would give them three-quarters Earth gravity. That would increase the drip rate of the reclaimed water. When I told Mom she kissed me on the head and told me that I was brilliant.

Erecting the stills was complicated and awkward, though, but the crew had a real incentive program. I talked one of the crew members through the process via the video screen. Sophie sat with me for a while and listened. She tried to hang out with me whenever I was doing some repairs aboard the ship, and she was learning fast. Very fast, actually, and a couple of times I asked her if she was messing with me because it seemed like she already knew how to use the tools. She said she was a quick learner. Even so, the problems on the other ship were way beyond her. She wanted to know everything she could about it, though, and she listened closely to everything I said.

"Will it work?" she asked when the tech put the call on hold to make some of the adjustments I recommended.

I chewed my lip for a moment. "I think so."

She squeezed my shoulder. "You're a genius, you know that?"

"I'm just a mechanic," I said, and I could feel my face going red-hot.

"No, *cher*, you and your mother are so much alike. You can see into all these machines. You're already smarter than Inga and Tony. You're going to be smarter than your mother. She knows it. I've heard her tell people. She's so proud of you."

"Please stop," I begged. "That is really not helping. I'm just trying to be useful."

The tech suddenly came back on the screen and from the expression on his face I knew that something was wrong.

"Didn't it work?" I asked.

"It's not that," he said grimly. And he laid more bad news on us. Inga's assistant had collapsed. He'd been trying to bull his way through a bacterial infection, but it caught up with him and between fever, chills, and seventy-seven hours without sleep, his body just couldn't do it anymore. That left Inga as the only qualified mechanical engineer. There were others who could hold a wrench, but there was no one else with her level of skill. That put more of a demand on my water reclamation project.

The tech ended the call and we stared at the blank screen. I felt like I'd been gutted.

"Are they all going to die?" whispered Sophie.

"No," I growled. "No way. The stills are going to work. We're really good at this. It's why they selected us above all of the other engineers who applied."

"How can they survive with only one mechanic?"

Instead of answering I got the tech on the screen again and began working with him to build a to-do list of adjustments and repairs that might help them get ahead of their growing problems. Mom and Tony were on the call for a while, but they dropped off to work on specialized aspects of the repair protocol, leaving me to do this part. It was problem solving, and that was something I was good at. I kind of zoned out, forgetting Sophie and everything else on *this* ship. Hours passed and we covered everything. The more I looked at the problems, the more sense they made, and the more obvious the fixes became. I wished I was over there because—egotistical as it sounds—I knew I could do some of this faster even than Inga. It was frustrating not to be able to get my hands dirty on this, to work the problem with tools instead of words.

Chapter 81

"It's working," I told Nirti and the others. We were sprawled on the low-gravity floor of the wheel, sipping tea from little sippy cups. Luther lay on his back and Zoé had her head on his flat stomach. Nirti sat cross-legged, her fingers twisting and knotting in her lap.

"A still?" mused Luther. "Did you used to make moonshine back in the States?"

"First off, dumbass, no. I don't drink and they make moonshine in the mountains of Kentucky. I think. We lived in Wisconsin."

"Kentucky, Wisconsin . . ." He shrugged as if it were all the same. "Wisconsin is near Illinois, and that is where Chicago is."

"So?"

"Prohibition. Al Capone. Bathtub gin."

"Jeez . . . how do you even *know* about that stuff?"

"I read. You should try it."

"Bite me," I suggested, and he laughed. "And Prohibition was like a hundred years ago. And besides—"

Zoé interrupted. "Will it work? Will they be able to purify enough water?"

"If the other systems come back on line? Sure. And it'll help them until then. It's only supposed to be a temporary fix. Inga's fixing the whole filtration system."

"What I don't understand," said Nirti, her voice dropping to an almost conspiratorial whisper, "is *how* it happened in the first place. My mom was talking with Dr. Sakai aboard the *Muninn* and you know what he told her?"

We all bent closer to listen.

"Dr. Sakai thinks somebody *did* that to the water system."

Luther frowned. "Did what?"

"Messed with it."

"What—deliberately?"

Nirti nodded.

"No way," said Luther, shaking his head and smiling. "That's paranoid. We're on spaceships with no escape craft. Who in their right mind would do something like that? And why?"

Nirti chewed her lip. "People can go crazy out here."

We all stared at her.

Zoé frowned at her. "You're serious?"

"I'm just telling you what my mom heard from Dr. Sakai."

"Which makes it third-hand paranoia," said Luther. "Sure, let's all panic."

"Do you have a better explanation, Mr. It's All Fine?" demanded Nirti.

Luther's eyes clicked over to me. "If a machine that

shouldn't break down breaks down, ask the person who inspected it."

"What's that supposed to mean?" asked Nirti.

"Ask him," Luther said, nodding toward me. "His mom's the one who—"

I pointed a finger at him. "You're going to want to be real careful how you finish that sentence, Luther."

Luther pushed Zoé aside and began to sit up. I started to get to my feet.

And then the alarms went off.

It jolted all of us, and then my mom's voice boomed from the speakers. "Tony and Tristan, report to the workshop. Now."

I shot to my feet. I wanted to leave Luther with some kind of gritty one-liner, like "this isn't over" or "later, your ass is mine," but instead I ran to the edge of the wheel, leaped out of the partial gravity, and soared toward the other end of the ship.

I made it to Mom's workshop a heartbeat faster than Tony Chu.

"What is it, Jean?" he yelled past me.

She turned toward us, her face tight with tension and anxiety.

"It's the *Muninn*," she cried. "Their life-support computers just went down."

"What about Inga?" barked Tony. "Tell her to—"

Mom didn't answer immediately. I looked past her and did not see Inga's face on the screen. Instead there was a guy who had been trying to help ever since the *Muninn*'s number two engineer got sick. And this guy's face looked gray and greasy. His eyes had that bright polished-glass look people get when they have a fever.

"Inga's down," said Mom. "She has a fever of one hundred and four. The medical team is treating her, but they are running short on antibiotics. And two of the crew, the astrobiologist Norquist and your friend Sophie's chum Marcel are in comas. This is bad. This is really bad."

"Oh no!" cried Nirti, who'd followed me into the workshop. I looked to see Zoé and Luther in the doorway too.

"How much of the repairs did she get done?" I asked. "Will it be enough to last them until—?"

The expression on Mom's face cut me off. "That doesn't matter anymore."

"What? Why? What *else* happened?"

"The *Muninn*'s life-support system has gone down," she said in a hollow voice. "And there's no one left to fix it."

Chapter 82

Director Colpeys called a meeting and all twenty of us gathered in the common room. Mom was next to Colpeys, her face as hard and cold as stone. Colpeys looked like he wanted to throw up. Several of the crew were crying as Colpeys and Mom explained the situation aboard the *Muninn*.

"Can they fix the life support?" asked Mrs. Mbede.

"If Inga was well enough," said Mom, "then yes. But she is critical. So are eleven of the crew. The rest are all busy working on the stills."

"How long do they have?" asked Sophie.

"Best guess is three days," said Colpeys. "They can cluster around the stills for warmth, but they are on batteries and those won't last more than seventy-two hours. They have enough oxygen for maybe two more days, but by then the temperature inside the craft will be minus two hundred, and it will continue to fall."

The gasps I heard made me flinch. Nirti took my hand and squeezed it.

"So what do we do, then?" demanded Mr. Mbede. "Let them all die?"

"No," said Mom. "That is not an option."

"Jean—" began Colpeys, but Mom cut him off.

"There is only one way to save the crew and that ship. We need to adjust the orbit of both ships using controlled burns, and then someone needs to go over with equipment, replacement parts, antibiotics, and as much fresh water as the *Huginn* can spare."

That statement was met with a profound silence.

"I thought we couldn't do that," said Nirti. "I thought it would burn too much fuel."

Colpeys said, "It would burn through most of our reserve."

"Not all of it," Mom corrected.

"Enough of it. It would take us to a dangerous level."

"We have enough to slow both ships into Mars orbit. Actually, we have three times as much fuel as we need for that. We made allowances for the overages because these are colony ships. Nothing was left to chance, Jurgen, you know that. Will a controlled burn slow us? Yes. It will slow both ships and allow us to get closer to each other."

"The ships weren't designed to dock with each other, Jean, and the EVA tethers won't reach nearly that far."

Mom said, "They don't have to. Once the trajectories are synced we can use a tether to get about half the distance to the *Muninn* and then we can use an EMU to free fly the rest of the way."

"Will that even work?" asked Nirti, her eyes wide with apprehension.

"We ran the numbers when the *Muninn* first started having troubles," Mom said. "And we got confirmation of the best set of procedures from Mars One." She nodded to the De Jaegers. "The numbers are good and we can make it work."

Only Mrs. De Jaeger nodded back. Her husband and daughter did not.

"It's too dangerous to even try," Colpeys said heavily.

Mom shook her head. "It's the only choice we have. It's that or we let everyone on board the *Muninn* freeze to death. Take your pick."

There was a horrified gasp at her words.

Tony Chu pushed off and floated over to Mom and Colpeys. "Then I guess I'd better suit up."

Mom shook her head again. "Sorry, Tony, but you're staying here."

"The hell I am."

"You are, and that's an order."

"Then who is going over to the . . ." His words trailed off and he gaped at her. "You're out of your mind, Jean. You can't risk it."

There was a flicker of something in Mom's eyes. Almost humor. Maybe reckless humor. "Tony, I love you like a brother, but are you going to stand there and tell me that you're a better mechanical engineer than me? Really?"

"I'm better in an EMU," he protested, but that was a weak punch-back because he knew as well as I did that Mom was better than all of us.

"I'll go with you!" I blurted.

A hard hand clamped around my shoulder and I turned to see my dad right behind me. "No."

It was the only word he could choke out of his throat.

Chapter 83

"There's no way in hell you're doing this, Jean," said Dad when we were all back in Mom's workshop. He didn't yell it, but his voice filled the still air. He gripped the edge of the worktable and glared at Mom in mingled shock, horror, and anger.

"This isn't a discussion, Cornelius," she said quietly.

"Then let's *make* it one," he countered.

"No, let's not."

"Hey," I said, "don't I get a vote here?"

"No," they both told me.

"Why not? I'm part of this family and I'm part of this mission. I'm not a kid anymore and I should have a say."

Mom continued to stuff equipment into a canvas bag. "There's nothing you can say, Tristan, that's going to change my mind. I have to go."

"I know," I said.

They both stopped and stared at me.

"Wait . . . *what*?" demanded Dad, clearly feeling betrayed.

"Mom has to go, Dad. Tony can't fix those systems half as fast as Mom. I mean, *I'm* faster than Tony most of the time, and Mom's ten times faster than me."

"Don't sell yourself short," Mom said under her breath.

"Look, Dad," I continued, "don't get me wrong . . . I don't *want* her to go. No way. But we're talking about twenty people dying over there."

"Maybe twenty-one," Dad countered.

"Or maybe none," I said. "Don't you know how good she is?"

Okay, that was maybe unfair. It was kind of a cheap shot, and I saw how it hurt him. But as terrifying as it was to think about Mom going out, untethered, in an EMU to a ship filled with mechanical faults and disease . . . there was no other option. None.

"It's that," I said, "or we go the rest of the way to Mars side by side with a coffin."

That's when Dad started to cry.

I'm not sure I ever saw him cry before. I never thought his emotions ran deep enough. He pulled Mom to him and she pulled me in, and the three of us floated there, crying, heads together, minds filling with blackness and thorns.

Chapter 84

I won't go into the math of how they calculated the timing and rate of burn on the engines to slow the *Muninn* by a fraction so that the *Huginn* could inch up. They fired fore and aft rockets in computer-controlled microbursts to align the ships. The computations were excruciating and when Zoé tried to explain it to Luther, Nirti, and me, we begged her to stop. All that mattered was that someone on both ships could understand it. And Mars One had to agree, verify the math, and then send commands to each ship to make sure the timing was absolutely precise. It was maybe the only bit of good luck we'd had so far in that the pilot of the *Muninn* was not too sick to work the controls. Our own pilot oversaw it all.

We all clustered along the wall of the common room, squeezing together to watch through the ports as our sister ship came closer and closer.

At first it all looked like it was happening in super slow motion.

And then it seemed as if we were converging way too fast.

Sophie was right next to me, and I could feel her body trembling with excitement and fear. I'd told her about the conversation I'd had with my folks, about how I backed Mom's decision to go. And about how scared I was to even open my mouth to say those things.

"Sometimes, *cher*," Sophie told me, "courage means breaking your own heart."

Mine. Sure. And Dad's.

That was fourteen hours ago. Now the ships were lining up. Both craft had lost some speed during the adjustments, and unless they could do another controlled burn to accelerate after all of this was over, it was going to tack another fourteen days onto our journey.

That was tomorrow's problem, though.

We watched in ghastly silence. We waited for what seemed like years.

And then the pilot, his voice as dry and casual as ever, spoke to us from the loudspeakers. "Parallel trajectory achieved. Everything is green across the board."

No one cheered.

We weren't there yet.

I spun around and began making my way to the main airlock. By the time I got there Mom was already in her white suit. Dad was there too, hanging back, pale and weary from stress. He did not say a word the entire time. Not one. No smiles, no jokes, no nothing. Maybe he'd said his good-byes to Mom before I got there, or maybe his fear was too big and held him too tightly.

Mom and Tony and the command crew checked all the fittings on her suit. Mom caught sight of me there and reached out a hand. I flew to her, took her hand, pulled myself close, kissed her cheek.

Neither of us mentioned the fact that this was probably going to be a one-way trip. Or at least it could be. If the ships drifted apart even a little it would be too dangerous for the EMU to fly her back. She saw in my eyes that I understood this.

"Trust yourself," she said to me.

Just that.

And then she pushed me back so Tony could place the helmet on her and connect it to the shoulder unit.

She touched fingers with my dad, and then stepped into the airlock.

Tony closed the inner door and I listened without hearing anything as they talked their way through the steps of depressurization, locking and unlocking, hooking onto the tether. All of it. I knew the steps, so I didn't need to hear the words.

I went to the portal and watched her step out of the *Huginn*.

My heart was filled with black ice.

Chapter 85

Mom made it look easy.

She unspooled the tether all the way, speaking calmly, describing everything she was doing. From the way she sounded she might just as easily have been describing shopping for Frosted Flakes and bagels. It sounded so ordinary.

And I had a thought.

Of *course* that was how she'd do it. Ordinary. That was Mom fixing a problem before it blew up. She made it sound like nothing, like it was no big thing at all to spacewalk on a small gas-powered rig between two spaceships hurtling through the black at insane speeds, all the while towing a tripled-up tether that would be used to haul over the supplies.

Thinking that . . . *knowing* that this was what Mom was deliberately doing, changed me. It made me smile, but it also melted the ice that clung to my heart and filled my chest. When Nirti and Sophie came to stand with me by the port, I began describing the steps to them in a voice that was every bit as calm as Mom's. And for exactly the same reason.

I could feel them begin to relax, to step back from their own fear, to accept that we *had* this.

And then it was over.

I know. Over.

Just like that.

Mom was at the airlock on the *Muninn*. She hooked the longer tether to the outside of the ship, clicked an autopulley into place, triggered it, but didn't even bother to look as the water, parts, tools, and medical supplies clipped to her line began to follow her. By the time the supplies caught up with her, she had the airlock open. Then she was inside, reeling her gear in as fast as she could.

Everyone in the common room began cheering. Pounding the walls.

We heard Mom's voice through the speakers, heard shouts and weeping from inside the *Muninn*.

Chapter 86

Tony and I began going over everything aboard the *Huginn*. Not because anything was broken but because after what happened aboard the *Muninn* we needed to be totally sure. It was now our job to keep this ship in perfect shape. And everything was. This was Mom's ship and she'd been over everything a zillion times since we left the Lucky Eight.

Also, working was a great way for me to keep from going totally bug-eyed crazy. I know I could have used some of that time to record a message for Izzy. Most of the crew were recording segments for one or another of the reality shows. Killing time. Each of us did it in our own way. My dad was in with his plants and hadn't said a word or showed his face. Somehow when Mom left for the other ship she seemed to have taken his sense of humor with him. Dad looked sad and had turned inward, closing me out. I had no idea how to help him. I tried, but all I got from him was one-word answers. He didn't even seem able to meet my eyes. It was a side of Dad I'd never known existed. A depression hidden beneath all the jokes and goofy humor.

It was nearly nine hours before Colpeys put Mom on the speakers so she could give her report.

"We have life support back on line," she said. That was her entire message. It was enough.

We all went a little bit nuts.

Chapter 87

I guess we all thought it was over, the crisis, the danger, the drama.

I know I did. I crawled into my bunk, snugged the straps around me, and fell asleep. Maybe the first good night's sleep I'd had in weeks.

Everything was going to be fine now.

Except that it wasn't.

Chapter 88

I was dead asleep when the alarms went off.

We had four kinds. A signal beep for meals. A gong for special meetings or interfaith church. An action buzzer when something malfunctioned. And a loud, continuous shrieking buzz if there was a fire.

It was that last one that slapped me awake, knocking me out of a dream of flying through clouds, my arms out like wings, my hair whipping, birds flying in a flock around me. One second I was there and the next I was awake. Stupid, bleary, but awake.

And then I smelled the smoke and the fog in my brain instantly burned away. I was alert, listening to the buzzer, stretching out with my senses the way Mom taught me to, allowing the moment to tell me what was happening.

A fire.

Fire!

There is nothing more terrifying in space travel than fire. We lived in a small metal barrel filled with flammable gasses. A fire could sweep through the ship, burn up the oxygen, choke us and kill us even before it burned us.

Smoke boiled from my left, from forward, rolling and twisting in the air like something alive. The galley was behind me, and this didn't smell like someone burned their powdered eggs. The engines were far behind my bunk, but there was no fuel stink. This was a smaller smell, if that makes sense. Something burning, but not the whole ship. And it smelled like plastic and copper.

Circuits.

I grabbed the tab and unzipped the canvas door of my bunk as fast as I could and rolled out. I caught a handhold and pulled hard and fast, propelling my body forward toward the hatch that connected the main habitat with the first of the systems compartments. Around me other people were opening their zippered doors and struggling out, some fast, some slow, all like bees emerging from a hive.

"Tristan!" called Nirti, her voice filled with panic. "What is it?"

I didn't answer, but instead grabbed another handhold, and another. A brown leg swung out of a bunk and I grabbed an ankle and used it to propel myself forward even faster.

"Hey!" yelped Luther. "What the hell are you—?"

I ignored him. I saw Sophie appear out of the smoke, her hands and face smudged, eyes filled with fear.

"Where is it?" I demanded.

"There," she yelled, pointing the way she'd come. "It's inside the wall. Oh God!"

Her English words disintegrated into hysterical French, which I couldn't understand. I pushed past her and dove into the smoke, chin tucked to keep it all out of my eyes, nose, and mouth.

Then I saw it. One of the panels was bent outward, the heavy-grade plastic warped by the heat. Dense black smoke poured from it, twisting in the air, pushed by heat and the energy released by burning oxygen. I slammed into the wall beside the buckled plate, felt the intense heat, recoiled, but kept moving.

The automatic fire control systems should have kicked in long before now. This fire should have been out before it even got started. It should never have gotten this bad. I fumbled through the smoke for the extinguishers that were clipped to the wall, but all I found were empty clips.

I saw Luther out of the corner of my eye. "Get another extinguisher. Find one. Do it *now*!"

He kicked off the edge of a cabinet and flew to the far side of the corridor, where another small extinguisher was hung, tore the unit free, kicked back in my direction.

"Douse it," I ordered. "Get inside the wall. Keep spraying until the smoke stops."

While he did that I opened the service panel. All the little green lights had turned red, indicating that there was damage to secondary systems. I began shutting them down, taking electricity out of the mix. The extinguisher hissed as Luther emptied it into the wall. Suddenly Tony was there too, and he had a second extinguisher. He pushed Luther back and took over, firing a fresh burst.

The fire, fierce as it was, died.

"Tony," I yelled, "the smoke's not venting."

"On it," he snapped. He let the extinguisher go and dove straight upward to another service panel. "It's jammed. Wait . . . wait . . . I think I—"

Suddenly there was a clunk and a mechanical gasp and then the smoke began funneling upward into the mouths of two vents in the north wall. I kept working, rerouting systems so that we didn't lose anything that needed to keep functioning. The lights in the room flickered and half of them went out. I switched to emergency lighting and then shut down every system I thought might be compromised.

By the time I was done the room was clear of smoke. It was inside my lungs, though, and I couldn't stop coughing. Tears welled but they clung to my eyes, making me waste precious seconds in clearing my vision. Tony came over and helped, and together we got the whole system settled down.

Then I sagged away from the wall and hung there, rubbing at my stinging eyes. Tony was examining the warped panel, bending close to it to study the burned plastic. He removed a penlight and aimed the powerful beam into the wall.

"I don't get it," I heard him say. "I don't get this at all."

"You don't get what?" snarled Colpeys as he pushed in

beside Tony. "What happened here? How *could* this happen?"

Tony looked at the melted plastic, then at Colpeys. Neither of them said a word, but I swear I saw them exchange a small, private nod. And after that no one was allowed in that part of the ship.

Later, when I asked Tony, all he said was, "I'm still trying to sort it out. Don't worry about it, kid."

People never really mean that. All it means is that they're worried about something and they're too scared to talk about it.

Chapter 89

"Tony was scared?" asked Nirti. We were back in our com-pod. After some careful tinkering I'd managed to turn the reality show camera mounted on the far wall to face the other way and muted the microphone. The port was now one of the few spots on the ship where we could actually be alone. "Are you sure?"

"I know Tony."

"But scared of what? The fire's out and you said it wasn't that bad."

"It could have been really bad, though. If the fire had spread inside the wall it could have destroyed the backup O_2 scrubbers. That would have left only the main system operational for the duration of the flight."

"Okay, that's bad," agreed Nirti, "but it didn't happen. You, Luther, and Tony stopped this right away, so what's there to be afraid of?"

"I don't know," I said. "Yet."

I tried to ask Tony again, but he was in the workshop with the door locked. I heard his muffled voice talking with my mom via the video-chat, but I couldn't make out what they were saying. I'd have to rig some kind of snooper device.

Tony wouldn't let me do any of the repairs, either. He told me that he'd handle it. He gave me the rest of the day off, which was weird, because I was supposed to be his assistant while Mom was away. There were no days off for engineers. Not right after we had a fire, for God's sake.

But orders were orders.

So I went to the wheel to work out my frustrations on the ARED.

Why was Tony so scared?

Why was he closing me out?

Why did the fire control systems fault out? Those circuits weren't in that part of the wall.

"What's going on?" asked a voice and I turned to see Sophie there. Her hair was a mess and she looked a little scared. Maybe a lot scared.

"Working on something," I told her. "Can't really talk now."

"The fire?"

I glanced at her. "Yeah. And other stuff."

"The *Muninn*?"

"Sure," I said. "That too."

"I heard that even with the antibiotics they're having a hard time getting ahead of the infections."

"Yeah." It was ugly and true. Three of the team, including Inga, were in very bad shape. Inga was on a respirator and had lost consciousness.

Sophie's eyes were huge and haunted. "Will they die?"

I added more weight to the ARED and settled back to do some bench presses. "I don't know."

As days go, this one truly sucked.

Chapter 90

That night I locked myself into a com-pod and recorded a message for Izzy.

Actually, I recorded fourteen messages, but I kept erasing, stopping and starting, getting it wrong. *Being* wrong. Finally I was so exhausted, I sat there for ten minutes and stared at the screen. It took me that long to realize that I was recording myself sitting there. I hit delete on all of the files I'd created, shut the system down, and began ripping open the Velcro straps.

"Damn it, Izzy," I said.

I hit record one last time.

"Izzy," I said, "I love you and I guess I always will. I'm sorry for dragging you with me all this way into the black. That's me being selfish. That's me being unfair. That's me being weak."

The red eye of the camera burned into me.

"You're braver and smarter than me and you tried to tell me, but sometimes I'm too stubborn to listen. Or maybe too scared. I don't know. I mean, I *heard* you, but I've been acting and thinking like we're still together. As if this is somehow going to work out. How stupid is that?" I laughed and wiped my eyes. "So . . . yeah, this is me finally getting a clue. This is me finally—hopefully—managing to say the right thing. But what's the right thing? How do I say it without being ridiculously corny?"

A couple of seconds burned away.

"Okay, I guess I don't care if it sounds corny. I'm just going to put it out there," I said. "Izzy, you were the best thing that ever happened to me. You brought color and light and music and laughter and love into my life. And those are things I can take with me, even out here, even all the way to Mars. I will always love you. Of course I will. But I can't bear to think of you there in some kind of suspended animation. This is not us being Tristan and Izzy anymore. This is us being *us*, each in our own world. I love you and you will always be my best friend. You've always been a better friend to me anyway. Sorry about that."

I placed my palm flat on the screen for a long, long time.

And hit the stop button on the recorder.

Maybe half an hour later I was able to record a second video. This one for Mindy. I said most of the same things, but in different ways. I had no doubt they'd edit it into a ratings winner.

Who cares?

I put my face in my hands and as the ship flew through the black I counted all of the things I'd left behind. Weighed them, valued them, and began putting them one by one on the shelves inside my head. Where they would have to be from now on.

Chapter 91

Next morning I rigged a listening device and attached it to the door of the workshop. Tony was already inside. Then I retreated to a com-pod and set it up as a listening station.

"What are you doing, *cher*?" asked Sophie, who seemed to materialize out of nowhere. She wore sweatpants and a T-shirt, and her hair was in a thick braid. She looked at me, at the pod, at the switched-off camera, and cocked an eyebrow. "You are acting very clandestine. Are you doing something sneaky?"

"Good guess," I said, and then on impulse I pulled her into the pod and shut the door. It was a tight fit. "Can you keep a secret?"

She gave me a sly smile. "I keep secrets very well."

"Good." I quickly explained what I was doing and switched on the speakers, leaving the mic muted. We immediately heard Tony in the middle of a conversation with Colpeys.

"Who would *do* something like this?" said Tony, sounding shocked and scared.

"No one," said Colpeys. "You were wrong and you need to recheck your findings again."

"I *have* checked. Over and over again and it always comes up exactly the same. This could not have been a mechanical fault. There's simply no way."

Colpeys dug in. "It has to be mechanical."

"It can't be. That's what I'm telling you. And that's what Jean was afraid was happening on the *Muninn*. Why do you think she insisted on going?"

"But . . ."

"Listen, Jurgen, this isn't us being paranoid, and there is zero chance we're wrong about this. Someone is—"

"No! Everyone is totally committed to this mission, Tony. Everyone knows that this is a lifelong commitment. Why would anyone try to jeopardize that? It would be pure suicide."

"Tell that to Jean. Tell that to Inga, for God's sake. That's if she doesn't die."

"Listen to me, Tony," said Colpeys, his voice hard and sharp, "you keep your wild speculations to yourself. I let Jean go over because the *Muninn* needed the medical supplies and parts. I did not send her over there to do a criminal investigation."

"But—"

"We're having a run of bad luck. That's all it is."

And that was all. Colpeys flung the door open and left Tony alone.

I turned to Sophie, who was staring. "What's going on?"

she whispered. "Do they think someone *did* this deliberately?"

"Yeah, Sophie," I said grimly, "that's exactly what Tony and my mom think."

"What do *you* think?" she asked.

I just shook my head. Not as an answer but because I didn't know what to say. My heart was beating so fast it hurt.

Chapter 92

While Tony was busy repairing all of the fire-damaged wiring, I sneaked into my mom's workshop. Door locks on a spaceship are a joke. They're mostly designed to keep doors from accidentally swinging open. Tony had rigged a spring lock, but Mom had me bypassing that stuff before I was out of grade school. I mean, please.

The workshop was one of the larger single-use areas on the *Huginn*. It had all sorts of tools, machining gear, a 3-D printer, and bins of raw materials. It was my playground. Mom's too.

I slipped inside and closed the door. The lights were already on but set low. I could find anything in that room in the dark, though, so it didn't take me long to find the burned and twisted piece of plastic panel Tony had removed from the wall. It still smelled. Tony had it in a drawer and I removed it and set it on the table, holding it in place with long rubber bands. The panel was sixteen inches by twelve, and it had four screw holes, one on each corner. The four screws were in a plastic Ziploc bag attached to one corner. There were no useful notes that would have given me easy answers. Tony would have entered everything in the computer and I didn't have his password. All I had was the panel.

I studied it for maybe ten minutes, turning it over, shining light on it at various angles. Then I went over the panel again, taking each item in turn—the weight, the degree of damage, the types of damage: direct burns, smoke smudging, melting from sparks, melting patterns from contact with hot wires, the marks from Tony's screwdriver scratches from when he removed it, the overall warping from heat buildup inside the compartment.

Then I stopped and stared at it for a moment. I pulled a magnifying glass over on its accordion arm and peered through it at the screw holes. Then at the screws.

"Crap," I said.

Tony Chu had exactly the same set of tools I had. Same exact make and models. I'd also worked with him enough to know how he approached a job. He's left-handed and so any scratches he made came in from that angle. I'm a righty, so my scratches would be from a different angle. Most of the time neither of us scratched a screw or plate, not unless it was stubborn. Or, in this case, in a moment of panic, dealing with smoke and fire. But here's the thing: I could find all of the marks of Tony's screwdriver, and in exactly the places where I'd expect to find them. Except they weren't the only marks on the plate. There were marks from a totally different kind of screwdriver. Thinner, narrower blade, and handled differently. Less force but leaving more damage. Not inept, but not as skillfully handled as Tony or Mom. Or me, for that matter.

A second screwdriver.

Tool marks can be as distinct as fingerprints. Mom taught me that. If you know what you're looking at you can tell the difference between them, and between handheld tools and electric ones. Tony, Mom, and I used electric screwdrivers, so I knew the kinds of scratches they left. But the other marks I saw were clumsier. The kind someone would make using a handheld screwdriver. No doubt about it. And whoever used that tool knew what they were doing but was doing it badly. Nerves? Haste? Maybe both?

All of Tony's marks were cut over those other marks, and the thin-bladed marks were cut over the last set of electric screwdriver marks. The last person I knew for sure opened that panel was me. With an electric screwdriver. Three and a half weeks ago, during a routine inspection. So who owned that thin-bladed screwdriver? And why had they opened the panel?

Or was that second question too obvious? Way too obvious.

I put the panel back in the drawer and searched for the small switching box that had been the source of the electrical fault. I found it in another drawer. It was so badly melted that it took me a long time to even make sense of it. The core was metal—aluminum-magnesium, copper, and some alloys—but the casing was dense industrial plastic. I spent an hour going over it, tracing each circuit, using the magnifier on each connection, looking at the points where the wires melted onto the housing. This was something Mom taught me to do—to assess damage in order to understand how the damage occurred. It was a kind of forensic science but before now I never expected to be doing it to understand an actual crime.

And that's what this was. I was absolutely sure of that.

And I was absolutely terrified.

But I was also really freaking furious.

Chapter 93

I needed to tell someone. Sophie was busy in the galley, so I went looking for Nirti and found her in the wheel, working out on the ARED. Problem was that Luther and Zoé were with her.

"Crap," I said. "Look, Nirti, can I talk to you for a minute?"

"I'm halfway through my set, Tris," she said. "Can it wait?"

"Not really."

She eased the wing bar back into place and sat up. "What's going on?"

"I just need to talk to you. Alone."

Zoé shrugged. She was on the stationary recumbent bike and was bathed in sweat. Luther was doing one-armed chin-ups, which looked very cool but the fact was that the wheel was still on Mars gravity. A ninety-year-old man could have done one-armed chin-ups there.

"Let me guess," he said. "Your girlfriend back home broke up with you because she found out you've been sliding it to Sophie Enfers, and you need a shoulder to cry on."

"Shut up, Luther," said Nirti.

"Oh, gross," said Zoé.

"Nirti, please . . ."

"And now he's begging," said Luther. "Very manly. Very attractive."

I wheeled on him. "One more word out of you, and I'll knock that grin off your face."

"I will try to be terrified later on."

I ignored him. "Nirti—?"

She stood up. "Okay, Tristan, but you're being very mysterious."

"It's important."

She wiped her face. "Is it about the fire?"

I hesitated. "Yes."

Suddenly Zoé was interested. "Wait, what about the fire?"

"Look, it's nothing," I said. "I just want to talk to Nirti. Is that okay with everyone?"

"Not really," said Zoé. "Not if it involves what happened to the ship. Everything keeps breaking down. If you have something to say, why not tell all of us?"

"It's not like that," I lied.

"Why not?" asked Luther, dropping from the chin-up bar. "This is all your mother's fault anyway. It's about time you stopped covering for her and—"

"Stop it," sobbed Nirti. "Both of you, just stop it."

I glared at Luther. "You can say whatever you want about me. Joke or not. But you don't talk about my mom."

I expected him to come right back at me with something sarcastic, but Luther surprised me and held up his hands. "My bad," he said. "Sorry. Everything's been so weird lately."

We studied each other for a moment, and then Luther held out a fist. I let it hang there for a long time before I bumped it.

Nirti cocked her head at me. "Tristan, what was it you wanted to say . . . ?"

"Okay," I said after giving it some thought, "but you guys have to promise not to tell anyone. Not your folks, not Director Colpeys . . . no one."

"What is it?" asked Zoé. "What are you talking about?"

"You have to promise."

None of them liked it, but they gave their word. I took a breath and then laid it on them. All of it. At first they didn't believe a word of it, so I took them back to the workshop. And I went through the other things. What happened on the *Muninn*, too. All the malfunctions and how improbable it was for them to happen the way they happened.

"Anything can break down," said Zoé, but she sounded uncertain.

"My dad says that it's all because the equipment isn't maintained right," said Luther, and then he realized what he was saying and stumbled to a halt. He muttered something in Zulu that I'm sure was directed at himself and was probably deeply obscene. Moments of self-realization can be nasty.

Zoé frowned at me. "You're serious, Tris? You actually think someone is trying to sabotage this ship?"

"No," I said. "Not someone. Not one person. I think there are at least two of them. Someone on this ship who set the fire and someone on the *Muninn* who sabotaged the water and the life support."

Nirti said, "If it wasn't for Tristan's mother, everyone on the *Muninn* would be dead."

"But . . . but . . . *sabotage*?" protested Luther. He looked to Zoé for help, but she nodded.

"It's the only logical answer, Luther. Someone's trying to kill all of us. Someone's trying to stop us from getting to Mars."

And that was when the alarm bells went off.

Again.

Chapter 94

But it wasn't another disaster. Instead Director Colpeys called us all into the common room to show us a video.

"What's going on?" I asked Tony as we hurried in.

He pointed to Colpeys, who was adjusting the settings on the big monitor. "Something just came in from Earth."

Before I could ask anything else, the face of Dr. Ilse Aukes filled the screen.

"Hello to you all," she said, her face grave and her tone very formal. "You are a long way from home but your journey will be over soon. I am gratified to hear that the crew of the *Muninn* is doing well and everyone is expected to make a full recovery. We were all very concerned, as was everyone here on Earth. Our thoughts are always with you."

We waited, knowing that this assembly could not have been called just for that.

Dr. Aukes took a breath. "One hour ago we received a message sent in confidence from the Chinese government. That message has also been shared with a select few space programs, including SpaceX and NASA. I will read to you a translation of that message." She glanced at the camera as if she could see us in real time. Maybe she was trying to decide how we would react to what she was about to say.

Nirti took my hand and squeezed it, and her fingers were like ice. "Oh God," she breathed, "they're dead. That's what this is going to be. They're all dead."

I held on to her hand.

Dr. Aukes read the message. "'Late last night our satellites were able to get their first good angle on the *Golden Dragon*. We have been able to confirm that the capsule is still attached and that no one has left the ship to descend to the surface of Mars.

"'However we have made a discovery,'" continued Dr. Aukes, still reading the note. "'While we do not yet know what happened to cause the *Dragon* to fail, or what prevented our astronauts from reaching the Martian surface, we know that at some point one or more of the crew accomplished a successful EVA.'"

We all waited, frozen where we clung or hovered.

The image on the screen changed as Dr. Aukes's face vanished to be replaced with a grainy, dark, badly lit satellite image. It showed the side of the *Golden Dragon*. Someone had gone outside the ship and attached a long piece of cloth to the outside, fastening it to handholds. Two words were written on it. In Chinese. In French. In Italian. And in a dozen other languages.

Including English.

"We don't know how long ago this was done," said Dr. Aukes, "and we don't know if it's still true. But it is a glimmer of hope. The Chinese expressed concern that the crew has not performed any additional EVAs, as far as they know, which suggests that there was additional damage, either to their suits or to the airlock. Or both. The real point, though, is what they accomplished with the spacewalk they were able to make."

Those two words changed the shape of the world.

They said, ALIVE INSIDE.

Chapter 95

"We have to save them!" cried Nirti. She was the first one to break the stunned silence that followed Dr. Aukes's message.

A few of the crew echoed Nirti, but most didn't. What happened was a very loud nineteen-way argument. Everyone began yelling their opinion, their reaction, the pros, the cons.

"We have no idea how old that message is," said Mr. De Jaeger, and that became a big point. He was right, too. By the time we reached Mars it would be more than three years since the Chinese ship left Earth and almost two years since they reached Mars's orbit. There wasn't enough food for that many people for that long a time.

As the adults' voices rose louder and louder, Nirti and I drifted to the edge of the crowd. After a moment Luther and Zoé joined us.

"We have to rescue them," said Nirti. "That's the bottom line."

"And kill ourselves trying?" countered Luther.

"We won't kill ourselves. Dr. Hart got over to the *Muninn* okay. We were able to get both ships together."

"It won't work."

"So, what? We just leave them to die?" Nirti yelled, then immediately dropped her voice. A couple of the adults glanced at us, then went back to their own frenzied conversations.

"I'm not saying I don't *want* to rescue the Chinese," said Luther, his voice low but urgent, "but we don't even know if they're still alive in there. I mean . . . look at the risk-reward thing. We could burn a lot of fuel and take all sorts of risks to get over there, and what if we find a ship full of dead people?"

"What if there are still survivors?" I asked. "How would you feel if we did nothing and they died?"

"Hey, I didn't say I like it, but we have to be practical. We need to use our resources we have to keep *us* alive. The *Muninn*'s a mess and bad things are happening here on the *Huginn*. We'd have to be crazy to go looking for *more* trouble."

Zoé shook her head. "We could do it, I think. It's not impossible."

"There's too much risk, though," Luther insisted. "Shouldn't we be smart and fix the problems at hand before we make it worse?"

"Why can't we do both?" asked Nirti.

"It's dangerous." Luther's voice was rising now and we all shushed him.

"Dangerous?" I said. "So is going to live on another planet. Come on, man, we're supposed to be intrepid explorers and colonists. Everything they've trained us for since we joined

Mars One was about doing a bunch of things at once. We're the ultimate multitaskers."

He shook his head stubbornly. "All of the risks we're taking on this mission have been thought through. We have safety margins. Going outside of the mission is nuts. How could we possibly justify it?"

Nirti said, "What if the Chinese were sabotaged like we were? If anyone's still alive over there they might know who did it and why. That could help us figure out who's doing it to us here."

Luther considered but still didn't like it. "That's thin. It's not enough of a reason."

"How about basic humanity?" I asked. "We're all trying to establish human life and civilization on Mars. Everything we do is going to be part of history. It's going to be part of our legacy."

"Legacy?" he said, almost amused by the word.

"Yes. What we do now is how we're going to be remembered. Saving other people while dealing with personal dangers. Tell me you haven't read about that kind of thing in history books before. Come on, Luther, you've been saying all along that you want to be the first person on Mars. How about being the first *hero* on Mars?"

He smiled. "Oh, man . . . that's corny even for you."

"Maybe," I said, "but am I wrong?"

I could tell that, corny as it was, I'd scored a point on him.

Even so, he wasn't sold. "It doesn't matter anyway," he said. "The *Golden Dragon* is orbiting too far out from Mars. If we rendezvoused with it we'd be at the wrong altitude for our landing vehicles to make their descent."

"We could course correct after," I said. "We still have some fuel."

"Sorry, Tristan," Luther said, "but we used up a lot of that fuel with your mother's scheme."

"My mother's 'scheme'?" I echoed. "You mean saving everyone aboard the *Muninn*? Yeah, I can see how that was a complete waste of time."

He faltered. "That's not what I meant."

"What *did* you mean?" I asked, moving closer to him, crowding his space.

He bristled immediately and puffed out his chest. "You want to do this again?"

"Stop it," snarled Nirti. Luther exhaled and looked away at the rest of the crew, who were all arguing as fiercely as us.

Zoé touched Luther's arm. "You're wrong about the fuel. We ran all the numbers when Dr. Hart went over to the *Muninn*, and even taking into account the retro firing and the acceleration boosts, we're still going to reach Mars with extra fuel. Not a lot, but enough. And none of the sabotage has hurt the engines or fuel tanks."

"But—" began Luther, but she cut him off.

"We have enough," she repeated. "That was always the

plan, don't forget. To make sure nothing would prevent us from getting here. The calculations are complicated and figuring it out will take a lot of time and resources . . . but we can do it."

We all looked at the adults, some of whom were yelling at each other. Everybody seemed to be speaking at once and no one was looking in our direction.

Nirti nodded and said, "They're not arguing about the fuel or about whether we should risk doing something with all that's going on here. That's not it at all."

"What, then?" asked Luther.

Nirti's eyes were filled with strange, sad lights. "I think they're upset because the *Golden Dragon* is a Chinese ship." When we stared blankly at her, she explained. "The Chinese government's always been private and apart. They keep their politics and science mostly to themselves. The rest of the world's been helping each other out. Even NASA and SpaceX have helped us, and we're technically competitors. But China didn't even tell anyone they were launching a ship. They hid their launch platforms. It was all secret. And, I guess, people resent it. I know my mom was really pissed at them when we all thought they were going to land people on Mars first. And, sick as it sounds to say it, I bet a lot of people—on Earth and on our ships—were glad when we heard that the *Golden Dragon* was lost. Or damaged . . . or whatever. People were glad—my own mother was glad—that something happened to them to keep that crew from beating us." She shook her head very slowly. "How sick is that? We're all ready to leave the crew to die because we don't like what their government did? How is that a good thing? How is that something we can be proud of? There were all those speeches about mankind heading out into deep space for the benefit of all mankind. Does 'all' mean what it's supposed to mean, or do we cut out the people we don't like? What does that say about us? What does that say about who we're willing to be?"

Luther and I stared at her, unable to answer those questions. Zoé, however, wrapped her arms gently around Nirti and kissed her on both cheeks, then hugged her for a long time. I glanced over at Luther. He was chewing his lip and there were deep lines between his brows. He cut me a look too.

"I'm still more freaked out about the sabotage than the Chinese," Luther said. "I'm sorry, but that's the truth. Not saying I don't want to help, but we can't help them if we're dead."

I looked past the crowd to the section of wall that was still scorched from the fire. One by one the others noticed me and realized what I was looking at.

"Maybe we can do something about that," I said.

While the adults still argued, the four of us went back to the wheel. Gravity seemed appropriate for the weight of what we had to talk about.

Chapter 96

Zoé looked up from what she was doing and laughed.

"What?" I asked.

The four of us were crowded into the workshop. It was the third day in a row we'd met there while Tony was busy doing other stuff. I'd rigged a tiny location tracker into the lining of his tool kit. It would let us know when he was heading back to the workshop. Simple stuff.

The project Zoé was working on was key to what we were trying to prove. There were reality show cameras everywhere on the ship, but the sabotage still happened. Since no one on either ship had been arrested or confined or whatever it was we'd have to do when we caught someone, there had to be an explanation. Zoé found it by hacking into the digital files stored in the cameras. These were collected all day, then uploaded to the Laser Communications Relay System. Twice each day the LCRS sent bursts of data back to Earth. The current rate of transfer was 925 megabytes of data per second, which was really fast, but not when you were talking about video interviews from twenty people on each ship. That's a lot of data.

Zoé was trying to hack all the way into the bulk storage so we could see what—if anything—was on the cameras in the hours leading up to each major malfunction. It was harder than it sounds. Mars One did a lot to protect the data it sent back to Earth, but the TV networks were ten times more paranoid about that sort of thing. Weird, I know, but Mars One was a public nonprofit corporation and TV networks were multi-billion-dollar companies who had a thing about proprietary information. I bet the CIA and NSA could have learned some tricks about cyber security from them. Cracking that level of protection takes mad skills. Zoé, on the other hand, was Zoé.

Even so, it took her a couple of long days, but she beat it. Then we had to watch those videos.

I thought that part was going to involve hours of boring footage of people floating around the hab, but I was wrong. Zoé ran the feeds at high speed and sat there like a statue, her blue eyes ticking back and forth between two screens, watching everything. And seeing everything.

"There!" she cried, and as we crowded around her she ran one feed back. The time code on the corner of the screen said that it was 04:16 a.m. on the morning of the fire here on the *Huginn*. The camera was in a fixed position and it showed a little more than half of the corridor. I touched the screen to indicate the panel, which was still undamaged.

We watched the seconds click by and then the screen went

blank. It wasn't static or an interrupted signal because the time counter was still there in the corner of the screen. But the image had gone weird. Dark gray and textured.

"Hey, what happened?" asked Luther.

"Run it back," I said, and we watched it again. Then Nirti suggested we watch it in slow motion. That's when we saw what it was. There was the briefest flash of a hand, or part of a hand. Two fingers and the edge of a palm. The rest of the hand was covered by a piece of cloth. The hand reached above the camera and then all we could see was the cloth. It was almost completely opaque, allowing just enough light through so we could see some of the texture.

We played it again just to be sure.

We were sure.

Someone had blocked the camera with cloth. It remained in place for eleven minutes, and then it was whipped away. Thirty-five minutes later smoke began leaking out through the seams between panels. We watched the heat buckle the corner of the panel and finally pop it open as denser smoke poured out.

"Turn it off," said Nirti, looking sick.

Zoé hit the button and the screen went dark.

"So," said Luther heavily, "we know."

"We know," I agreed. "But we don't know who."

"We know enough to tell Director Colpeys," said Zoé.

"Maybe, but not enough to help him do anything about

it." I sucked a tooth for a moment while I thought it through. "Zoé, can you access the feeds from the *Muninn*?"

She considered, shrugged, nodded. "Sure. It'll take a couple of hours, but I can do it."

"It's going to be the same thing, isn't it?" said Luther. "If there's two of them, they'll both be careful. The other guy will have blocked the camera too."

"Yeah . . . I guess. And I just thought of something else. I think we're actually wasting our time with this."

Zoé bristled. "Why?"

"Because the reality TV people already have these files. They'd have seen this stuff."

"No," she said.

"What do you mean?"

"Look at this." She pulled up one of the pages she'd been looking at earlier. It showed long lists of coded file names and corresponding numbers. "This is the transmission log from the LCRS system. The cameras belong to the reality show network, but the LCRS belongs to Mars One. Director Colpeys has the right to withhold any video files that he feels are inappropriate. They did that in case there were things like fights aboard the ship, technical discussions that they didn't want to share, or if . . . you know . . . a couple of people were . . . you know . . ." She cleared her throat and her face was flaming scarlet. "If someone forgot they were on camera."

Luther looked at his nails, suddenly finding them endlessly fascinating. Nirti blushed too. I kept everything off my face.

"Okay," I said. "Go on."

"So the transmission logs all have to be approved by Colpeys. If he flags anything for any reason, it's indicated here by his personal code. C1746."

She pointed to several instances where C1746 was entered.

"You're saying he flagged the videos that show the sabotage?" asked Luther.

"Yes."

"Sure," he said, "but look at all the times he did that. They can't all be part of this."

Zoé touched one entry. "This is the senior staff meeting. That was flagged. That one is when he was having another of those arguments he used to have with Tristan's mom while she was still on board." She pointed out a dozen ordinary events that Colpeys had chosen not to broadcast. "But this . . . that one is the file we just watched. And these others? Those are when Tony Chu was working on the panel, you know . . . when no one else was allowed in there."

"So what you're saying is Colpeys already knows what's on the video," I said.

"I think so."

Luther sighed. "Which means he probably also flagged the videos from the *Muninn*."

"Which is why it hasn't made it into the reality shows,"

said Nirti. "He's been messing with the feed, so all that the network people back home know is that we're having a lot of technical problems."

We all thought about that for a while.

"If Colpeys knows, why did he argue about it with my mom?" I asked, but then I answered my own question. "He probably didn't know about it at the time."

"He's slow running the bases," said Luther, and then he cut a look at me. "That's the baseball phrase, right?"

"He's slow getting to first base," I corrected, "but yeah. Colpeys doesn't want any of this to be true."

"He knows it's true now, though," said Nirti.

"Sure, he can't help but know. But he's keeping it on the downlow."

"Well, if we can't be the ones to break the news to him," said Zoé, "what can we do?"

I spread my hands. "There's only one thing we *can* do," I said. "We need to set a trap for whoever's doing this."

Chapter 97

Setting a trap was easier said than done. I had to steal a crap-load of electronics from Tony and hope that he wouldn't notice. I felt bad, too, because I thought that Tony would be on our side. But on the other hand he hadn't taken me into his confidence, which meant that Mom wasn't willing to bring me in on it either.

Well, trust either goes both ways or it doesn't. So I sneaked around and didn't tell them. The plan was absolutely going to get me—all four of us—into serious trouble. But we'd deal with that later.

I removed the small cameras from half of the space suits we had in storage, and then filched some more from the equipment lockers in the workshop. These cameras were crucial to the mission, but not until we were actually on Mars, so I figured, what the heck. Using them now might help us get *to* Mars. The problem was that they were green. So once I had them all I took them to one of the heads and locked myself in while I painted the cameras white. We had several drums of paint on board—white, green, blue, and black—for staining landmarks once we were on the surface. The Martian landscape is red, so bright colors would stand out from miles away. We obviously wouldn't use it until we were on the ground, so no one would notice some missing now.

Why paint the cameras? Everything inside the *Huginn* was pretty much white, so once painted, the cameras would simply blend with the white walls. After that there was the matter of the paint smell, but that wasn't a serious problem because I did the painting in the bathroom and . . . well, it was a bathroom. Paint smells had no chance in there. To make sure, though, I added some of the deodorizers Nirti brought.

With that done I divided up the cameras among the four of us and we began positioning them around the ship. It took two days to do it, because it was hard to find moments when there was no one around. Plus Colpeys and Tony always seemed to be in the vicinity of the wastewater system and life support, looking for anything that was not as it should have been.

"They're not being very sly about it," observed Luther.

I shook my head. "They're trying to prevent what happened on the other ship."

"There are lots of other things people can sabotage," he said, which was both true and scary.

We eventually got the cameras in place, and Zoé channeled the feedback to her own laptop.

That night, after spending the rest of the day doing maintenance chores Tony gave me, I recorded a reality show segment that was a total pack of lies. Talking about how we were all getting along so great and having fun and looking forward to getting to Mars. The two bits of actual truth were the fact that Mars One back home approved us doing a controlled burn to get both ships moving faster again. They actually came up with some numbers that would shave five days off the total trip, and it wouldn't use up all of our fuel. That was great news, because it meant that we would reach Mars and still keep alive the possibility of rescuing the Chinese.

If there were any Chinese left to rescue.

The other bit of good news was that the crew of the *Muninn* were all beginning to recover. Even Inga was awake and able to speak. I raved about that for the reality show crowd, but there was still a cold spot in my heart. "Recovering" wasn't the same as "recovered." The danger was far from over.

Just like the fact that there hadn't been any new malfunctions on the *Muninn* didn't mean the danger was over. My mom would be watching things like a hawk, and she'd be better at it than either Tony or Colpeys. But she couldn't be everywhere at once. If there was a maniac aboard the *Muninn* he'd be waiting for the next opportunity, and there were a lot of very bad things you could do on a spaceship.

I left the com-pod and went back to my bunk, and had just closed it up when I heard someone knock. When I rolled back the privacy cover Sophie was there, looking tired and stressed. "I was looking for you. Can I come in?"

"Sure. What's up?" We sat on opposite ends of my bunk and once we were settled she fixed me with a penetrating stare.

"I'm just wondering what you're up to, Tristan?"

I said, "Um . . . up to . . . ?"

"For the last few days you and your friends have been very secretive. You haven't said two words to me or anyone. And you have a look in your eye."

"A look? What kind of look?"

She took a breath, then said, "A guilty look."

"No I don't."

Her eyes glistened as if she was trying not to cry. "Tristan," she said with gentle urgency, "if there's something going on—if there's something you need to *tell* me . . ."

"Um . . ."

"Something you want to confide," she said carefully. "Or confess . . . I promise I won't judge you."

I smiled. God only knows what she thought my big secret was. I never asked because there was no way it wasn't going to lead us anywhere but a weird conversation. Instead, I told her what was really going on. My theories and all of it. Well, almost. I left out the bit about the hidden cameras. I was afraid that if she knew, she might get paranoid and jumpy and keep looking around for them, which would probably make it way too easy for our bad guy to accidently find out about them. She listened without comment until I was done with the story, and then she gave a single, slow shake of her head.

"Non," she said. "I cannot believe this."

"Why not? We saw the video, we know what happened. You were with me when we overheard Colpeys and Tony talking about this stuff. Someone on this ship is a spy. Someone wants to kill all of us."

"I know . . . but I still find it so hard to believe," she said. "I mean, why would anyone want to *do* such a thing? It's preposterous, grotesque. It can't be what you think."

"I really don't know why, Sophie, but it is happening. And whoever's behind all this . . . they're absolutely insane."

"Or," she said with a very French kind of shrug, "they're dedicated to a different ideology."

"Like what? Murder isn't an ideology, last I heard."

"Is it murder if it's something that supports what you believe?"

"Of course it is," I said, but she shook her head.

"What about holy wars? The Crusades? Those were people fighting for what they believed God wanted them to do."

"Yeah, maybe, but that doesn't make it right."

"It doesn't make them wrong, either," she said. "Not in their own view. If someone absolutely believes that God—and by 'God' I mean whatever they truly and deeply believe in—requires them to raise a sword, then they are obeying God's will. The Torah, the New Testament, the Koran . . . they are filled with stories of saints and holy people killing in the name of their god."

"That still doesn't make them right."

"What about *jus bellum iustum*?"

"What's that?"

"It is a philosophy as old as history. In the Indian epic the *Mahabharata*, there is a discussion of a 'just war.' It's presented in a story where five brothers who are all rulers enter a debate about war. One of the brothers asks if the suffering caused by war can ever be justified. You would think the answer would be an easy 'no,' but really, Tristan, who has ever completely argued with effect against war?"

"Is that what they said in that story?"

"It's complicated. You should read it. I'm sure Nirti has a digital copy. But there are two aspects to the argument. One is a discussion of when, if ever, war is acceptable. The general feeling there in the *Mahabharata* and much later in the writings of Saint Augustine and others is that war is justified in defense or to protect the innocent. However, this is at odds with much of the Bible because the Israelites are told many times to conquer another people because it is God's will that they do so, and who are mortals to deny the will of God? In Islam the people are encouraged to spread their religion through the use of violence. They call it jihad. There are many other examples."

"So you're saying we have jihadists on the ships?"

She almost smiled. "No, I don't think so. I'm not talking about radical Islam or anything like that. We're having an abstract conversation about motivation, *cher*. We are speculating."

"Uh-huh. So what are you saying? That whoever is doing this believes that God wants them to?"

"Probably."

"How can you even know that?"

"I don't know it," she said, "but it fits the circumstances."

"How?"

"Whoever is doing these things must be aware that they, too, will die."

"Sure, but that just means they're nuts."

Sophie shook her head. "You are sometimes very young, Tristan. Very naive. Don't you know anything about martyrs?"

"Sure. But what you're talking about are suicide bombers. People like that."

She traced a heart shape on my chest. *"Jus ad bellum, jus in bello,"* she said. "There are two kinds of acceptable behavior in war. The first is the right to go to war. *Jus ad bellum.* This is the morality of war, of killing. This is the justification of raising a sword . . . or strapping on a bomb. No one would do this unless they believed."

"Or unless they like to hurt people?"

"No. I do not believe anyone who would lay down their lives for what they believe would ever—*could* ever—be filled with hatred for others. No, they do these things because they are filled with love."

"Love?"

"For what they believe in. It's not about harm; it's about protection."

I shook my head. "What was the other kind of 'acceptable' behavior?"

"Jus in bello," she said. "That is how one acts during war. When countries go to war they have agreements about what is not allowed. No firing on civilians."

"Sure, the Geneva Conventions."

"That becomes irrelevant when it is not a clash of countries but a collision of beliefs. When a group is fighting for their beliefs but has no country, no flag, they also have no rules. They are labeled as terrorists because they need to fight in a completely different way."

"By different you mean blowing up busses full of school kids or sabotaging spacecraft?"

"Yes."

"And you think that's what we have here?"

"I cannot think of anything else that makes sense."

I thought about and had to admit that it did make sense. "But who's doing it? What ideology are they trying to defend? We're not a political party, Sophie. We're astronauts. We're trying to help mankind."

"Perhaps," she said, "not everyone believes that."

"Ah. You mean nutcases like those Neo-Luddite freaks."

She shrugged. "Why not?"

"But they don't even say what it is they believe in. All they do is blow stuff up."

"They would not do that, *cher*, if they did not believe in something."

"Like what? Give me an example."

Sophie shrugged. "Perhaps they do not think anyone should leave Earth."

"Why not?"

She shook her head. "That's a question you'll have to ask them."

Chapter 98

That night, after I crawled into my sleeping bag, I lay awake for a long time. Thinking about Izzy. Missing her so much that I wanted to cry, to bang my head on a wall. I might have done it if I thought it would actually help. Breaking up is a kind of grief, and though I'd read all the pamphlets during the training, there's a big difference between knowing something and getting through it.

Not sure when I finally drifted off to sleep, but it took a long time. I dreamed that I was on the Drakes' porch roof with Izzy, watching falling stars and making wishes. Suddenly Izzy tensed and then she turned to me and began to scream.

It was the sound of the explosion that woke me up.

Chapter 99

I flew the length of the ship, back to the workshop, following smoke and clouds of debris. Everyone was coming out of their sleeping pods, and terror was as thick as smoke.

The explosion hadn't been in the workshop, though.

With absolute horror I saw fire crawling along the ceiling through the open door to my father's greenhouse. Two shapes—smeared in black soot and red blood—hung in the smoky air.

Dad.

And Tony Chu.

I screamed as I kicked off of a handhold and shot toward them. They looked so bad. Droplets of blood filled the air and I smashed through them to get to my father. He hung limp, eyes closed, his face flash-burned, half the hair on his head melted away. But as I reached for him, his hand closed around my wrist with surprising strength.

"The . . . the . . . ," he tried to say. Then the last word came out as a faint whisper. ". . . *vent*."

I didn't understand. Other people were there now. Nirti's parents were pulling Tony out of the smoke.

"Help!" I yelled. "My dad!"

Suddenly Nirti was there, pushing me to one side, a medical kit slung around her neck. I tried to fight her, to hold on to Dad, but Luther's big arms wrapped around me and pulled me back. He had a firm grip on a handhold and I had no leverage at all.

"Tristan," he yelled. "*Tristan!* Let her work. She knows what she's doing. Come on, we have to stop the fire."

That snapped me out of it and suddenly Dad's words made sense.

The vent.

Jesus . . . the *vent.* There was a control vent in the greenhouse that moderated the gasses necessary for hydroponics. If the vents were open they'd continue to feed the fire, and if it went on long enough the flames could back up into the main tanks. That would destroy the entire ship.

"Okay, okay," I bellowed. "Let's go."

Luther released me at once and gave me a hard shove toward the greenhouse. He followed fast and we ducked under the flames and had to grope our way through clouds of toxic fumes as the heat tried to fry us.

The greenhouse was one of the largest parts of the ship, and though I was not in there very often, I knew the layout. I knew every inch of the ship.

With Luther clinging onto my ankle, I pulled us both over tables of heat-withered barley and rye to a pair of heavy valves set into the far wall. These were emergency cutoffs. The fire control system should have triggered them to close automatically, but while reaching in, my hand encountered something strange. Someone had wedged pieces of metal into the works, effectively dogging them open.

"Luther—help me." I coughed my way through an explanation of what we had to do and he got it right away. Even so, we had to work more by feel than sight because the fire and smoke were getting worse. The pitch of the alarm had changed too, which meant that the main tanks were in danger of being compromised.

We had no time. No margin of error.

He grabbed the metal jammed into one valve and I grabbed the other. We braced our feet on the wall, and with smoke filling our lungs, we pulled.

We pulled. And we screamed.

Both pieces of metal came loose at the same instant and the release of resistance flung us all the way across the greenhouse. I hit the wall and Luther crashed into a group of confused people. We cursed and elbowed the people who were grabbing us, thinking they were rescuing us. This time Luther got free first and pulled me away from helping hands, and with a growl like a bear hurled me back toward the valves.

I found them by crashing into them.

Pain owned me. It was everywhere; it screamed inside my

skin. But I found the valve and began turning. Then Luther was there, turning the other valve.

The hiss of gasses changed in pitch. Faded, faded . . . and stopped.

And then there was the clunk of machinery as someone found the control for the oxygen intake, which sucked the smoke out of the air. People filled the room with fire extinguishers, but the flames were already dying.

Luther and I hung there, holding on to the valves, gasping.

Chapter 100

It was bad.

Dad was badly burned. Tony Chu had a concussion and a broken arm from hitting the wall during the blast. Six of the crew, including Luther and me, were treated for smoke inhalation.

The greenhouse, though . . . that was gone. Dead. Every plant and half of the seed stock Dad brought with him.

While I lay in my sleeping bag, half hopped-up on drugs to calm my system, Sophie came to check in on me. She had a few burns too, and her hair smelled of smoke. She sat and held my hand and we didn't say much.

While all of this was going on, Nirti and Zoé went and checked the feeds from the cameras. Except that's not what they did because they couldn't. Instead they found that the cameras I'd placed near the greenhouse had been removed from the wall and someone had crushed them. The debris was floating around, mixed in with blood, soot, and charred plants.

We were back at square one.

The day wore on and the drugs brought me in and out of a set of very weird and ugly dreams. I remembered when Sophie left. She kissed my cheek and whispered, "I'm sorry." Then she was gone.

The next day I was awake but I felt like a smoked sausage. Everything hurt. Even my hair and teeth hurt.

I checked on Dad, but he was groggy. They'd given him a whole lot of painkillers.

I spoke with Mom, though. And I leveled with her. Told her everything. When I was done there was an odd mix of expressions trying to fit onto Mom's face at the same time: pride and approval, disappointment, anger, and a cold shrewdness.

"No. You *can't* keep out of it," she said. "Can you?"

"I don't think I should."

"No," she said, "I don't think so either."

I told her about my conversation with Sophie, about the "just war." She nodded.

"Terrorists always need to justify what they do. I guess we all do," she said. "But when what you want robs someone else of what they want, then it's not justice. You understand that, Tristan?"

"Yeah," I said. "I really do."

"Be careful," she told me. "These people are going to try again. You understand that?"

"I do. I'll be ready."

She frowned at that, but then she nodded. "Don't give them any chance at all."

It was the strangest advice I'd ever gotten from my mom, but perhaps it was the best.

Chapter 101

The ships flew on. Inga had a relapse, which meant that Mom had to keep at it with almost no rest. I spent a lot of time with Dad. We talked about the sabotage and the dangers. We talked about the *Golden Dragon*. We talked about hatred and radicalism and we talked about being afraid. We talked about dying. But we also talked about fighting back, taking a stand. Dad was a gentle guy who wasn't much into politics, but he had a strong sense of right and wrong. If I got my skills and focus from Mom, I got my compassion and tolerance from him.

He did not try to talk me out of continuing to hunt for the saboteur. He wouldn't have done that. Instead he told me to be careful and to be smart.

There were no more attacks.

Probably because Colpeys changed his approach to security. He put adults in pairs to patrol the ship while everyone slept. He tried not to pair the same people up two shifts in a row, but he had limited resources. Tony and my dad were still on light duty, and Colpeys wouldn't use any of us kids. With Mom gone, that meant there were only thirteen healthy adults on the *Huginn*.

Everyone knew about the cameras I'd placed. Colpeys found the debris and put two and two together. He yelled at me for a long, long time about how stupid it was to take things into my own hands. Everyone heard it. I tried to argue with him and tried to be reasonable with him but he was too mad. Maybe he just needed someone he could unload on and that was me. I didn't dime out my friends, though. No reason to do that. I gave up arguing when it was clear it wouldn't do anything, and then I apologized and told him I'd try to rebuild some from the parts I could salvage. They hadn't worked like I'd wanted anyway.

Things became routine again.

Then one morning we got word that a NASA satellite had made contact with the *Golden Dragon*. We all crowded into the common room to hear the news. Dr. Aukes looked very excited as she explained what happened.

"Late last night," she told us, "at eleven fifty-one Greenwich time, NASA's Arthur Clarke communications satellite detected an anomalous signal coming from the *Golden Dragon*. The pattern was processed and analyzed and it was determined that it could not be an automatic signal because the pattern was irregular. Computer analysis was able to verify that it was Morse code."

I felt my heart leap into my throat.

"The message was in Mandarin, using the old Chinese telegraph code, which is similar to Morse code, and was channeled through a short-range communications system that they believe was taken from a rover. The sender was only able to send electronic pulses. There is no audio or video, and the satellite was only able to pick up part of the message during its flyby. However it will be back in range at the same time tomorrow. An attempt will be made to transmit a message to the *Golden Dragon*, but we are not certain whether they can receive."

"What was the message?" yelled Nirti. "Are they okay? How have they managed to survive? What happened to their ship?"

When Nirti realized she was yelling at a video sent with a twenty-two-minute delay, she shut up. Dr. Aukes picked up a clipboard and read from it. "This is the transcript of that message. It is a partial message, as I've said, and it is both encouraging and deeply disturbing."

That quieted everyone in the room, and I could imagine the same silence falling over the people on the *Muninn*.

"I quote," said Dr. Aukes, "'. . . survivors aboard ship. All others dead. Ship is damaged. Inner working of airlock damaged. Cannot EVA. Space suits damaged. Supplies and life support low. Twenty-nine days food left at minimum rations. There are eight crew left. I am engineer Ting.'"

Dr. Aukes paused and her face became very serious, very grave. "The person who sent the message is a young girl. She is the last surviving teenager of the three aboard."

"Ting . . . ," I breathed.

"NASA was able to pick up one last part of the message," Dr. Aukes continued. "It is a single word, a warning from the girl before the satellite went out of range, but I think it tells us what we need to know." She paused as if anticipating how bad that word would taste in her mouth. Her lips curled as she said it. "Neo-Luddite."

Chapter 102

We were horrified, but we weren't shocked.

I mean . . . by now, how could we be?

Dr. Aukes gave us all a long talk about cooperation, about caution and protection, about keeping focused on the mission while also trying to ferret out who among our crews wanted us all dead.

We'd all been screened so many times. We'd all trained together for years. For someone to infiltrate us, they'd have had to infiltrate the whole Mars One program. And to guarantee that there would be at least one of them aboard each ship. Zoé said that the statistics made sense only if the Neo-Luddites had a lot of people in the candidates program.

"Otherwise the math is too absurd. There's no telling how many of them applied and how many of them made it to the top one hundred."

"And none of them got flagged?" said Nirti. "How's that even possible?"

"Well," I said, "it's not like the screening program weeds out fanatics. 'Cause let's face it . . . we're all more than a little nuts for wanting to do this."

"Right, but wanting to do it and wanting to kill everyone isn't the same thing."

"Yeah, sure, but who's going to answer 'yes' to a question like 'are you a murderous fanatical psychopath?'? These Neo-Luddites, whoever they are, aren't stupid. Even if they don't dig technology, they understand it enough to sabotage it."

"That's weird," said Zoé.

"No," said Nirti, "it makes sense. When people back home are fighting, they always try to understand their enemies. I mean, how else can they figure out the best way to hurt them?"

Chapter 103

The next couple of days were filled with a thousand variations of the same conversation. Who were the Neo-Luddites? Why did they want to stop the space programs? Who among us were trying to kill us? What would they try next?

And how did a teenage girl like Ting keep her people alive all this time? What happened aboard the *Golden Dragon*? Who lived? Who died? Was the saboteur one of the living or the dead?

The messages from the ship were the same and it became clear that Ting had rigged some kind of repeating loop.

That, though, was not good news. Not really. Because there was no way to tell when she'd rigged that message to start. Her estimation of how much food they had left might refer to some day that had come and gone. The crew of the *Golden Dragon* could be dead already.

Those arguments were what Colpeys used to try and convince everyone that we should not try to rescue the Chinese ship. There were so many arguments, and so far Lansdorp, Dr. Aukes, and the other people back at Mars One hadn't made a decision about what to do.

It was driving us all crazy.

We were getting closer and closer to Mars.

Instead of months away, instead of weeks away, we were now only days away.

If we were going to make courses corrections to rendezvous with the *Golden Dragon* we'd have to make a decision in the next three days.

Izzy kept sending video messages and sometimes even actual e-mails, but now all of her messages were about the *Golden Dragon*. The news stations on Earth were saying that the Chinese ship had been damaged by a collision with a micrometeoroid. Nothing about the Neo-Luddites at all. I didn't tell her the truth. Not her, and not Herc.

I talked about it with Sophie, though. We talked a lot about it. She knew her politics and philosophy. Much better than I did. She joked once and said that every café in Paris is filled with people arguing over political issues. She made it sound fun, but that was Paris, not the *Huginn*. The politics and philosophy of what the Neo-Luddites were doing filled me with such hate that I had to watch what I said. Sometimes I slipped, though, and then I told her exactly what I wanted to do to the psychopath who hurt my dad.

"If I ever find out who it is . . . I'm going to kill them."

Sophie looked sad. "Tristan," she said, "don't you realize that you're not talking about a stranger? You're talking about someone you already know. One of this crew. It could be Luther, for all you know."

I said nothing to that, but I shook my head.

"Or Zoé or Nirti. It doesn't have to be a man."

"No."

She shook her head. "Tristan, for all you know it could be Tony or even your father."

"What the hell are you talking about?" I yelled, but she shushed me with fingertips to my lips.

"Shhhh, just listen. The explosion in the greenhouse could have destroyed the whole ship. It would have if you hadn't been there. The two people caught in that blast have been mostly confined to bed ever since and in that time there have been no more attacks. It is not unreasonable to suggest that one of them is responsible. And before you answer, think about the *Muninn*. Most of the crew are still recovering. Some are still confined to bed, and there have been no new attacks there, either. Could it not be that the Neo-Luddite aboard that ship is too sick to do any more mischief?"

I shook my head. "Maybe that's true over there, but here . . . no. It's not my dad and it's not Tony. My mom trusts them."

"When we left Earth, *cher*, we all trusted each other. And look at us now."

A soft *bing-bong* rang through the ship. The signal for the change of watch. Sophie sighed.

"I have to go," she said, and kissed me. "Get some sleep and dream of Mars."

And then she was gone.

I lay there, secure in my Velcro straps but totally unsecure in my thoughts. She had to be wrong. Definitely not Dad. That was just plain nuts. And it couldn't be Tony.

It couldn't be.

I tried to sleep but it wouldn't take me down.

Chapter 104

After three hours of faking sleep and trying to convince myself I was asleep, I unstrapped myself, quietly undid the zipper on my microbedroom, and floated out into the corridor. The lights were down low and I could hear the loud snore of Director Colpeys and the softer, buzzing hum of Luther.

I felt weirdly alone, like a caretaker in a crypt. Even with the sounds of people sleeping it was like being among the dead. And that thought didn't scare me so much as it made me sad. I thought of Ting over on the *Golden Dragon*. A girl not much older than me, an engineer, trying to keep a handful of survivors alive with no way to know if her message had been heard. No way to know if anyone was coming.

Then it occurred to me that maybe she *did* know. Or hoped, anyway. The Chinese may have kept their launch secret, but the whole world knew about Mars One. The timetable had been set years ago, and we were almost exactly on time. Ting must have known that, so was her message for us? Maybe the NASA satellite would get an update soon. An adjustment to the days of food left. Ting was clearly very smart and resourceful. If all of the survivors on the *Golden Dragon* were equally sharp, then they figured some way to stretch their resources, hoping for a rescue. Maybe hoping for exactly what was happening—the arrival of two ships from Earth.

My sadness dropped away and I got so excited I needed to tell someone immediately. Sophie was probably in the hab with whoever was on watch with her. I was grinning like an ape as I kicked off and flew through the ship to tell her, and I knew it would make her every bit as happy as it made me.

I was flying, flying, inside and out.

And I flew right into something dark and wet.

It smacked me in the face.

I snaked a hand out and caught a handrail and used the other to paw the stuff out of my eyes, thinking that someone had hocked a loogie and didn't clean it up.

But then I looked at my fingers.

The dark stuff looked as black as oil.

Oil?

Oh, God . . . no. Not another . . .

The thought ground itself to nothingness in my head because I floated into a small downspill from the night-lights. My fingers were slick with something, but it wasn't oil.

No.

It glistened a dark, horrible, angry red.

It was blood.

Chapter 105

I looked up and saw other droplets of it. They filled the air, drifting toward me. From the direction of the hab. My own blood turned to ice and I breathed a name. *"Sophie . . ."*

Imagining her up there. Dead. Victim of the monster who had gone into space with her. It made me so mad and I suddenly wanted to find the maniac who had come out here just to hurt us. The person who'd hurt my dad and nearly killed everyone else.

I'd never wanted to kill anyone before, but I did now. I hurled myself away from the handhold, grabbed another and pulled, another, another, accelerating through the still, cool air of the ship, meeting no resistance in the microgravity, dragging my hate with me.

With a bellow of rage I burst into the common room, saw two figures struggling amid an asteroid field of blood particles. Saw Sophie's braid swinging loose. Saw hands scrabbling at a ruined throat. Saw the glint of a knife in a tight fist. Saw the locking mechanism to the command module entry hatch hanging open, wires trailing out, circuits floating free. Saw the big security airlock door gaping wide.

Saw the world—the universe—crack and fall sideways off its hinges. Sophie was there, locked in a deadly battle with Garcia, the ship's security officer. Blood flew like red jewels. From the edge of the knife. From the terrible, terrible wound in Garcia's throat.

I screamed.

Sophie looked past the man she had just killed and saw me. I saw her face—that sweet, beautiful face—as it really was. Not the face of my friend. Not the face of someone I loved like a sister. Not the face of the gentlest person among us.

It was the face of madness. It was the face of a killer.

It was the face of a Neo-Luddite.

A bunch of expensive tools floated around her. I saw them with a bizarre clarity. Wrenches, socket drivers, and a set of thin screwdrivers. All the tools that she had pretended not to know how to use but had used so easily. All the tools with which she had sabotaged our ship and bypassed the security on the command module. Once inside she could have fired the engines, burned off all the fuel, sent us crashing into the *Muninn*, or killed us all in a hundred ways. Garcia had tried to stop her, and paid for it.

I said, "No . . ."

Sophie shoved Garcia aside and he floated away, dead or dying.

"Sophie," I whispered, "please."

Her eyes were chips of dark ice. There was nothing in them that I recognized. Everything had been a lie. Everything.

"Why?" I begged.

She put a hand out to steady herself by the airlock. "You wouldn't understand," she said. "You're incapable. All of you."

"Tell me. Please. I have to know. Why are you doing this? What do you people *want*?"

She hesitated and edged closer to the entrance to the command module. If she got in there and closed the door, she could do enough damage to prevent any of us from getting down to Mars. *Was that what happened aboard the* Golden Dragon? I wondered. Probably.

"Tristan," said Sophie, "I told you about the just war. I told you that there are times people have to fight, have to go to war, do you remember?"

"Of course. You said it was because of God and—"

"This isn't about God," she said. "This is about *Earth*."

"I don't—"

"We are failed custodians of our planet, Tristan. That was a sacred trust given to us. To mankind. It's a common truth that our world is the gift from God, or the Goddess, or whoever you want to believe in. But the gift came with a challenge, a burden. We were to nurture and care for our world. We were supposed to be shepherds in its fields. We were never supposed to rape it and abuse it and tear the heart out of it. And now, having failed to protect our sacred trust, we dare—*dare*—to go and ruin another pristine world? What sin could be greater than that?"

I stared at her. "Are you serious?"

Her lips curled into a sneer. "I knew you would never understand. This is why we don't hold press conferences. This is why we don't issue press releases. All that matters is action. All that has ever accomplished anything is action. We are dedicated to one goal—to keep mankind on Earth in order that we humans may fulfill our sacred trust."

"That's . . . that's . . . insane . . ."

For a moment I thought I saw the Sophie I knew look out of those eyes. Her sneering mouth seemed to soften, and her expression seemed to change to something else. Not love. No. Maybe sadness. Or was it pity?

She whirled around and threw herself through the hatchway. If she got that airlock closed and secured it from the inside we were all dead.

She was so fast.

But I . . .

I was faster. And the suction of air pressure from the open hatch jerked me forward. I reached for her as she tried to pull the massive door shut. I tried to grab her shoulder.

Missed. Instead my fingers tangled in her hair. She was moving fast away from me. I was pulling her back with all my strength.

The sound.

Oh, God, the sound her neck made.

Please, God . . . let me forget that sound.

Chapter 106

I let her go and she drifted away from me. I watched the light go out of her eyes, and she floated there, her head tilted too far over, lips parted as if she wanted to ask me a question. The silence was enormous.

The rest of the crew heard my screams.

Everyone heard them. They came flying like ghosts out of the shadows. They found Garcia. Dying, not dead. They found Sophie Enfers. A broken doll floating among the worlds of blood she had spilled. They found me a few yards away from her. Also broken, and in ways that I don't think can ever be fixed.

It took a long time for me to tell them what happened.

Director Colpeys called my mother immediately, to warn her about Marcel.

But Marcel was already gone. He had died in the night. So had three others, including Inga, who had relapsed and faded. The infection had taken its toll.

Forty of us had left Earth. If Garcia lived it would mean that thirty-five of us would reach Mars. That was math I could understand. And the sums were horrible.

Chapter 107

We buried Inga Holstrom, Matthew Peake, and Hiro Tetsudo. "Buried" isn't the right word, not out here. They were wrapped in sheets and placed in the airlock aboard the *Muninn*. Everyone on the *Huginn* stood at the ports and watched as three silent forms floated out into the big black. In time they'd be pulled down into the gravity of Mars and burn out as they fell. Colpeys said a prayer and we all wept.

I don't know when Marcel was sent out of the airlock. Not then, and not when anyone was watching. The same with Sophie. It was all taken care of without letting the crew know. She was wrapped in white and fired into the black.

We mourned our dead as we approached the Red Planet that was going to be our home.

The next day I got a long message from Izzy. She'd met a boy. She liked him. And . . . he was there. On Earth. With her. She looked so scared as she asked me if it was okay.

Okay?

It crushed me.

God.

But I hit the record button and sent her a return message.

"Izzy," I said, "I couldn't be happier for you. Don't worry about how I'm taking this. We both know that this is nothing but crazy. Now it's up to us to do the sane thing, right? So . . . of course it's okay. I hope he's good to you. Tell him I'll be watching." I paused and wondered if it was wrong to say it . . . and decided to say it anyway because it was always going to be true. "I love you, Izzy Drake."

Two seconds later I was recording another message. This one was for Herc. I told him to check this new kid out. Grill him. Make sure about him. And if he ever hurt Izzy, I wanted to know where the boy's body was eventually buried. Herc messaged back that he was already on it.

Chapter 108

We flew on, getting closer and closer to the moment when we would have to decide what to do about the *Golden Dragon*. We waited for the Mars One command team back home to send us a directive.

Mindy ran an online poll for a week and the results were pretty hard to ignore. Eighty-six percent of the 7,600,000 people who responded to the poll said that we needed to rescue the Chinese astronauts. People all over the world were wearing T-shirts and buttons with the face of Ting Chin.

Then we got the official word.

We were all in the common room when Colpeys played the video from back home. We were to proceed with the mission and not risk the crew or ships in an attempted rescue.

Dr. Aukes's face was like stone and I can guess that it hurt her to give that order. Maybe it hurt everyone who was involved in the decision process.

But it hurt us more.

When the message was done there was a long, long silence. A crushing silence that made it hard to breathe.

"We can't," said Nirti's mom.

"We have to," said Zoé's dad.

"It's inhuman," said Zoé's mom as she turned to stare at her husband as if he were suddenly a stranger. "You've seen the news—the whole world wants us to save those poor people."

"We can't."

"We can. We have to."

"No," growled Colpeys loud enough to cut through the din. When everyone turned to him he said, "It's sentimentality. None of those people are here with us. None of them have suffered the losses we have, and none of them have as much to lose. I cannot and will not condone this action."

Which was when I stood up. Well . . . floated up. "I want to say something."

"I've made up my mind," said Colpeys.

"I have a right to speak my mind," I told him. "With Tony hurt and my mom on the *Muninn*, I'm the chief engineer aboard the *Huginn* and—"

"You're seventeen," he cut in. "And while I appreciate everything you've done, Tristan, this is an adult discussion and an executive decision."

My dad, swathed in bandages and looking haunted, said, "Now wait just a damn minute, Jurgen. If it wasn't for my son we'd all be dead. How about you show a little respect?"

There was a murmur from the others. A lot of nods. Colpeys sighed. "Very well. Speak your piece, but it's not going to change anything."

I pulled myself up and grabbed a handhold on the west wall so I could face them all.

"Look," I said, "I know the dangers. I get it. But we have a chance here. We're right on a line between the two ways we can go. We can say screw it and let them die. We can do that and no one would blame us. After all, there's so much risk in going over there. We could die trying to save people who might already be beyond helping. Sure. That could happen. And even the history books will forgive us, I guess. They'll write it as a tragedy. Unavoidable. Nothing we can do."

I looked around. No one said a word. Not even Colpeys, because so far I was backing his argument.

"Or," I said, "we could risk it. We could cross the line the other way. We could roll the dice and go over there and see if we can save them. Back on Earth, China and America and Russia and everyone else shake with one hand and hide a gun behind their backs with the other. That's how it's always been. That's the history of the human race. Name one country back home whose map wasn't drawn with blood. Seriously, tell me."

Nothing. Absolute silence.

"We're about to colonize a new world. Look at us. Thirty-five people in two ships. We could write a whole new chapter in the history of the human race. And that's what it's really all about, isn't it? We're about to set foot on Mars. On a *new world*. On a planet that's named after the God of War but there's never been war there. It's like a blank piece of paper. Do we start our life on Mars with an act of cruelty? Who do you want to be the first people on that planet? Cowards who let suffering people die? Or do we start the next chapter in human history by doing everything we can to save lives?"

Silence washed around me.

"Luther and I have been fighting since before we left. If you want to know the truth, I don't even know why." I looked at him. "And I'm sorry. Whether it was my bad or yours, it's over. You're my brother, man."

I held out my hand. After a long moment—so long I thought he was going to leave me hanging—he took it and we shook.

I turned back to the crowd.

"So how do we play this? Do we keep doing the same stuff we've always done or do we change the game? Isn't it worth trying to start all this with courage and mercy and do something great?"

No one moved. No one spoke.

"Besides, what's the whole point of us coming to Mars in the first place? Mars One was started as a way to help humanity. Maybe even save it. That speech Dr. Aukes gave when we left—that wasn't her just blowing smoke. She believed it and we do too. I mean, we're *here*; we have to believe in something bigger and better, right? Remember that plaque that Buzz Aldrin and Neil Armstrong put on the moon when they got there? 'We came in peace for all mankind.' Well, that's why we're here too. Colonizing Mars isn't enough. Don't we have to represent something more than that?"

Then Nirti pushed herself up so that she could be seen by everyone. "Earth is a beautiful, violent, spoiled, wonderful, tragic, horrible, confused, messed-up ball of craziness. But it's where we're from."

"Yeah it is," murmured Luther. A few other people nodded.

Nirti turned and looked at me. "But we're not earthlings anymore," she said, her eyes searching mine. "Are we?"

I smiled. It almost hurt to smile, I was that scared. "No," I said.

"Then what are we?" she asked.

I cleared my throat. "We're Martians."

She grabbed my wrist, pulled herself over, and kissed my cheek. "Mars is a peaceful, beautiful, perfect place," she said as she faced the crowd. "It's a gift. It's a promise."

Zoé came over and hugged Nirti and then me. After a moment's hesitation, Luther joined us. They didn't have to say anything. It was said in ways clear enough for everyone to hear and understand.

For a few long, dangerous seconds it was just the four of us kids there. The faces of the adults were hard to read. Some people didn't even want to meet our eyes. But I saw doubt on a few faces, and tears.

It was my father who spoke first. He'd been sitting on

a bulkhead and he straightened, kicked off the wall, glided over, and he kissed me too. On the forehead. Then he turned and faced the others.

"Give me one good reason why not," he said.

The moment stretched.

And stretched. And then everyone except Colpeys rushed forward, yelling, shouting, screaming. Grabbing, hugging, squeezing. Weeping. Laughing.

Being human.

Together.

Chapter 109

I didn't envy Director Colpeys. Even though he was the last person to agree with us, once he did, it was up to him to sell it to the people back at Mars One. He broadcast the message back home with all of us in the common room with him. Showing that this was *our* decision. The message took twenty minutes to travel all that way and the response took an hour to come back, and I can imagine the conversations—and arguments—that our message ignited.

We sweated it. None of us wanted to hijack the ships and we definitely didn't want to derail the future of the Mars One project in any way. This was an enormous risk and while we waited that kind of sank in.

Then Bas Lansdorp came on the screen. He had a bunch of the senior staff behind him, including an unsmiling Dr. Aukes. Them against us?

He said, "You are all crazy." Then he wiped at tears in his eyes. "How do you want to proceed?"

After that we got to work. I spent the whole night in the workshop, coming up with the best plan to reach and enter the *Golden Dragon*. My mom was with me on the video monitor, but we didn't work like mother and son. It was different from that. Our relationship had evolved over the months. We were colleagues. Two mechanical engineers working a problem.

Other people were working out the math, here and on Earth. Lansdorp called NASA and then they conference called the Chinese. I kept expecting someone to push back, to start acting like jerks about this.

They didn't.

However, the top brains did warn us that we had left it almost too late. There would be all kinds of problems to solve. But again . . . *top* brains. All over the world and on board our ships. The cooperation we saw was amazing. I wonder what things would be like if we could work together like that on everything that was important.

The controlled burns were being programmed. We would go to the Chinese ship first and bring back anyone who was still alive. If anyone was. Then the *Huginn*'s lander would be launched. The *Muninn*'s crew would follow in one sol—one Martian day. We were on that time schedule now and forever.

There were people alive on the *Golden Dragon*. At least that's what I believed. Not everyone agreed with me. Colpeys still thought that whoever put the ALIVE INSIDE sign up had to be dead by now. Even with rationing, he thought the math was against them. And, he said, that last message had said their airlock was damaged, and he felt that should have been that.

I didn't accept that. No way. Airlocks were machines, no different from any other. Machines can be fixed. Mom hadn't trained me to accept a repair job was too hard, and "can't do it" isn't an acceptable answer. Not to her.

And not to me.

Satellites were looking at every inch of the *Golden Dragon*, including the airlock. It looked mostly intact, and the seal had to be good or there would have been no one to send that message. So the airlock mechanism was probably damaged from inside. There were plenty of ways to do that, but every single item—down to the last washer on the least important nut—was made to be repaired or replaced. You don't do it any other way if you plan to fly millions of miles from a hardware shop. Spacecraft were also designed to be repaired from inside or outside. The Neo-Luddites clearly hadn't damaged the outside, which meant that all of the access panels on the exterior of the ship were intact. I'm not saying it would be easy to access the workings and open the door without making whatever damage was inside worse. Not saying that at all. But I'm also not saying that it was impossible. Not for the son of the best mechanical engineer on two worlds. Not for a Hart. No, sir.

So, yeah. I got this.

I went through it all with Mom, and we discussed everything that had to be done. She told me to describe every step, list every tool, describe every procedure. Three times. In great detail. When I was done, she stared at me for so long I began to wonder if she was working out the best way to tell me that I had screwed up, that I'd missed something.

Instead she said, "I love you, Tristan."

That was the conversation we had the day the *Huginn* settled into orbit alongside the *Golden Dragon*.

Chapter 110

The computers did the controlled burn.

The pilot and copilot glided us up to the sweetest soft dock in the history of space travel. I make that part sound easy. It wasn't. But our pilots are as good at their jobs as Mom is at hers.

This time we could slide right up close. The first stage is to initiate a soft dock by making contact with the International Berthing and Docking Mechanism—the IBDM—which is what's called an "androgynous" low-impact docking mechanism. That means it can dock with all kinds of spacecraft, large and small. The docking connector is extended out to the target vehicle and once the soft connection is secured, both spacecraft are pressurized. We couldn't do it that way because of the damage to the *Golden Dragon*. If I managed to bypass the damage and access the internal systems, then the key would be to establish an airtight hard dock seal, pressurize the dock, and then open the door.

It went by the numbers.

We docked. I was with Director Colpeys and several other crewmembers, including Nirti's parents. All of us in spacesuits, ready for any emergency. For any horrors.

The docking collar was pressurized.

I opened the airlock on the *Huginn*. The outside airlock of the *Golden Dragon* was there. Right there. It took me sixteen minutes to free the manual lock and open the hatch, and another two hours to deal with a lot of torn wires, melted circuit boards, and other damage. The Neo-Luddites aboard the Chinese ship had really messed things up. Mom was in my ear, talking me through some of it; but for most of it I had to make decisions based on what I saw, I thought, I believed I could handle.

A heavy mechanical shudder suddenly went through the skin of the *Golden Dragon*. I could feel it. It was as if a body that had been in a coma so long everyone thought it was dead suddenly took a breath. Then, I felt a series of impacts from inside. I placed my hands on the broken airlock and tried to "hear" through a sense of touch. There's no sound in space, but I swear I heard the *bang-bang-bang* of something happening on the other side of that door. We all froze, looking at the airlock, expecting the absolute worst.

Suddenly a valve opened. Not on my end, but at the other end. Inside the ship. It was as if someone in there understood what I was doing out here and was trying to help.

Gas blew out. Slow at first and then with great force. My suit read it for what it was.

Air.

I yelled for the team on board the *Huginn* to start pressurization and, between the two jets of air, we established a hard dock.

The door was still closed, though. The lock didn't want to open.

Too bad. I wasn't about to fail now. I wasn't going to let that stop me. No way. I used my tools, I used every trick I know, and then I used muscle. After a moment of hesitation, Colpeys came up beside me, grabbed hold of one of the safety rings inset along the outside of the hatch, put his shoulder against the hatch, and pushed. I could hear him growling, muttering, swearing under his breath as he pushed. I turned and looked at him, caught his eye. He paused for a moment and then he smiled. We smiled at each other. I nodded, set myself, and together we pushed with everything we had.

The others joined us. It took all of us to push it in because the big steel airlock door was a mess.

But it moved. Yeah. It moved and it swung inward.

And there she was.

A slim figure, wrapped in stained blankets, shrunken to scarecrow thinness by malnutrition. Young and scared. Holding a hammer in one hand and a screwdriver in the other.

Ting.

And she was alive.

Chapter 111

We celebrated.

Not just the crews on the ships. The whole world.

It was all so strange. First there was all that fear and sickness, all the pain and death . . . and then there was life. Our crew and the Chinese crew were suddenly one crew. It's crazy how fast and how completely it happened. They stopped being *them* and became part of us. Ting was so happy to see other kids, and we were so happy to adopt her and her companions into the *Huginn* and *Muninn* family. We had no idea if China would send a ship to bring them home, but that didn't seem likely. They were going to be part of our colony until the Chinese established their own. Or maybe it would come down to one colony. Maybe this was going to change how we viewed the whole "us and them" thing. I mean, what do nationalities and borders matter on Mars?

Like all of the survivors, Ting was rail thin, so everyone took turns trying to fatten her up. I wished I had a pizza, wings, and some onion rings, because that girl needed junk food. Unfortunately all we had was really healthy stuff, so we gave her a lot of that.

Language barriers somehow didn't matter much. We all understood each other because we were all out there for the same reason.

During the party my dad told me that I had messages waiting from Herc and Izzy, and I went into a pod to play the video files. They were crying and laughing because the news services had picked up images from my helmet cam during the rescue and it was all over the Internet. The airlock opening. Ting's face. Life.

We'd all worked together to save the last crew members of the *Golden Dragon*, so it wasn't fair that my name and my face kept showing up everywhere. I tried to tell Herc and Izzy that, but I don't think they heard me.

Before she signed off, Izzy smiled at me across all those millions of miles and said, "I'll always love you, Tristan Hart."

It wasn't something she said with a broken heart. No. This was different. This was my friend Izzy Drake. Even so, I kind of broke down and cried.

Good thing those pods had doors.

That night—the last night of the voyage for the *Huginn*, the night before our crew would crowd into the landing craft and leave the transit vehicle behind forever, to be followed a day later by the crew of the *Muninn*—Colpeys gathered everyone in the common room. We all knew what was coming. Luther, Zoé, Nirti, and I were holding hands when Colpeys explained how it was going to work.

"Despite what the rumor mill's been saying, this isn't a meritocracy," he said, cutting a look at Luther.

Luther sighed but he was smiling. We all were. Nervous smiles, sure, but still smiles.

"As much as *I* would like to be the first person on Mars," continued Colpeys, "it was always our decision to make this completely fair. We have a computer program that will make random selections from among the crews of each ship. The names will be printed out and those persons will represent Mars One and all of Earth as the first people to step onto our new world. We on the *Huginn* have the special honor of having one of our own be the very first of all the colonists to make that step. Onto Mars . . . onto our new home. The following day the first person from the *Muninn* will step out. And then the rest of the crew per our standard work assignments. Setup crews and so forth. First things first, though. Let's find out who will be the first Martian."

He looked around and everyone was nodding. The excitement in the room was incredible. Palpable. My mouth was totally dry.

Colpeys took a breath and then pulled himself across the room to a computer terminal. The screen display showed the crew of the *Muninn*. Mom was there, looking pale and worn, but she was smiling too. Colpeys punched in a command code and then paused with his finger over the ENTER key. He glanced around at all of us.

"Best of luck to everyone," he said. "You all have my love and my greatest respect."

Nirti squeezed my left hand and Zoé clutched my right. Ting stood near us, looking small but very much alive.

"Good luck," I said to my friends. We looked at each other and shared a nod.

Colpeys pressed the button. There was a moment where nothing seemed to happen as the computer algorithm cycled and cycled and then suddenly a piece of paper ticked its way out of the printer. Colpeys snatched it and all I caught was a flash of black letters on white paper. That page, I knew, was going to be famous. It would be an artifact that would belong to history. We all held our breaths as Colpeys studied it, lips pursed. Then he turned it around to show us.

LUTHER MBEDE

Everyone gasped. And then everyone burst into applause.

If there had been enough gravity I think Luther would have collapsed. Zoé and Nirti released my hands and they hugged him. People flocked around to pat him on the back and kiss him. His parents were weeping. I waited my turn and offered my hand, then pulled him into as tight a hug as I could give.

"Congratulations," I said, having to yell above the shouts.

But then Luther pushed me back, turned, soared over to Colpeys, and took the paper from him. Colpeys offered his hand, which Luther shook. Colpeys, beaming at him, turned to the crowd.

"Please, everyone," he yelled, "if you would all settle down for a moment. Our Mr. Mbede would like to say something." To Luther he said, "I suspect you had something planned all along."

Luther looked at him for a long moment, then nodded. The room grew quiet and everyone on both ships listened to what the first Martian was going to say. A live feed would be sent back to Earth, where billions would be hanging on every word.

Luther's face was serious. He was the only person who wasn't smiling, and there were tears in his eyes.

"I've wanted this more than I've wanted anything in my entire life," he began. "Ever since my family joined Mars One it's all I've been able to think about. I've worked so hard for it, and maybe I worked a little too hard." There was a small ripple of laughter from our crew. "And all along I really believed that the selection was going to be about merit, about who deserves it most. I wanted to be that person. I still do." He held up the paper and showed it to us. "And it came down to a random computer pick. A random pick."

Luther shook his head.

"But it shouldn't *be* random."

He looked at the paper and smiled as he wiped the tears from his eyes. They sparkled in the air as they floated off.

"It *should* have been about who deserved it most," he said. "It should have been about who earned it."

Nobody spoke. Colpeys looked confused.

"My name's on this page," said Luther, "but it shouldn't be. It's a mistake."

"What do you mean?" asked the director.

Luther turned and pointed across the room. "His name should have been on this page. And . . . as far as I'm concerned that's what this page really says. *He's* the one who really earned this."

One by one every person in the common room turned.

He was pointing at me.

Chapter 112

A lifetime later, I stood on the lowest rung on the ladder.

Everyone was watching. Everyone in the first lander, everyone else back aboard the other ship still in orbit. Thirty-five plus eight. Forty-three humans on two ships. Everyone on Earth, too, though by the time they saw the video feed history would have already changed.

My suit was regulated for temperature but I was sweating and my hands were ice-cold. My heart was beating so hard I could hear it.

Through the radio I heard my mom's voice. "I love you, Tristan," she said. In the back of my mind I remembered the way Izzy smiled at me in her video.

I bowed my head and rested the visor against the ladder.

The whole universe seemed to stop. All those worlds, all the stars and galaxies held their breath.

I knew what the mission people wanted me to say. It had been scripted for whoever was chosen to be the first. A long speech about the glories of mankind and the benefits of imagination and cooperation. We all knew it backward and forward. It's what we were supposed to say, and maybe some historians and reporters had already drafted it into the headlines because they'd been given copies by our PR people. Historic words.

But no, I've never liked scripts.

I took a breath, blinked tears out of my eyes, and stepped down.

My foot crunched onto the hard, flaky red soil of another world.

Then the other foot.

My knees were trembling but I felt fifty feet tall.

I knew that whatever I said was going to be remembered forever.

"I am a Martian," I said. "And I'm home."

Izzy's Going-to-Live-on-Mars Playlist

2 Skinnee J's: "Pluto"

Aimee Mann: "It's Not"

Ash: "Girl From Mars"

Ayreon: "Into the Black Hole"

Babylon Zoo: "Spaceman"

Beastie Boys: "Intergalactic"

Belle and Sebastian: "A Space Boy Dream"

Billy Bragg: "The Space Race Is Over"

Blink-182: "Aliens Exist"

Blondie: "Rapture"

Bruno Mars: "Talking to the Moon"

Chris Bell: "I Am the Cosmos"

Clutch: "Escape from the Prison Planet"

Crookers featuring Kid Cudi: "Embrace the Martian"

Daft Punk: "Technologic"

David Bowie: "I Took a Trip on a Gemini Spaceship"

David Bowie: "Life on Mars?"

David Bowie: "Loving the Alien"

David Bowie: "Space Oddity"

David Bowie: "Starman"

David Bowie: "Ziggy Stardust"

Destroyer: "The Space Race"

Devo: "Space Junk"

Dinah Washington: "Destination Moon"

Donald Fagen: "Tomorrow's Girls"

Drive-By Truckers: "Puttin' People on the Moon"

Electric Light Orchestra: "Ticket to the Moon"

Ella Fitzgerald: "Two Little Men in a Flying Saucer"

Elton John: "Rocket Man"

Ernie from *Sesame Street*: "I Don't Want to Live on the
    Moon"

Feist: "My Moon My Man"

Flight of the Conchords: "Bowie's in Space"

Frank Sinatra: "Fly Me to the Moon"

Frank Zappa and The Mothers of Invention: "Dwarf Nebula
    Processional March & Dwarf Nebula"

Gorillaz: "Every Planet We Reach Is Dead"

Hawkwind: "Silver Machine"

Ian Brown: "My Star"

Incubus: "Stellar"

Janelle Monáe: "Many Moons"

Joe Cocker: "Space Captain"

Jon Anderson: "Flight of the Moorglade"

Julie Brown: "Earth Girls Are Easy"

Justin Timberlake: "Spaceship Coupe"

Kanye West: "Spaceship"

Kate Tempest: "Hot Night Cold Spaceship"

Katy Perry: "E.T."

Klaatu: "Calling Occupants of Interplanetary Craft"

Komputer: "Valentina"

Kool Keith/Dr. Octagon: "Aliens"

Lou Reed: "Satellite of Love"

Megadeth: "Hangar 18"

Mike Oldfield: "First Landing"

Moby: "We Are All Made of Stars"

Modest Mouse: "Space Travel Is Boring"

Morrissey: "Fantastic Bird"

Neko Case: "I Wish I Was the Moon"

Nick Drake: "Pink Moon"

Patti Smith: "Space Monkey"

Peter Schilling: "Major Tom (Coming Home)"

Pixies: "Bird Dreams of Olympus Mons"

Pink Floyd: "Eclipse"

Pink Floyd: "Set the Controls for the Heart of the Sun"

Portishead: "Wandering Star"

Powerman 5000: "When Worlds Collide"

Prism: "Spaceship Superstar"

Radiohead: "Black Star"

Radiohead: "Subterranean Homesick Alien"

R.E.M.: "Man on the Moon"

Schoolhouse Rock!: "Interplanet Janet"

Simple Plan: "My Alien"

Skillet: "Alien Youth"

Smog: "Teenage Spaceship"

Snow Patrol: "The Planets Bend Between Us"

Styx: "Come Sail Away"

Sun Ra: "Space Is the Place"

The Aquabats!: "Martian Girl"

The Beatles: "Across the Universe"

The Byrds: "Mr. Spaceman"

The Firm: "Star Trekkin'"

The Flaming Lips: "Yoshimi Battles the Pink Robots Pt. 1"

The Game featuring Lil Wayne and Tyler, The Creator:
"Martians vs. Goblins"

The Killers: "Spaceman"

The Kinks: "Supersonic Rocket Ship"

The McGuire Sisters: "Will There Be Space in a Space Ship"

The Misfits: "Teenagers from Mars"

The Misfits: "I Turned into a Martian"

The National: "Looking for Astronauts"

The Neanderthals: "Martian Hop"

The Only Ones: "Another Girl, Another Planet"

The Police: "Walking on the Moon"

The Pretenders: "Space Invaders"

The Prodigy: "Out of Space"

The Rocky Horror Picture Show soundtrack: "Science Fiction/
Double Feature"

The Rolling Stones: "2,000 Light Years from Home"

The Steve Miller Band: "Space Cowboy"

The Tubes: "Space Baby"

T.Rex: "Ballrooms of Mars"

Voivod: "Forgotten in Space"

Yes: "Starship Trooper"

Zager and Evans: "In the Year 2525"